THE LIFETIME OF A SECOND

THE TIME SERIES BOOK THREE

JENNIFER MILLIKIN

ISBN-13: 978-1-7326587-0-7
www.jennifermillikinwrites.com

1

BRYNN

I BLINKED, AND THEY DISAPPEARED.

The Saguaros, I mean.

The tall, multi-limbed cactus only grow in the Sonoran Desert. I only grew in the Sonoran Desert, too, until it became clear Phoenix could no longer be my home. All I had to do was climb into a car and point it north. Such a simple ending following a catastrophic journey.

Me and the Saguaros. We've disappeared.

The vehicle I'm in does a terrible job absorbing the black tar road. The road noise rushes in, whirling around us. It doesn't even matter. The air is already thick with awkward silence. What does a little road noise hurt?

Through a wide-open swath of nothingness we drive on, and the car climbs higher. A small sigh escapes my lips at the first pine tree. In less than a mile we lose the tall, scrubby bushes and there are only pine trees, some clustering together and others spaced far apart. I feel somber at the sight of some that are barren and blackened by previous fire. It seems unfair they're left standing, bearing the marks of how they were ravaged for all to see.

At least my marks hide on the inside.

My shoulder bumps the hard plastic door as the driver changes lanes and speeds up to pass a semi-truck. He sends the massive truck a couple beeps from his horn as we go by, grumbling under his breath about the left lane versus the right.

I should've known someone who spells his name Geoff would be a bad driver. The moment I saw his name I wanted to call him *Gee-off* but resisted the urge. Leaning forward, I open my mouth and say the first words spoken to one another in two and a half hours. "It should only be twenty more minutes." Looking down, I check the map on my phone again.

I look up, catch his gaze in the rearview mirror, and immediately avert my eyes.

"I've never been asked to drive this far before," he says, his tone curious.

He's fishing for information, but he's going to come up empty. The phrase 'Life or death' used to be said by my dad when I complained and he wanted me to see how inconsequential my complaint was. But this is not like that.

This is actually a matter of life or death.

And to make this all work, I have to trust a stranger who drives too fast and wants to know why he's taking me to a small town in the woods.

If he recognizes me, I'm screwed.

I pull the ball cap lower onto my forehead. Without thinking I reach for my hair, held back in a ponytail. My fingers keep reaching, curling against the cloth interior of the seat instead of my hair. I've done that so many times since I chopped off my long, blonde strands two days ago. I wonder when that will end? The hair is gone.

Another sacrifice. Or, perhaps, a penance. If giving up

my hair could atone for what I've done, I'd be bald in a heartbeat. Nothing can change what happened, the judicial system decided I wasn't guilty, but in my heart?

Guilty.

Guilty.

Guilty.

We're almost there. "Number forty-seven," I tell the driver. He crawls down the street at the same time I'm filled with an overwhelming urge to arrive. *So now you go slow?*

My nails dig into my palms as I will myself to calm down. To distract me, I study the homes we pass. They are small, squat, and each one has a chimney. The front yards are tidy; some of them have flowers rising from terra-cotta pots. I lean in, focusing on the house on the corner. The tip of my nose pokes the window. The house is nondescript, no flowers or bushes in sight, and the door is black. Shiny, midnight black.

That door screams its message loud and clear—*Stay away*. I want that door. Too bad my rental agreement won't allow me to paint. Or install an alarm system.

"Here you are," Geoff says, slowing to a stop.

I undo my seatbelt and hop out. By the time he makes his way to the rear of the car, I've pulled out my two bags and placed them on the ground. This is the first time I've seen him standing. He didn't get out when he arrived to pick me up from the gas station. Geoff's left leg is missing, and in its place is a metal rod. Now I feel like an ass for disliking his name.

"Accident when I was a kid," he explains, pointing down. He shrugs. "Sometimes I forget it even happened."

I nod because I don't know what to say, and I still feel awful. I was a terrible companion for that long car ride, but that's the thing about disappearing. It comes with stipulations. Starting with: Don't be memorable. I can't tell a funny story, or have a meaningful conversation. I can't be a vibrant color in someone's memory. No magenta, or teal. I am beige. Endless, insignificant beige.

I used to be lemon yellow. Happy, outgoing, ebullient.

One second of time turned me into a neutral shade, and it will be my color forever. I've come to accept that. It's one of the reasons I decided to run. Well, that and the other thing. The thing that will always have me looking over my shoulder.

"Good luck, Ms.—"

"Brynn," I say quickly, not wanting Geoff to say my last name again, in case one more passage of it through his lips prompts it to stay in his mind longer than necessary.

Already I regret not using a fake name. My middle name seemed like enough of a deviation, but I'm not so sure now. Last week this was all just an idea in my head. I received his most recent hate mail, and after I placed it alongside his other letters, thought *I should skip town.* From that one tiny thought came big choices. I began searching for places to rent in northern Arizona, and when I found a place ready for immediate move-in, I snapped it up. Ginger, the owner of the eleven hundred square foot cabin, was chasing her dream of backpacking through Europe, and would be gone for six months.

Perfect, I told her. What I didn't tell her was that I'll be long gone by the time she comes home. Three months of wages is all I need. Just enough to pad what my parents will give me when their season is finished. I arranged a property manager for my place, packed my bags, gathered all my important documents, and Elizabeth Brynn Montgomery dropped the Elizabeth. I did not pass Go, I did not collect two hundred dollars.

I ordered a car and had it pick me up two blocks from my condo. Now that car is driving away, and I'm here in Brighton—a town dwarfed by sprawling, sunny Phoenix—standing on the sidewalk, and staring at the small home in front of me. The yard is neat, the grass a deep green and trimmed. Three stairs connect the front walkway to the porch, and each step is buffered by a small pot of geraniums. On either side of the front door hang two rustic lights that resemble lanterns.

"Here we go," I mutter, and *bump bump bump* my rolling suitcase along the cracks in the short driveway. Ginger said the house key would be under a pot of flowers. I lift one after the other, and on my fourth try I find one gold key on a silver key ring.

The inside of the home looks much like the outside. Tidy, modest, and sparsely decorated. Ginger must have a thing for apples. The curtains are blue and white gingham with red apples lining the bottom and top. A large, framed picture of apples hangs on the wall in the living room. Fake apples are piled in a basket on top of the fridge.

It takes only a few minutes to walk through the place. In the hallway I find a locked closet and assume that's where Ginger has stored her personal items. There are no photographs in the place, no books, or anything that tells me even a morsel about Ginger as a person. They all must be in that closet, and it strikes me as sad that these things can mean enough to take up space in our homes but can so easily be locked away.

Is that the way it is for everything? Are things only as important as we make them?

The thought depresses me, but the feeling isn't new.

I won't take those pills the therapist gave me. At the request of my parents, I went to see someone. She kept calling what happened *the accident*, but I argued it wasn't an accident. The therapist said she understood that, but for my sake, they would call it an accident because, from my standpoint, it was one.

I rub my eyes, an attempt at banishing the thoughts. Thinking them won't help anything. What's done is done. It can never be undone.

Instead, I search the place. Open every cabinet, sift through every drawer, until I'm certain I know every inch. After that, I dump my suitcase on the bed and put everything in its proper place. The master bedroom is large, Ginger said, because she'd knocked out the wall between the two bedrooms.

"When you're single, one large is better than two small," she'd explained, then asked me if I was single.

"Yes," I answered her quickly. "And I plan to keep it that way."

Besides, nobody will want me now.

Not after what I've done.

I don't remember falling asleep. Or what woke me up.

Rolling over, I place a hand over my eyes and take a deep breath. I know what I'll see when I open my eyes, but I'm not ready to see it. The unfamiliar walls, the furniture that isn't mine.

Tap tap tap tap tap.

I sit up, my heart banging in my chest. Instinctively, I know it's not him. He wouldn't knock. Standing, I glance in the mirror above the dresser and swipe my fingers under my eyes. The mascara streaks don't budge. Another knock drifts to me, this one soft and out of cadence. Turning away from my reflection, I hurry to the door and peer through the peephole.

A woman.

My lips twist, thoughts rushing through my head. Meeting people is unavoidable, but so soon? I planned to hide out as long as possible, living off the protein bars I brought with me, until I felt ready to venture out. Grocery shopping and finding a job have to happen soon, but I wanted a couple days to hole up and absorb what I've left behind.

I gulp in a breath of air and open the door.

The young woman smiles and lifts a hand, waving. "Hi. I'm Cassidy Anders. I live next door." Her thumb points to my left. "This is Brooklyn," she adds, looking down.

A child. I hadn't noticed a child. She stands only three feet tall, her head barely reaching her mother's mid-thigh. Gripping the door handle, I try not to slam the door closed. I want to be away from these people. My therapist taught me what to do in these situations, when panic grips me, and I feel like my world has tilted off its axis. Breathe in *one, two, three, four* and out *one, two, three, four*.

"Are you okay?" Cassidy asks, eyes squinting with concern.

"Yes," I bark, wincing at the harshness in my voice.

Brooklyn hides behind her mother's leg, and shame fills me. Like the depressed feeling from earlier, shame is not new to me either.

"Yeah, okay. Well, I, uh..." Cassidy holds out a silver tin with a clear plastic lid.

I don't want what she's offering, but my hands reach for it anyway—a reflexive response. Looking down at what is in my hands, I assess it, then glance back up to the woman. She is young, very young, maybe my age. Smile lines frame her eyes, lines that I don't have. A swipe of flour dusts her forearm.

"You made me a pie?" The astonishment in my voice is embarrassing. Baking a pie is not a new concept, but someone being kind to me? That hasn't happened in a while.

Innocent until proven guilty are words we use to remind us not to judge too quickly. But let's be honest. It's really guilty until proven innocent, and even then, the guilt leaves behind traces. Like smudges of ash following a fire, or particulates floating in the atmosphere after an explosion. The slate is never fully wiped clean.

"You're our new neighbor, right?" Cassidy offers a friendly smile, but I can't seem to reciprocate.

"Uh-huh."

"And your name is?" She cocks her head to the side, her eyes tentative. Her smile falters. Maybe she has that sixth sense mothers develop. My own mother claimed to have one.

"Brynn," I answer finally, balancing the pie in the crook of my left arm and offering her my right hand.

She seems relieved by this customary display of normalcy. We had a rocky start, but perhaps I've passed her test after all.

"Mommy, can I go play now?" Brooklyn's little voice floats up from her hiding spot behind Cassidy. Her head is stuck out and she looks up at her mother, eyes big and wide, waiting.

"Sure, sweetie, but not for too long. Taylor will be here soon."

Brooklyn yells with excitement and jumps down each stair, landing on them with two feet and a solid *thud*. When she hits the grass, she bolts for her own front yard.

Cassidy turns back to me. "She loves her babysitter. I, on the other hand, do not like needing a babysitter."

"Oh," I say. I could make conversation. Ask Cassidy why she needs the babysitter. Ask her about Brooklyn. *How old is she? Is she in school? What's her favorite color?* Hell, I could even ask Cassidy what filling is in the flipping pie.

But, no.

I'm not in Brighton to make friends.

I'm here to blend in, make money, and run.

2

CONNOR

My biggest worry in life is that I'm washed up before I ever made something of myself.

It has been months since I've sold a painting.

It has also been months since I've painted anything new. I haven't been inspired, for one, and I've been busy. Too busy to pursue my passion. The blank canvas in my living room taunts me every day. I leave it there, leaning on its wooden easel, for a reason. I need something to remind me I can't give up on my dream, even while I'm keeping someone else's alive.

It's a lot to ask of a person. Keeping enough faith for one dream is difficult. Two? Tall order.

It's early in the morning. The birds have only just begun to sing. Back when all I did was paint, I'd stay up all night—that's usually when inspiration struck. Now I'm in bed by ten, alarm set for six.

My dad was diagnosed last year. It started with some tremors. He didn't tell anyone about those, but my mom noticed. She called me crying, and said it was hard for my dad to turn a screwdriver. I wrote it off as age-related arthritis. I think he did, too, because that's what we wanted it to be.

Then he fell from the ladder while he was on a job. He'd only been on the second step, thank God. He was supposed to be changing a lightbulb in a ceiling fan for Old Lady Linton, and lost his balance. He got off easy with a bruised hip, but it was only the beginning. Eventually came the diagnosis of Parkinson's Disease. After that, we had to tell him he couldn't work. Hands down, I'd take a double root canal over having to do that again. Telling my dad he could no longer run his business was the spoken equivalent of delivering a punch to his gut.

The only person who could run Vale Handyman Services? Me. The artist. Who knew next to nothing about fixing things, despite having grown up around tools. I'd never shown an interest in the business, and Dad didn't push me. To get up to speed, I read books. *Home Repair for Dummies* and things like that. The first few homes I visited, I sent pictures of the repair to my dad. He'd study the photos, then call me and walk me through it.

I still have to call him from time to time, but mostly I'm good on my own. I expanded the business to include interior painting. Might as well do painting of some kind. I feel better with a brush in my hand, even if I'm not creating art.

Every Monday morning I hop into my truck and head to my parents' house. This Monday morning is no different. My mom prints out my schedule for the week and I look it over, adding the tools I think I'll need from Dad's workshop if they're not already on my truck.

She sends me off with a thermos of coffee. Dad nods, then thanks me. I hate when he does that. I don't want him to thank me. I don't want him to have something for which to thank me. I want my dad back. The way he was before the neurons in his brain started wreaking havoc. I didn't know how much I liked watching him walk up the driveway with his toolbox until it became an image I'd never see again.

I finish putting the new tools in their spots, and close the toolboxes that line the bed of the truck.

"Connor, honey, hang on a second," my mom calls, just as I'm climbing into the cab. She makes her way across the yard, to the end of the driveway where I'm parked. She wears a sweater even though it's May. Always cold. She has a sweet smile and a caretaker's heart.

"What's up, Mom?" I close the door, roll down the window, and lean on the window frame.

"Are you doing okay, Connor? You didn't say much this morning." She lifts a hand, shielding her eyes from the bright morning sun.

"Just tired," I tell her. I stayed up late, daring the rush of creativity to come flowing in. It never did.

"Do you want to hang on a second? I can make you a lunch. I have leftover chicken from dinner last night. It will make a good chicken salad sandwich."

"No, thanks, Mom. I need to get to Old Lady Linton's. You know how she is." I give her a knowing look and she laughs, then puts a hand over her mouth because she feels bad for laughing.

"She's lonely, that's all." Mom steps closer to the truck. "Something I imagine you know a little about."

Lifting my gaze to the ceiling, I take a long, slow breath.

"Don't get bent out of shape," she scolds. "It was just an observation."

I look back at her, remembering she only wants the best for me. A little of my irritation evaporates.

"You know," she says, smacking my forearm once with her palm. "It might not hurt for you to hire a helper. I have you booked for the next two weeks already. Things are picking up. Getting a lot more business now that it's summer." Her lips twitch as though trying to hide a smile, but she's terrible at it.

"What?" I ask, fiddling with the dial on the radio. It's not on, but I want something to do with my hands.

"Oh, nothing. Just that a lot of those calls are coming from families with girls home from college. Some for the summer. Some have graduated. You never know—"

"Alright, alright, that's enough," I say, turning on the truck and putting it in reverse.

She takes a step back. "You'll have to get over her sometime," she shouts, cupping her hands around her mouth.

"I am over her," I yell back, reversing into the street.

I DRIVE ON THROUGH TOWN, AND OUT ON ROUTE FOUR TO Old Lady Linton's.

I sip my coffee, and when I'm not sipping, I'm muttering. Mostly about what my mom said. She doesn't know anything. It took a long time to get over Desiree, but I did it. It helped that once she left Brighton, she never came back. She called twice, each time she was drunk, crying and carrying on about how hard it was to make it in L.A. She was mistaken, thinking she was going to receive sympathy from me. The second time was eight months ago, and I asked her not to call back. She hasn't.

I haven't dated because I haven't had the desire. By the time I was over Desiree, my dad was diagnosed, and I started working the longest days of my life. Doesn't leave a lot of time for dating. Not to mention this is a smallish town, and I know nearly everyone who lives here. Mostly, anyway.

The people in the summer crowd are strangers to me. Many of them are families, and many of them have college-age daughters. Those girls, paired with Brighton girls coming home from college, are the ones my mother would love to see me going on dates with, but she must think I'm still twenty-two and interested in girls like that.

Every summer they arrive, and every summer they do the same stupid shit. They walk through town, staring down at their phones, and nearly walking into traffic. Or sit in the coffee shops in their tiny shorts and talk loudly. Not that I have anything against tiny shorts. It's the people filling the shorts that bother me. They are shallow. I don't think they could ever experience the kind of emotion I feel when I paint. I'm twenty-six years old, and I want someone who *feels*.

I'm perfectly content with where I am right now. I'd love to paint more, but other than that, I'm fine.

Happy, even.

I'm not lonely.

Not at all.

OLD LADY LINTON WAS A HANDFUL. SHE WANTED TO TALK TO me about Rufus. How he jumps from his cat stand and hides behind her chair. Of course I needed to see it firsthand, but she couldn't catch Rufus, so I had to do it for her. Reaching down, I run a fingertip over the new scratch on the back of my hand. *Damn cat.*

I couldn't finish the second job I went to, not without a visit to the hardware store. Before that, I need lunch. I need a Cuban, and I need it from Mary. She's been at the diner for as long as I can remember, and she's my mom's best friend.

"Mary," I call as I walk in, the bell above the door chiming. She's standing at the long counter, placing two platters of steaming hot food in front of a couple guys.

"The Cuban or the Monte Cristo?" she asks, pouring my iced tea and setting it down at an empty spot.

"Cuban," I say, tossing my keys down on the Formica countertop and swinging a leg over the circular seat. Mary walks away and sticks a ticket in the window, yelling back to the cook that it's for me. Saying my name is code for *Give him extra fries.*

I take a long sip from the tea, drinking all of it in nearly one gulp. Brighton might not be the desert, but it's still warm here.

Cassidy Anders walks by, her arms full of dishes. She's a nice girl. Graduated two years after me, but made the mistake of getting involved with a guy from the next town over, and he got her pregnant. Five months in, he left her high and dry, swollen belly and all. *Dick.* Brooklyn is a sweet kid though.

"Hey, Connor. Working hard today?" Cassidy drops her dishes in a big brown plastic tub and circles the counter, picking up a pitcher of tea on her way.

"Always," I answer. She refills my cup and I thank her.

"Want to hear some good gossip?" She pushes her bangs from her eyes and laughs softly. "Not that you'd be interested in gossip, but it's not the bad kind."

I lean back in my seat and cross my arms, my interest piqued. "I suppose so."

She sets her elbows on the counter and leans forward. "I got a new neighbor yesterday," she says, voice lowered. "Ginger went to Europe to sow some oats, and rented out her place. A girl, probably around our age, arrived in a car, but the car left. *It left her there.* Isn't that odd?"

"So she doesn't have a car?"

"No. She arrived in a new town, without a way to get around. I took a pie to her, just to be neighborly, and you know I make one heck of a peach berry pie."

My stomach grumbles when she mentions her pie. "Uh huh," I say, and nod Cassidy on.

"This girl was...cold, I guess. That's the best word I can think of. She wasn't friendly to Brooklyn." She gestures with her palms up, showing her consternation. "I mean, who isn't friendly to Brooklyn?"

I don't think it's a question that needs an answer, so I lift my shoulders and let them drop.

"She wasn't interested in chatting, and getting her name out of her was like pulling teeth. The whole experience struck me as odd." Cassidy pulls her bottom lip into her mouth and chews on it. "You know—"

"Order up," yells someone from the kitchen. He has already disappeared from the window, so I can't see if it was Mutt or Grizzly. Nice names, I know, but the cooks nick-named themselves.

Cassidy spins around, spies my sandwich, and grabs it. She sets it in front of me, along with a bottle of ketchup. "I'll let you eat. Just keep an eye out for the new girl in town. I think she's nice under that layer of spikes, but," Cassidy pauses, her eyebrows pulled together, "I guess you don't always know when someone is batshit. And maybe the people who seem like they could be, aren't." She throws her hands up and laughs at herself. "I don't know anymore. I have mom brain."

"You must," Mary says, passing through as fast as her considerable, sixty-three-year-old body will carry her. "Table twelve has been out of tea for about five minutes."

"Crap!" Cassidy grabs the half-full pitcher and hurries away.

Mary rolls her eyes and throws my check down next to my plate. I place my customary twenty on top of the slip of paper, and tuck into the sandwich I would never admit to having dreams about.

The rest of my afternoon is nothing to write home about. A trip to the hardware store, talking an expectant mother out of painting her nursery neon green, and then putting the crib together for her. I didn't know it, but cribs are really hard to assemble. The pressure of knowing what was going to lay inside it made me go three times slower than I needed to. I only charged her for the hours my mom quoted for the job, but that means now I'm late meeting Anthony.

My best friend won't care. He's probably already three deep.

I'm on my way to the bar when I realize how close I am to Cassidy's street. Curiosity fills me, and I swear it makes me turn the wheel. It's mid-evening, but thanks to the summer sun the sky is a muted blue, with streaks of deep purple and fading pink. Slowly I pass Cassidy's small home, then Ginger's.

It doesn't look any different. I don't know why I thought it would, or why I'm curious at all. Stopping at the end of the street, I peer at the house with the black door. Some people say that house is like a body, and the black door is the heart of the old man who lives inside.

Maybe somebody should warn this new girl about the cantankerous old guy living at the end of the street. A young girl should be aware of someone off his rocker. I'll remind Cassidy the next time I see her.

The street is only a few blocks from where town really gets started, with its maze of shops and restaurants. Warm air pours into my open windows as I start down the main street in the middle of all the action. Bluegrass music drifts in from the amphitheater one block over. Brighton in the summertime is a magical place. Sun-stroked Phoenicians flee the valley, sometimes for just a week, looking for a respite from the oppressive heat. Tonight, even though it's a Monday night, the sidewalks are crowded with people. The bar where I'm meeting Anthony is at the end of all this, so I continue my crawl through crowded downtown.

A family with young children step into a crosswalk. I slow and wait for them, and return the dad's wave. When they are through, I let off the brake and lift my jug of water, drinking deeply. I don't think I had enough water today, and dehydration is a bitch to deal with.

My eyes are on the road. I'm still drinking, but I can see what's in front of me. There's nothing but open road, cars parked along the sides, and a green light up ahead.

Suddenly, that's not all there is.

A girl steps out from behind a parked SUV, and darts into the road. She freezes, staring at my truck, *at me*. The water drops from my hold as two hands grip the steering wheel, and somewhere in a small part of my awareness I register the water soaking my passenger seat. My foot jams the brake, but there isn't time. I wrench the wheel right to avoid her, and my front tires jump the curb, ramming right into a fire hydrant.

"Fuck," I yell, throwing it in park.

The girl is still standing in the middle of the street. I jump out, leaving the door wide open in my haste.

I storm toward her. "Are you out of your mind?" I yell.

Her eyes swing up, meeting my anger. "Yes," she whispers.

If she yelled back at me, my anger would be increasing.

If she'd denied responsibility, I'd be livid, but it's her eyes, aghast and disbelieving, that stop the white-hot anger I had when I catapulted from my truck.

I come closer until I'm two feet from her. She has blonde hair hidden beneath a baseball cap. Her cheeks are sallow, her eyes red-rimmed—evidence of previous tears.

"Are you okay?" I ask. She's still standing in the middle of the street, though I guess now I'm in the street too.

"I'm alive," she answers.

What a weird response. I'm not sure what to say now.

At once, the street fills with light. She blinks up at a shining streetlight, and it's like the sudden addition of light has awakened her. Despite the ball cap hiding a third of her face, I can see how stunning she is.

She looks past me, to my truck with its front bumper wrapped around the yellow fire hydrant, and her open palm flies to her lips.

"I am so sorry," she says, walking a wide arc around me and coming to a stop a few feet from the truck. "I...I...don't know what to say. I'll pay for the damage." She shakes her head in disbelief and puts her hands on her hat.

"Don't worry about it. My friend has an auto body shop. He'll give me a good price."

"No." Her eyes are blue, like deep water, and they churn with a storm. For some reason I think of rough seas, tidal waves, salty spray smacking my face.

"No," she repeats, stronger this time. "I'm taking responsibility for this. I *will* pay for the damage, even if your friend gives you a deal. It might take just a little time, though. I need to find a job."

She purses her lips and looks around at the storefronts, like maybe a *Now Hiring* sign will magically appear in the window.

I'm aware of the irony. She needs a job. I need help.

I'm probably going to regret this. "Do you know how to use a screwdriver?" I ask.

Her eyes squint with her confusion. "Yes. Why?"

I point back at myself. "I'm hiring. I'm nice, only a little crazy, and I pay cash. Summertime is busy, and I need help."

She eyes the logo on the side of my truck. Her eyebrows lift. "Vale Handyman Services?" Her tone is skeptical. "I'll keep looking."

My muscles tense. She's one of those holier-than-thou girls home from college. She doesn't want to ruin her manicure by actually working hard. The baseball cap threw me off, but I should've known better. She has the tight jean shorts, a signature part of the uniform. Her white tank top has something written in black Old English lettering, and it takes me a few seconds longer to read it, which is awkward because now it looks like I'm staring at her chest.

"Are you getting a good look?" She crosses her arms in front of herself.

"I was reading your shirt. I'm guessing that's why you're wearing a shirt that has words plastered on it. So people will read it." My tone is snappy, matching hers. I'm not a Neanderthal. I know how to surreptitiously check out women.

She tips her head to the side and smirks. "And what does my shirt say?"

I have to bite my lip to suppress my laughter. "It says 'Fuck Off.'"

"Uh huh," she nods.

"Is that what you're telling me to do?"

She gulps, watching me, and her lips twitch while she blinks a few times. I can almost see the wheels turning in her mind. "Yes," she says.

A short stream of air leaves my nose. I walk to my truck,

lean in the open door, and retrieve a card from the center console.

"Here." I hold it out to her.

She takes it cautiously, her gaze going over the words. "Connor?" she asks, looking up at me. Her voice is sweeter now, wrapping around my name, like the attitude she had one minute ago never existed.

I nod. "And you are?"

She opens her mouth to speak but hesitates, closing her lips. "Brynn," she finally says, nodding once as she says it.

"It was nice to meet you, Brynn. Call me if you can't find a job that lets you take selfies and post them all day." I keep a straight face, even though her jaw drops. Her eyes are rough waters in an instant, as though all I had to do was snap my fingers.

She gives me a nasty look and stomps past me. For a second, I fear she's going to reach out a hand and rake her fingernails down the length of my truck. She disappears around the bumper and then I spot her on the sidewalk. She walks quickly, her head ducked.

"Fucking ridiculous," I mutter, climbing into my truck and slowly peeling it off the fire hydrant and back into the street.

Now there are two crazies for Cassidy to warn her neighbor about.

3

BRYNN

Fucking hell.

I've been all over this town. Nobody is hiring. At least not for what I'm qualified to do. Fat lot of good my degree in event planning is doing for me now. All the jobs that don't require some type of education or degree have been snapped up by college kids home for the summer.

I have some money socked away, but I need more. I can't just depend on my parents' money. Their fishing business is lucrative, but there's a chance they'll have a bad season. It's unlikely, but there's always a chance. I need to cover a few bases without them. Namely, just enough to get me on a plane to somewhere in South America. Probably the Brazilian beach town I visited a few times as a child.

I'll figure it out more once I get there, but my plan is to buy a bunch of beach chairs and rent them out every day. Same inventory, new money. I saw it happening when I went to Costa Rica for Spring Break my sophomore year of college. At the time, even dazed from shots of a liquor I didn't know the name of, I saw what was happening and thought *duh*. This person knows what they're doing down here.

It's not exactly my dream job, but when life goes to shit, choices must be made.

Connor Vale's business card has been staring at me for three days. I put it in the trash when I got home the night I played chicken with his truck, but the next morning I dug it out. Now it's sitting on the kitchen counter, reminding me of a man with light brown hair and kind eyes.

And a job that pays in cash.

That means no W-2's, no social security number needed, and most importantly, no background check.

The last thing I need is someone up here knowing what happened.

"Uggghhh," I groan, taking my cell from my back pocket. I type in the number on the front of the card and stare at it, my thumb hovering over the screen. With a swipe, I cancel the call and put the phone back in my pocket.

I can only imagine what Connor thinks of me. I stepped in front of his car, for goodness sake. He might think I was frozen, the proverbial deer in the headlights, but no. It wasn't a good night. I'd wandered through town, watched the families eating ice cream from the hand-dipped place, and listened to the music. It was too much for me. My mind raced, wondering what she was thinking that day. How someone could make that choice.

So I tried it too.

I saw the truck coming, the driver nothing but a shape behind a wheel. I wasn't trying to kill myself, even though I knew that could be a consequence. I've never been able to understand why she stepped in front of my car *on purpose*. She didn't trip in the street. She wasn't a distracted pedestrian. Through the windshield, she met my eyes. She knew what she was doing. She made the decision.

It cost me everything.

My life, my job, my friends. It didn't matter that I was innocent. That's the day I learned the life-crushing impact held by headlines. Nobody reads the whole story when the soundbite is so sensational.

All my dirt came to the surface, like sunken ships resurrected by a hurricane. Troubled youth. Underage drinking citation. And then, the big one. Cited for driving under the influence. It didn't matter that I was stone sober when it happened. My name was dragged through mud, spit at, and desecrated. The worst headline of all got the most clicks. They must have delighted in watching the numbers tick higher and higher.

Baby-Killer.

It didn't matter that I was innocent, and due process had understood that from the beginning.

The article made it clear I didn't kill the baby, but nobody reads the article. All it took was one unflattering photo taken at a college party, alongside a picture of the scene of the accident, complete with the stroller crushed like an accordion, and people assumed I had been drunk-driving and killed a mother and her baby.

In the court of public opinion, I was toast. The lowest of the low. Scum of the Earth.

My life disappeared the day that woman pushed her stroller in front of my car.

Now all I want is to disappear too.

I CHOSE GINGER'S HOUSE BECAUSE IT'S CLOSE TO A GROCERY store and a pharmacy.

I need places I can walk to. I haven't driven a car since the day it happened, and I hope I never have to again. The problem, of course, is that I can only carry so much. I could push a grocery cart home, and then back to the store, but then I'd be the girl pushing a grocery cart down the street. On top of being new. Talk about giving people a reason to notice me.

The walk to the grocery store isn't that bad, and it's nice out. I take a deep breath. The scent of pine and clean air is invigorating. I spent all day in the small house, cleaning the same surfaces, and trying to keep the memories at bay. There's a modest garden in the backyard that Ginger asked me to maintain. I told her I lacked a green thumb, and she asked only that I not kill it. I hung up on her when she said that, out of shock not anger, and when she called back I blamed it on a bad connection.

The nightmares have decreased. It helps I'm so far away from where it happened. I'm still in Arizona, but nothing looks the same here. The elevation changes the landscape, and it was enough to help me. I wish I'd known a long time ago that all I needed to do was go *up*.

On my way home I pass the house with the black door. A large window faces the street, just like my house. The curtains ripple, swing aside, and a man's face peers through. His deep wrinkles are evident from my place on the sidewalk. So is the scowl. For a reason I don't fully understand, I lift a hand and wave, the grocery bag waving with me. He disappears from the window.

Why did I do that? Maybe I felt a kindred spirit. He looked like how I feel.

I've taken three steps forward when the sound of a door

opening stops me. The old man steps out, walking to the end of his short porch. His fingers curl around the railing, using it for support as he slowly steps down the stairs. His steps are quicker once his feet hit a flat surface, and in no time he's close to where I am on the sidewalk.

"Hi," I say, stepping forward to greet him. I've always had a thing for old people.

"You're on my lawn," he growls, pointing down.

I follow his hand, the back of it dotted with age-spots, and look down.

Sighing, I step off the grass and back onto the sidewalk. "Happy now?"

"Hardly. Why were you spying on me?"

I snort. "You were the one peeking out your window. What size binoculars do you have? Are they military-grade? Or the kid's kind that come in bug-catching sets? Because—"

"Argh," he rumbles, throwing his hands out in my direction. "You're one of those chatty types, huh? Well, keep your chit-chat away from me. I'm not interested."

"Then why are you still standing here?" I don't even try to hide my smile. Grumpy old men are my favorite.

"You were on my lawn."

"No, I wasn't. Not when you first came out."

"Don't you argue with me, young lady. That's the problem with youth. You don't have any respect." He goes on and on, and I let him. I know his type. My grandpa was one of them before he passed away. This guy is lonely.

When he's finished, I ask for his name.

"Walt," he answers, his tone still as gruff as it was when he came out of his house.

"I'm Brynn," I tell him. If I held my breath waiting for him to ask I would probably pass out first.

He gives me a skeptical look. "Sounds an awful lot like Bryan."

"It's not." I take a step away. "Have a nice day, Walt." Two more steps.

"Why did you get dropped off last weekend?" he calls out. "Don't you have a car?"

I turn back, and I can't help my grin. "Obviously those binoculars you're using are military-grade. Do they have infrared?"

"Bah," he grumbles loudly, turning around and heading up to his house. I continue on to mine.

When I get home, I unpack the groceries. Connor's card is still in the same spot it was when I set it down two days ago, after deciding not to call him. Today's trip to the grocery store was a good reminder that I need funds. I don't particularly care for ramen, and that's exactly where I'm headed.

I pick up my phone and dial the number, glancing at the card to be sure I've typed it in correctly. This time, I don't hesitate. No hovering thumb. *One, two, three, push.*

"Hello?" He answers on the third ring. He sounds frustrated, and I almost hang up the phone. Rock music blares in the background.

"Um, hi. It's Brynn Montgomery." My teeth catch my lower lip and I look at the ceiling. *If this job didn't pay in cash, there's no way I'd be calling him.*

"Oh, so you have a last name?"

I frown. *That's* what he says to me? "Most people do." I exhale loudly after I say it.

He laughs. "You're a bit like a bear, you know that? Grumpy and ill-tempered."

"Oh, really? I just met someone who fits that description far better than I do." Cradling the phone between my ear and my shoulder, I open a cabinet and pull out a saucepan.

"Let me guess," he says warily. "You met Walt Jenkins."

I pause. "He didn't give me his last name, so I can't say for certain. Apparently that's common among us grumpy and ill-tempered people."

"Old guy, lips turned so far down it's like an upside down horseshoe on his face?"

"That's the one," I respond, taking a can opener to the three cans of tomatoes I just bought. I'm going to make marinara and freeze half.

"You should stay away from him, Brynn."

My eyes meet the ceiling as I roll them. "He's harmless, and besides, it's kind of hard to stay away from a neighbor."

Connor is silent. If it weren't for the music still playing wherever he is, I'd think he hung up.

"Still there?" I ask, pouring olive oil in the pan and adding diced garlic.

Connor clears his throat. "Do you live next door to Cassidy?"

I picture the tiny blonde mom and her cute little girl. I've heard Brooklyn in the backyard every morning, laughing and shrieking. She does it again every evening.

"Yes. Why? Do you know her?" Leaning over the pan, I take a deep breath. The warmth of the oil has released the fragrance of the garlic, and it's kicking my salivary glands into overdrive.

Connor doesn't answer. Not with words. He laughs and laughs.

"What's funny?" I ask, irritated.

"Nothing," he answers. "Maybe I'll tell you someday."

"Whatever," I reply frostily, ready to be off the phone. I don't care if he never tells me. I'll be long gone as soon as I can manage it. "I called to see if that job was still available."

"Nope," he says, the answer coming so quickly it's almost on top of my question.

Shit. What am I going to do now? The oil pops and a drop lands on the pad of my thumb. I suck my thumb between my teeth, my mind racing.

"Just kidding." Connor laughs. "It's available."

My eyes squeeze shut as I try not to hang up on my new boss.

"Pick you up tomorrow morning? Eight?"

"I'll be ready," I say, dumping the cans of tomatoes into the pan. "How did you know I need a ride?"

"Estimated guess. Brynn?" Connor's voice is suddenly serious.

"Yeah?"

"I mean it when I say to stay away from Walt. He's dangerous."

What am I supposed to say? There's already someone who wants my head on a spike, so the crotchety old guy can get in line behind him?

"Thanks for the warning. See you bright and early."

I hang up and finish the sauce.

For the rest of the evening, I try hard not to think about the man who wishes I were dead instead of his family. It's always a futile effort, and tonight is no exception. When hate is strong enough, clear enough, it's easy to feel. He may as well be next to me, with his raw and unfettered hate radiating from his pores.

That night the nightmares return.

4

CONNOR

This Monday is not like other Mondays.

Well, it is, but only sort of.

I got up at the ass crack of dawn, went to my parents' house, and got the week's schedule. I said hi to my dad and sat down to have a cup of coffee with him. His slurred speech wasn't as prominent this morning as it sometimes is, but I've learned not to get my hopes up. Some days are better than others, a result of the medicine doing what it can for him.

I can't stay for much longer, not if I want to make it to Brynn's on time. At twenty minutes to eight, I stand up to leave. My mom pulls biscuits from the oven at that same moment, using one hand to hold them and another to wave their buttery scent my way.

"I know you're not starting the first job until nine." She turns around, sets the sheet pan on the stove, and takes three plates from a cabinet.

"I have to be somewhere at eight, Mom. I hired someone and need to go over some stuff before we start work."

"Good." She smiles and takes out two Tupperware containers. "Where did you find him?"

"Her," I correct.

Her eyes widen. "Her?"

Dad chuckles, but it's a stilted sound.

"I met her..." *in the street... in front of my bumper... after she caused a minor accident that left my car in need of bodywork...* "downtown."

Mom finishes wrapping up two portions of biscuits and ladles her sausage gravy into a stainless steel container.

"Breakfast," she says, pushing the food into my arms. "For you and your new *employee.*" She lifts her eyebrows a few times to make sure I get her drift.

"She is just an employee, Mom."

I know what she's getting at. My mom is as transparent as a glass door, and she can't keep a secret to save her life. Maybe I should tell her Brynn might be as crazy as Walt, just to get her off my back. If I did that, she would insist I fire Brynn, and I don't want that to happen. I'm curious about her. I want to know why she's in Brighton.

It must be her vibe that has me interested. She's kind of mean. She puts out these 'stay away' signals, the kind I'm sure most people listen to. Unless she causes an accident that dents their car and actually looks like she feels really bad about it. For three seconds, anyway. Then something happened, and she froze over.

Probably a good thing. A girl like Brynn needs to be left alone. And a guy like me? She's the last thing I need.

"Bring your new employee by sometime soon, Connor. We'll need to at least meet her." Mom places a hand on my arm. "Not that I don't trust your judgment, but I would like to know who's representing the Vale name."

"Will do. Gotta go, Mom." I nod at my dad and back out of the kitchen, trying not to run to my truck.

I'm late. I send Brynn a quick text at the number she called me from yesterday, letting her know I'm on my way, and drive off.

Nerves eat at me on the way, and that annoys me.

Okay, yeah, Brynn is gorgeous, but she also has an attitude bigger than Alaska. And as hard as I tried not to appreciate those cut-off jean shorts, I liked them a little too much. Her lips were sumptuous, and I don't think I've ever used that word to describe someone's lips. They are full, pink, and I'm certain kissing them would be like enjoying a lavish feast. Until she opens her mouth and slices me with her sharp tongue, anyway. Honestly, it might not be too high a price to pay.

I don't know why I'm doing this.

So, so stupid.

I am definitely smarter than this.

My truck rolls to a stop in front of her house.

Apparently I'm not that smart.

With breakfast in tow, I hop out and walk to the front door. Two knocks. Wait thirty seconds. Two more knocks.

Ummm...

Finally I hear the sound of locks clicking and sliding out of the way. The door opens a few inches and an ear-piercing sound fills the air.

"Shit! Sorry, sorry," she says from the other side of the door.

Something gets pushed aside and the sound stops. The door opens all the way and Brynn's standing there, sleepy-eyed. Her hair falls to her shoulders and it's a mess.

"Not a great way to start your first day," I tell her, stepping inside.

"Come on in, you're invited." Her tone is acerbic. Didn't she just wake up? How can she be ready to spar sixty seconds after she has opened her eyes?

She crosses her arms and stares at me. Sleep is crusted in the corners of her eyes, and it reminds me that she's human. In my head, I've built her up to be some kind of ridiculously attractive, hostile robot.

"What?" she asks.

"Nothing." I hold out the food. "My mom sent me with breakfast."

Her lip curls. "Do you live with your parents?"

My chest warms instantly. Not in a good way. This girl knows just what to say to get a reaction from me. And I give in. Every. Fucking. Time. "No, I do not live with my parents. Obviously you think I'm a hick loser with no ambition."

She rises on her toes, ready with her response. "You think I'm a bimbo who wants to blow kisses at the camera and post them online."

Okay. She has me there.

"Correction, that's what I used to think." I sigh, setting the containers on the ground between us and extending a hand. "Truce?"

She eyes my hand first, then lifts her gaze to my face. Her features soften, her eyes swim with something I have no name for. My chest warms again, but in a way that's opposite from before.

"Truce," she murmurs, placing her hand in mine.

Palm to palm, her grip in mine, she swallows hard and her lower lip trembles. She recovers quickly, taking her hand back and swiping the food from the floor.

"Come on," she says, turning and walking away.

I watch her make her retreat and think of what I just saw.

How long has it been since she has been touched?

THIS IS WEIRD.

I'm tasting familiar flavors, in a house I've been in before —those handles on the kitchen cabinets and drawers were done by yours truly—but I'm with someone I know nothing about.

And Brynn doesn't give anything away. I've asked her about her family.

I'm an only child.

I asked why she's here.

Just needed a break.

Okay. Sure. I understand that. Her evasiveness doesn't bother me at all.

Nope.

So we eat in silence. It's unpleasant. I'm not usually a talkative guy, but eating in total silence is annoying, and it's killing me. In a last-ditch effort to make conversation, I ask her if she's upset. Her eyes look worried, like she's holding more than someone her age should carry.

She sighs and points to her shirt. I noticed it the second she opened the door, but I didn't say anything.

"Fine, I get it." I hold up my hands and read her shirt. "You don't wanna taco 'bout it. Because it's nacho business."

She points one bright blue fingernail at me. "It's *nacho* business."

"Yes, yes, I understand." Irritation creeps into me. This girl is not like anyone I've ever met before.

She stands, pushing aside more than half her food. "I'm ready to start."

I pause, my fork suspended inches from my mouth. It's

loaded with flaky biscuit and lukewarm gravy and it's going to be as delicious as my previous ten bites. "I'm not done."

"You eat like a horse," Brynn whines, flopping back down into her chair.

I take my bite and point the now-empty tines at her plate. "You eat like a bird."

"I don't have much of an appetite this morning." Her words are soft, an admittance. She looks down, to the hands folded in her lap.

"Everything okay?" It's an automatic question.

Her gaze flies up to my face, eyes bulging.

"Forgot. Sorry. Taco, nacho, funny shirt, blah blah blah."

We stand, and I rinse the containers in her sink after she knocks the food into the garbage. She leans an elbow on the counter and watches me. "Please tell your mother I said thank you. It was delicious."

Using a kitchen towel to dry my hands, I inform Brynn she can compliment my mother herself. "She wants to meet Vale Handyman Services newest employee."

"When?"

"Sometime soon."

"Right. Um, okay." She clasps her hands in front of herself, twisting them. "I need to brush my teeth. I'll be right back." She turns from the room. In a moment I hear water running, then the faint sounds of bristles scrubbing teeth. I walk to the living room and look around. There are no decorations, no pictures, nothing to show that a person with a personality like Brynn's lives here.

Weird.

Brynn's silent on the drive to work. She stares out the window, but her muscles are tense. Normally I'm fine with quiet drives, but it's hard with a near-stranger sitting in my truck. Especially one who confounds me as she does.

"Brynn?"

"Hmmm?" She looks at me.

I had no question, really. No reason to say her name.

"What's your last name again?" Lame. I already know it, but I seized.

"Montgomery." She continues to look out the window as she answers.

"Thanks. That will help me when I Google you later." I smile because it's a joke, but to Brynn, it's obviously not a joke. Her head whips toward me, her face pale.

"Hey," I say softly. Without thinking, I reach over and find her, my fingers brushing along the outside of her forearm. "I was just kidding."

She nods, a quick, almost manic motion. "Sure," she says, her voice shaking. "No big deal."

The hand that was touching her goes back to the steering wheel, even though I really don't want it to. I want to keep touching Brynn. I want to sink into her obvious agony and shoulder some of the burden. I don't even know why.

THE NEXT FOUR HOURS ARE SPENT CHANGING LOCKS. THE house we're working on is a new-build, and the homeowner wants new locks now that they are moved in.

Brynn is smart, strong, and a quick learner. Teaching her what to do isn't as hard as I thought it might be. Her eyebrows furrow as she listens to me, and she purses her lips. When she concentrates, the tip of her tongue darts out and rests against her upper lip.

By the time we're done it's later than I thought, and my

stomach is rumbling. I find her finishing the last lock. "Lunch?" I ask her.

She tucks her hair behind her ear and steps back. "Can you check this, please? I want to make sure it's done right."

I reach out, testing the lock, and nod. "Good work. It'll keep the bad guys out." I wink at her, but somehow I've misstepped again. Her eyes cloud with fear. *Dammit.* Every time I open my mouth, I'm saying the wrong thing to her.

She clears her throat. "Lunch would be good."

I find the homeowner and say goodbye, letting them know my mom will send them an invoice.

We head for my truck and climb in. "Where to?" she asks. "I haven't explored much past my house."

"Route 66 diner. They make my favorite sandwich. My mom's best friend works there, and so does your neighbor, Cassidy."

I slow to a stop at a red light and look at Brynn. She's drumming a beat on her thigh with her fingertips and gazing out the windshield. It's not hard to see what Cassidy saw the day she met Brynn, but I see what Cassidy missed. The hollows in her eyes, and the fear that slips through the cracks of her tough exterior. There is far more to her, and I don't think she will ever give it away.

From our handful of interactions I've learned not to ask her personal questions, so if I want to learn about her, I'm going to have to get creative.

"What did you think of today?"

I'm shooting for a casual tone as we get out of my truck and walk to the diner. She's one step ahead of me and gets to the door first. She reaches for the handle, but I'm faster, reaching around her and pulling open the door. She stiffens, looking up at me before stepping in.

"This isn't a date. I can open a door." Her voice is quiet,

matching the volume of the diner. It's late for lunch, and there are only a few people in here eating.

Irritation surges. "It's called basic manners, Brynn. It doesn't mean I think this is a date."

"Sorry," she mutters.

Her apology takes me by surprise. I was expecting a scathing reply.

Snagging one menu off the small hostess stand, I lead her to a nearby open booth. "Let's get you fed. I think you might be hangry," I say, sliding in.

Brynn laughs, and then covers her mouth with her hand. She slides in across from me, dragging the menu with her as she goes.

"You're slipping," I tell her, sitting back and resting my arm across the top of the booth.

She looks up. "What are you talking about?"

"Your tough girl act. It's slipping a little. You just laughed," I point out. "Next you might smile, and then a pig will fly by the window, and who knows what else might start happening."

"Hell might freeze over?"

I shrug. "Anything is possible."

She looks back down to the menu. "I've been known to smile a time or two."

"I'll be on the lookout for that," I tell her, waving at Mary as she comes out from the kitchen. Mary's hands are full, but her eyes grow wide as she takes in the beautiful girl sitting across from me.

I usually eat here alone, or with my mom, sometimes with Anthony, but definitely never with a girl. Not since Desiree. After she left town, Mary informed me she never liked her anyway, and promised next time she'd tell me what she thought about someone. There hasn't been a *next time*, but the way Mary is hurrying over it looks like she's remembering her promise. This ought to be interesting.

"Well, hello there," Mary says when she arrives. She sets down two glasses of ice water and Brynn looks up. Mary grins and Brynn actually has a normal response. She *smiles*.

"Is it cold in here?" I ask, teasing her. Her foot swiftly connects with my ankle.

Mary gives me a curious glance and refocuses on Brynn. "I haven't seen you in here before." She sticks out a hand. "I'm Mary."

"Brynn Montgomery," she answers, shaking Mary's hand. "It's nice to meet you."

Brynn and Mary make small talk, and I try not to fall out of my seat. Since when is this girl nice? I don't know what to do with nice Brynn. Mean Brynn is better. Mean Brynn can be kept at arm's length. Mean Brynn—

"Connor?"

"Huh? Sorry, I—" I shake my head. "Never mind. I was somewhere else. What did you say?"

Mary scrunches up her eyes, like she's trying to figure me out. It's the same face she makes when she's looking at her iPhone.

"I asked if you wanted your usual."

I shake my head. "Monte Cristo this time. Thank you, Mary."

"Umm hmm." She gives me an extra long look before she turns to Brynn.

Brynn holds the menu out to Mary. "I'm not sure where he went just now," she says to her, but she smirks at me. She's enjoying this far too much.

"I think I know where he went," Mary says as she turns to go.

Brynn either didn't hear Mary, or she's acting like she

didn't. "Today was fun," she says, reaching for her straw and pushing the ice around her cup.

"Fun?"

"Yeah. It's useful knowledge."

"I suppose so. You really only need to change locks after you've moved in somewhere."

"Sure," Brynn agrees quickly. I think maybe she's placating me.

"Or you could buy some of those floor alarms like you have," I say as casually as I can, trying not to make eye contact with her. Pushing my straw aside with one finger, I drink from the cup and keep my gaze down. I'm trying not to look interested in her answer. *Nope, I haven't been dying to know why you have that floor alarm ever since it blared in my face this morning.*

When she says nothing, I try again. "Those are pretty cool." *Those are pretty cool?* That might be the dumbest thing I've ever said.

She looks at me, her face blank, but the nearly imperceptible twitch of her lips tells me she's trying not to show emotion. Whether it's laughing, frowning, or smiling is anybody's guess.

I switch tactics. "What do you do for fun? When you're not learning handyman skills from someone as devilishly handsome as me, I mean."

She rolls her eyes, but they look happy. At least if she won't crack a smile, I can see her eyes glimmer.

"Back home, I was a nightclub promoter. I taught a barre class, and I went to Mexico to visit my parents." Her voice gets softer, so I lean in to hear her. Something takes over her whole face as she talks. Wistfulness, I think, and maybe despondence. Fear of her clamming up keeps me from asking why.

"My parents retired to Mexico five years ago. They have a sport fishing tour company, and they take people out and help them fish. They fish themselves, too, and sell it to local restaurants. I loved going, but..." Her eyes lift, meet mine, and it's like there are steel shutters dropping down over windows. Looking away, she takes a deep breath and asks, "What about you?"

Her voice has changed. She is eager to turn the question to me and relieved that she didn't keep talking. Like she caught herself from whatever she was about to say. I start slowly, thinking about what just happened, but soon I'm talking at a normal pace as I tell her about my dad.

"It's hard to see him this way, but there's nothing anybody can do about it. It might actually be more difficult to watch my mom. She has always been caring and nurturing, but I doubt she ever thought she'd have to care for her husband this way."

"In sickness and health, Connor." Brynn tips her head, watching me.

"I know. I just... I don't know." I sigh. How can I say what I mean without sounding like a jerk?

"You wish she didn't have to go through this?"

I nod. "More than anything, I wish he didn't have to. This might sound awful, but," I pause, watching her. I've never said the words out loud, and I'm afraid to now.

Brynn reaches out, placing her hand on mine, and I don't even think she knows she's doing it. "I won't judge." She exhales softly. "Believe me, I'm in no position to."

The warmth of her hand spreads out, circulating through me. Her gaze is kind, her eyes rapt.

"I feel angry at him. His body, I mean. Resentful, too."

One side of her mouth curls up. She squeezes my hand. "That's normal."

"Do you know from experience?"

Her touch disappears, her hand returning to her lap, and she shakes her head. "It's normal to resent what other people do, and the effects it has on you."

"How do you know—"

"Are there any other ways it's affecting you?"

She has barged into my question, and I know what she's doing, but I allow it.

In my mind, I see my house, the blank canvas in the unfurnished living room, the pristine drop cloth. The place looks like it's waiting for an artist to arrive, not like one lives there already.

"I used to paint. On canvas. But he got sick, and the family business needed to be run. It's their sole source of income."

Mary swoops in quietly, sliding our lunches across the scratched table and refilling our waters, then ducks out. I think it means she likes Brynn. The place is nearly empty now, and there can't be much for Mary to do. She would stay and chat, but she wants Brynn and I to be alone.

Brynn lifts a French fry to her mouth. "What did you paint?"

"Everything. Anything. Whatever resonated with me."

"Did you sell them?"

"A few." I hear the pride in my voice. There's an incredible feeling that comes with knowing someone wants your work in their home.

"That's great, Connor." She bites into her sandwich and sighs contentedly. "I didn't realize how hungry I was."

Picking up my sandwich, I take a bite. An idea forms in my head, and I chew on the notion at the same time I'm chewing my food. It might be stupid, and when I say *might be* I mean it definitely is, but would it really hurt to try?

"You can see my work sometime, if you want." Using a napkin to wipe breadcrumbs from my lips, I look at her with what I hope is nonchalance. My insides feel the opposite of that.

She takes another bite and chews slowly. Is she aware that across the booth I am dying a slow, painful death brought on by extreme hope?

She swallows and reaches for her water. "I don't think that would be a good idea," she says, wrapping her mouth around the straw. Her gaze drops to the table, avoiding mine.

She says nothing after that, and I fall silent too. The air is thick and filled with awkwardness. We finish lunch without another word. Our second silent and annoying meal of the day. When I'm done, I hop up and go to the cash register where Mary sits reading a paperback book.

"How was everything, hon?" She takes the credit card I'm holding out.

"Great, as always."

"I like your new employee." She laughs at my confused look and winks. "I called your mom. I needed to get the scoop on who was with you."

"Just an employee," I say, taking back my card and slipping it into my wallet.

"She seems nice. That's all." Mary gives me a pointed look.

Brynn arrives beside me and thanks me for lunch. We say goodbye to Mary and head for my truck.

Mary called Brynn nice.

Nice Brynn put her hand on mine and let me tell her all about my dad.

I really like nice Brynn.

I hope she goes back to being mean Brynn soon.

5

BRYNN

That was close.

What the hell was I thinking?

It's him.

Connor Vale.

Extensive knowledge about the inner and outer workings of a home, and now I've learned his painting skills were honed by a canvas, not a wall.

Today I watched his hands. I couldn't help it. He touched me with them. Twice. And I touched him once when he was talking about his dad. I snatched my hand back as soon as I realized I'd done it.

Our afternoon job consisted of rehanging an in-cabinet garbage can. It sounded ridiculous to me at first, but Connor explained that the garbage can places too much weight on the brackets and that's why they were bent. He suggested a whole new system where the can rolls on gliders installed on the bottom of the cabinet, and the homeowner agreed. We went to the hardware store for the pieces that weren't in one of the built-in toolboxes in the bed of his truck, and the whole time he was showing me what to do, I watched his hands.

He has strong, deft fingers, certain of their movements. Capable. The skin on his palm, just below the start of his fingers, is slightly hardened. Callused, I guess, but not in the way I've always thought callused hands would be.

His hands are where I focused my fixation, because I cannot afford to have my gaze travel anywhere else. It was hard enough to sit across from him at lunch. Holding his gaze when I wanted to hide my face? That took strength. There's one surefire way to make him look away from me, but then he would know about my past, and that's completely off-limits. It's a good reminder to keep my head down, make as much money as I can until fishing season comes to Mexico and my parents can make enough to help me get out of the country.

As much as I don't want to be, I'm intrigued by Connor. A man who takes over his family business, even though he is good at the same thing he happens to be passionate about? He's a genuinely good person. Of course, I already knew that. I did step out in front of his truck and he hasn't said a word to me about it.

It's still dented. I noticed it but didn't say anything. I don't have the money to pay for it right now anyway. I'll have to ask him about it soon. I have no idea how much something like that will cost.

What a way to start my temporary life in Brighton.

I've managed to cause an accident, get a job doing something I know zilch about, and anger an old man. On the plus side, Cassidy said hi to me when I was out front watering Ginger's flowers, so I guess my first impression didn't terrify her too much. I said hello and nodded, still not sure how friendly I should be. Friendliness comes naturally to me, and snuffing it out takes work. I was voted friendliest person and nicest smile in high school, something Connor would probably never believe. It's also how I got my old job. Club-promoters don't scowl.

It's funny what tragedy will do to a person. The smiles it will rob you of, both present and future. The present smiles can't be summoned, and future ones never surface for fear of perceived happiness. *How dare I be happy?*

One of his letters said exactly that. I know he hates me, but I don't think he understands how much I hate myself.

I'VE MADE TOO MUCH.

I wasn't paying attention, and I poured the entire package of noodles into the boiling water. I could save it and eat it again tomorrow night, but I don't want to. I want the company of another person. Someone else's thoughts, the sound of their breathing, simply existing nearby me.

Cassidy comes to mind first, because she's closest. But, no. I can't deal with Brooklyn.

Definitely not Connor. There's only one person left.

He opens the door as I'm walking up. "What do you want?" Walt grunts.

"World peace. The end of child hunger. I could really go for a sea salt brownie if you have one."

He makes an undistinguishable sound and waves a hand at me.

I make my way up his steps and hold out the spaghetti. "I hope you're hungry."

He eyes the food. "I already ate."

"The early-bird special is more of an afternoon snack, don't you think?"

Walt cracks a small grin, and I'm close to one myself. Breaking through his wall feels like a victory.

He backs up, holding open his door. "Come in, then."

I step in, and the harsh click announces the door being closed behind me.

"Wasn't expecting anybody," he mutters, shuffling around. He picks up a folded newspaper, stares at it, then sets it back down in the same spot.

"Please, Walt, don't worry about clean-up. I made too much spaghetti and I want to give you some. I don't need to stick around." I look down at the containers, one for the noodles and one for the sauce I made last night, and stay in my spot, just a few feet in the doorway.

From the outside his house looks to be only a few hundred feet bigger than mine, but on the inside, it feels smaller. Muted photographs in thin wooden frames hang from the living room wall, and his recliner takes up a large portion of space. The lamp on the table beside his chair is huge, and so is the old TV in the corner of the room. Knick-knacks and a full collection of encyclopedias are crammed onto a dusty bookshelf.

Without thinking I walk forward, balancing the food in one hand and running my hands over the spine of one encyclopedia. "My grandparents had these."

"Oh yeah? Did they have the whole set?" There's pride in his voice.

"Nope. But my grandma wanted the whole thing." I can still hear her voice, telling my grandfather that an incomplete set was like leaving out a letter of the alphabet.

Walt walks over. He smells funny, kind of like how my grandpa smelled. It's hard to describe. Back then, when I was fifteen, the only word I could come up with was *old*, which wasn't very nice, or descriptive. Nine years later, and I'm still struggling for a better word.

"My wife didn't care about the books. I did, though. Guess I just like to know things."

I hold the spaghetti out to Walt. "Here you go. I just wanted to drop this off."

Walt takes it, walking away. "You might as well stay. The kitchen table has a motor on it, so we can't sit there, but there's a table out back that's clear."

I follow him and see he wasn't kidding. An actual motor is on the table, lying in parts on top of newspaper. At least he gets points for protecting the table first.

I want to say something about having a motor in the kitchen, but I keep my mouth shut. If I tease him now, I might never be invited back.

He stops for a fork and napkin, then I follow him out of the screen door. His backyard is an even bigger mess than the inside of his house. Random junk lines the fence, and in the very back is a large piece of ride-on equipment. I have no idea what it is, except to say it looks like it could flatten someone into a pancake if it drove over them.

He directs me to sit down at the glass-top patio table. Steam rises from the sauce when he takes the lid off the container. He leans in, sniffing, and tells me it smells good.

"Was that a compliment, Walt?" I grin. I can't help myself. Reaching over, I add the sauce to the noodles for him, then sit back.

"Don't let it go to your head." He takes his fork and sticks it in the spaghetti, spinning it around. "It might taste like crap."

I can only laugh. My food doesn't taste like crap. I'm a lot of things, but a bad cook is not one of them. He takes a bite and doesn't say a word, but he does take another bite, and I'll accept that as praise.

His hair is cute. It's mostly white, but there are strands of black here and there, a lot more salt than pepper. The top is messy. He has a bit of a natural wave, and his combover isn't terrible. It's obvious he's hiding some baldness, but it's a suitable hairstyle. Anything that's not a toupee is acceptable.

He's chewing now, and he looks at my shirt.

"Why does your shirt say that?" He points a gnarled finger at me.

I wink at him. "It's nacho business."

He glowers and takes another bite. "I don't get it."

"It's a play on words." I look down, pointing at each word as I say them out loud. "Now do you get it? Taco is like saying *talk* and nacho is like saying *not your*. Ha ha ha?"

Walt wipes his mouth with his napkin and places a palm on the table. "In my day, jokes were funny."

I'm pretty sure I can't even picture Walt making a joke. He's the crankiest man I've ever met, but I have a feeling he has a soft spot located somewhere deep down in the murky depths.

"Walt," I say, looking out at his yard while he finishes up. "What is that?" My chin is tipped toward the big piece of machinery in the yard.

"It's a roller."

"A...roller?"

"That's what I said."

"Why do you have a roller in your backyard?"

"Why did you get dropped off this afternoon by a guy in a work truck?"

I peer at Walt.

His lips draw together in a straight line, and I see a petulant fifteen-year-old somewhere in there.

Smacking the table with one hand, I say, "You are such a busybody."

He pulls back his shoulders, his expression offended. "I am not, young lady. It is my right to know the comings and goings of this neighborhood. Keeps everyone safe."

I arch an eyebrow. "Does everyone know you've appointed yourself the role of sentinel?"

Walt ignores me. I stop myself from asking him to turn up his hearing aid. He's not wearing one, and he may not think my joke is funny.

Using his hands on his armrests, Walt pushes himself out of his seat. "Thank you for dinner."

I stand too. "Anytime." I get the feeling Walt is finished with our visit, so I gather the empty sauce-smeared container, nestle it in the noodle container, and stack the lids.

Walt leads me back through his house and opens his front door. I pass him, stopping on the wooden planked porch.

"What's your favorite meal?" I ask him.

"Sour beef and dumplings."

I wrinkle my nose. "I've never heard of that."

He shrugs. "It's a Baltimore thing. I grew up there."

"Shouldn't you like crab cakes then?"

"I like those too."

I step down, pausing on the bottom step. "Maybe I'll learn how to make sour beef and dumplings."

Walt sticks his hands in the pockets of his pants and nods. "I haven't had that in years."

"If I make it, will you tell me about your wife and the roller?"

Walt eyes me, giving me a long look. "I suppose so."

"It's a deal, then."

I retreat to the sidewalk and walk home. Instead of rushing into the house before someone can talk to me, I sit down on the rocking chair Ginger has on the front porch. I spend only two minutes out there, listening to the breeze pushing the pine needles, the cawing of a nearby hawk, and Brooklyn shrieking in her backyard.

This place is only temporary, but at least it doesn't suck.

THIS TIME, I'M READY FOR HIM.

I'm dressed, fed, and properly caffeinated. No more embarrassing messy-haired wake-ups and piercing alarms.

I can tell he thinks the door alarm is silly, but he wouldn't think so if he'd read one of the letters. The last one was the final straw for me. I was gone within a week, and the more I think about it, the more I realize I had no reason to stay anyway. My parents don't live in the country, and my friends hit the road when everything started to spiral even more out of control. Nothing weeds out fake friends like crisis. And, it turns out, they were all fake, almost every last one of them.

The letter came, sounding even more desperate and irate than the others. I'd dealt with his resentment and anger plenty of times before, and I let him say what he wanted because he needed someone to hate. I swallowed his hate, let it sink down into my stomach and join the guilt that never left me, and the two ate at me like battery acid. The real person he hated was his wife, but it would hurt him to acknowledge that, so I shouldered his hatred for her. It was the very least I could do, and it made me feel the tiniest shred better to do something, *anything*, for her. But the last letter had a fantastical, hysterical edge to it.

"Maybe one day I'll show you what it feels like to have everyone you love taken away," he'd written.

The previous letters went on and on about the terrible human being I was, how one day I would pay for my sins. He called me party-girl, drunk, waste of space, scum, and that I should be in the ground instead of his wife and baby. Even though I know I didn't hit them on purpose, even though I know I never had a choice, I agreed with him.

I've gone over and over the moments leading up to that one second, and I see how many things I could've done differently to not be there, driving down the street at the exact moment that Amy Prince decided to end her life, and the life of her four-month-old, Samuel.

Every day I'm haunted by what happened. It took only one second to alter the course of my future. To change Eric Prince from a loving devoted new father, into a vengeful, bitter man. His grief morphed, became malignant with hatred, and he changed the narrative. All he needed was ammunition, and I had it in spades.

Never mind the eyewitnesses who saw Amy Prince do it.

Or me, who met her eyes just as she decided to go through with it.

Or the hours of questioning by the police, only to be released without charges filed.

Eric Prince needed someone to hate, and naturally, that fell to me. I really didn't mind, until his letters turned threatening.

So, yeah, the door alarms are necessary. I think I did a good job of covering up my destination when I left Phoenix, but I can't be too careful.

After locking my front door and double-checking it, I wait for Conner in the rocking chair. The outdoor sounds are the same as they were last night, but the bird is different.

Not a hawk, but twittering, sweet birds. Prey, instead of predator.

I hear Connor before I see him. His truck growls, turning a corner. The dent is still there, not that I really thought it would've disappeared overnight. I feel bad that I put it there. Connor thinks I was careless and froze in a moment of danger. What would he think if he knew the truth? He might fire me, and he definitely wouldn't like me.

Assuming he does.

I mean, I think he does. He's kind, and his eyes stay on me for a few seconds longer than they should sometimes. Yesterday he was patient with me, and very good about where his body was in position to mine when he was showing me how to do something. But still, there were those touches that came when he sensed my pain.

He pulls up to the curb, engine idling as I come down the steps and walk to his truck.

"Good morning," I say, opening the door and climbing in.

"Hello," he says, reaching for a thermos. He takes a drink and offers it to me. "Coffee?"

I stare at it until he sets it back down in the cup holder. I'm still not used to his kindness.

"I don't have cooties." He shifts into drive and the truck eases forward.

"You might," I respond, instantly piqued. What is it with this guy? Why am I so ready to charge into battle with him?

"I promise, I don't," he mutters, looking both ways before turning left onto the main road.

"Anyway," I say brightly. I'm determined to be at least civil and keep my job. "How was your night?"

His jaw clenches. He reaches up, his hand gripping his jawline, and rubbing in a circular motion.

"What happened?"

He lets out a short, frustrated sound. "Nothing happened. Again. Night after night, I stand in front of my canvas, and nothing happens." He shakes his head, his brown hair bobbing around with the movement. "Maybe I've lost it."

"Lost the..." I pause, confused. "What? Talent? I don't know if you can lose talent."

"Not that, exactly. The muse. The excitement. I have the desire, but not the capacity. It's like...like...having all this love and nowhere to put it." He glances at me from the corners of his eyes. His cheeks pink when he catches my gaze and he looks back to the road. "Sorry," he says, clearing his throat. "You're probably praying I stop talking about feelings and say something manly."

I snort. "Hardly."

"You don't like manly men?"

My nose wrinkles. "No. I mean, yeah, if that's how they are naturally. Not if they're only pretending to be manly."

"Who pretends to be manly?" A deep 'V' forms between his eyebrows.

Connor takes a turn and sunlight streams through my side of his truck. I look down at my legs. A spot I missed shaving last night glints in the light. *Damn knobby knees.* I almost always cut myself and I never do a good job.

"Well," I say, running a finger over one knee. "The guys in the clubs I promoted, for one. They were never who they said they were. They would only be what they thought the ladies wanted them to be. Like a chameleon, or an octopus."

"Do octopuses change color?"

"Yes."

"Hmm." Connor grabs the coffee and sips from it. "I'll just have to take your word for it."

"I'm reliable."

He takes another turn, this time onto a smaller road. "Yesterday at lunch you said 'back home,' but you didn't say where."

My thigh muscles contract. Should I tell him the truth? Would that be like giving him one more piece of the puzzle? In the end, I decide it's safe. He still doesn't know my real first name.

"Phoenix."

He nods. "Sounds about right. So you're moving up here for good then?"

This, I cannot tell him. He might fire me. Who wants an employee with a set timer? My mind is racing, concocting something on the fly, when he sends me a wary glance.

"Never mind. I may not want to know."

I slump in my seat, the air gone from me. "I'm sorry," I whisper, and I am.

I'm sorry I can't be more normal.

I'm even more sorry I can't stick around and form real relationships.

6

CONNOR

I'VE NEVER BEEN HAPPIER TO WAKE UP AND KNOW IT'S Saturday morning.

I don't mind working. I like it, actually. Fixing things is kind of cool, and there's always something new to learn about a house. A house has secrets, and they won't be revealed until it breaks or you go looking for them. Yesterday we were removing wallpaper from a living room, and discovered three layers of previous wallpaper. Brynn was amazed by the styles as they came off, trying not to laugh at the paisley in shades of brown. It ended up being an all-day job. Thank god I remembered my portable speaker, because Brynn doesn't talk much. When I turned on today's hits from the app on my phone, she flashed a disbelieving look at me.

"You don't like the top forty?" I asked.

"Too mainstream."

"What do you like?"

"Everything," she replied, then she climbed onto a ladder and learned how hard it is to peel off decades-old wallpaper.

That answer didn't shock me. She was like that all week. Evasive. Non-committal. At first, it irritated me. Why the hell does she act that way? I didn't understand. By Friday, I expected it. Anything different would've been shocking.

We stopped at the bank at the end of the day, and I pulled out cash from the business account. When I put the envelope in Brynn's hand, she slipped it into her purse and leaned her right shoulder against the truck window, murmuring her thanks. Her chest filled up with air, which she let out slowly and silently. Her relief makes me curious. Other than the obvious reason of food and rent, why does she need the money so badly?

I roll over and punch the pillow, groaning. I can't lay here and think about her any longer. She's a puzzle I don't have the pieces to.

My phone dings on my nightstand. I grab it and see Anthony's name and a message.

Let's hit some bags after I'm done fishing.

I'm not surprised he's already at the lake. It's his Saturday morning ritual. I respond, telling him I have to go to my parents' house first. My mom needs a reconciliation of all the work I did this week so she can start the billing. Normally I do that on Friday nights, but last night I wasn't in the mood.

I'm not much in the mood now, either, but it has to be done. At least today I'll be able to slam my fists into some bags and break apart the tension that has my body and mind in knots.

Knowing I have something to look forward to forces me from bed. I get ready slowly, enjoying not having to be somewhere at a specific time. I drink coffee on my back porch, wearing only my jeans, while the sun spills onto me and warms my skin. As hard as I try not to think about Brynn, my thoughts wander to her.

What does someone like her do on the weekend? Not only is she new in town, but she's reclusive. It's not like I could go to Chambers, the best bar on Main Street, tonight and find her there. She wouldn't go shoot pool, she wouldn't go to a movie, she wouldn't go...anywhere. I can't picture her feeling comfortable in any of those places.

I shake my head, hoping to push Brynn and her blue eyes from my mind. She's certainly not thinking about me. I need to stop thinking about her.

WHEN I GET TO MY PARENTS' HOUSE MY MOM IS ALREADY AT her desk, waiting for me. She leans back in her new, ergonomic desk chair when she sees me.

I sink down onto an old folding chair she keeps in the corner. "Hey, Mom."

"Hay is for horses!" She chuckles at her terrible joke.

I shake my head and try again. "Hello, Mom."

She grins. "Better."

"Where's Dad?" I lift an ankle over the opposite knee and pull out my phone. I need to access the log I keep in my notes app to remember where I was and how long. Sometimes all the homes blend together. *Except for this week, when Brynn was with me. I was hyper-aware of every step I took, every breath, every glance, every everything.*

My mom frowns at the ceiling, to where their bedroom is on the second floor. "He's lying down."

"Everything okay?"

"He didn't sleep well, and neither did I, as a consequence." She lets out a heavy breath and shrugs. "Oh well. Gotta keep on moving, right?"

I smile. My mom hates complaining. I think she was a saint in a different life.

"Mary called me and told me about Brynn." She grins impishly. "She said Brynn seemed like a little more than an *employee*, and that she's so pretty it's hard not to stare. She also said that you had no problem staring at her."

Never mind. She's not a saint. She's nosy, and so is her best friend.

I keep my gaze on my phone and act like what I'm doing is important. "I'll be sure to appropriately thank Mary the next time I see her," I say calmly to my screen.

"Oh, please." Mom waves her hand. It catches my attention and I glance away from my phone. "Don't be so touchy," she admonishes. "Brynn's beautiful, so what? You can still do your job."

When I don't say anything, she narrows her eyes at me and leans forward. "Right? You can do your job? Brynn won't be a distraction to you?"

I stare at her for another moment, drawing it out, and then palm my forehead with a dull smack. "I just forgot I didn't do half my work this week because Brynn blinked and I was captivated."

Mom gives me a dirty look, searching her desk for something to throw at me. A balled up napkin is all she has that won't cause real physical damage, so she tosses it. It bounces off my knee and lands on the ground. I grab it off the floor and shoot it into the wastebasket beside her desk.

"Mom, I'll be fine. Trust me. Brynn has less interest in me than she does one of the pine trees in her backyard."

She gives me a disbelieving look.

"I promise," I add, thinking of the way she practically

leaped from my truck when I dropped her off yesterday afternoon, after we were done for the day.

"Well, now I want to know why she doesn't like you. She would be lucky to have you, and I'm not just saying that because I'm biased. You're handsome, loyal, talented, responsible..."

I let her go on for fifteen more seconds. After the week I had with Brynn, I need an ego boost. Although considering the source, I'll have to discount fifty percent of what she said due to motherly preference.

I hold up a hand. "Okay, Mom, I get it. I don't think it's that she doesn't like me. Brynn is kind of like Fort Knox. She plays things close to the vest, and that includes most emotions, almost all thoughts that aren't snarky, and a lot of details about her life. She's told me some things, but..." I shake my head, recalling what she's revealed, but I remember more what she hasn't told me. *Like why she came to Brighton and how long she's staying.* "She doesn't give much away, that's all I'm trying to say."

Mom nods slowly, thinking. She pulls a piece of hair from her cheek, tucking it back into her low bun. "Sounds to me like Brynn experienced something very painful."

The thought sends a jolt through me. In my mind I see and hear the piercing door alarm.

Brynn is scared of something. Or someone.

"Shit," I mutter. "You're right." My head rocks from side to side sluggishly as I work through how I missed something like that. She doesn't have an attitude problem. She's hiding behind a wall, erected to keep her safe.

My mom's voice breaks through my thoughts. "Whatever happened to make her that way, I'd say she came into luck meeting you."

I look at her, eyebrows pinched. "What do you mean?"

"You're the best person I can think of to help coax someone from their hiding spot."

I nod as though I'm agreeing, and change the subject to the reason for my visit. I can't talk about Brynn anymore. The thought of someone hurting her sends anger coursing through me, and the thought of consoling her makes me want to jump in my truck, speed to her house, and show her how she deserves to be touched.

Clearly, that's never going to happen.

"Connor? What do you want?"

I draw in a quick breath, surprised Brynn answered her phone. "How is your weekend going?" For real? Did I just say that? *Lame with a side of extra lame.*

Brynn knows it too. The line is quiet for a moment, then she sighs. "I think you called me by accident."

"Maybe," I respond, tipping my head back against my truck's headrest. My ego is a tad bruised. Can't she sound at least a little pleased to hear from me on a Saturday?

She snorts. "Connor, did you mean to call me or not?"

"No," I say, lying through my teeth. "But since my butt decided to dial you, I figured I might as well make conversation."

Oh my God. No. No no no.

All I can do now is pray she doesn't think I'm making a crude junior-high joke about bodily functions.

"Ummmm okay?"

I have to recover from this. "I'm on my way to do something manly." I glance at my boxing gloves as I say it.

"Oh yeah?" She sounds completely uninterested.

Even though she hasn't asked me what manly thing I'm on my way to do, I tell her anyway.

"Boxing?" Her voice perks up. "Is there a boxing place around here?"

"The Knockout," I answer, stifling my surprise. "It's about twenty minutes away, in Still Creek."

"Oh." Her excitement disappears. "That's too far."

Right. The car thing. Another question I want to ask but I'm too afraid.

"Maybe I could take you there sometime?" I offer.

"I'll check out their website. Maybe I can take a lesson..." Her voice drifts, dropping low on the last words.

"What are you up to this weekend?" I ask, changing the subject.

"This morning I walked to the grocery store. I needed ingredients for a new dish I'm trying."

"Oh yeah? Need a tester?"

"Not unless you want to eat sour beef."

I make a face. "Sour...beef? Why would you eat sour meat?"

"It's not for me."

My whole body tenses. There's someone else? Have I missed something entirely? I hate having to ask the natural follow-up question. "Who's it for?"

"Walt. It's his favorite."

Angry breath pushes through my pursed lips. "Brynn, I told you about him. He's crazy."

"He is not." Her volume increases, and she sounds irritated. "I ate dinner with him last Monday. He is lonely, and grumpy, but he is not crazy."

"Brynn, you just arrived here. Take my word for it, okay?"

"No. I make my own judgments, and I say he's sane."

I smack the heel of my hand on the steering wheel. Why won't she listen to me? Wouldn't most normal people hear the word *crazy* and automatically turn in the opposite direction?

"A few years ago, Walt backed his car into a young girl's car at a red light. *On purpose.* They both got out of their cars, and Walt told her that she deserved to be hit, and then," I shake my head, angry I even have to say this part to her, but if she's not going to listen to my warnings, she needs to hear this. "He told the girl he was going to rip her fucking heart out."

True to form, Brynn is silent.

"I'm sorry," I finally say.

Her response shocks me, but maybe it shouldn't. I should be shocked at myself for expecting her to be anything other than oppositional.

"Were you there?" she asks, her voice angry.

"No, but—"

"Did you talk to Walt about this yourself?"

I sigh. I see where she's going, I just don't want to follow her there.

"No."

"Have a nice day, Connor." The line goes dead.

"Fuck," I yell into the empty space and toss my phone onto the passenger seat. Why is it everything I do manages to push Brynn farther away? I thought we could at least be friends, but now I don't even see that happening.

I press down a little harder on the accelerator. Now I really need to punch something.

7

BRYNN

My phone rings again, and I'm certain it's Connor, calling to apologize.

He should be apologizing. To Walt, not me. Connor doesn't know what he's talking about, and he's as bad as the people who judged me. Doesn't he know you can't judge a person based on what other people say about them?

"What?" I snap into the phone.

"Honey?" My mom's voice is fuzzy and far-away sounding.

"Mom, sorry." I switch the phone to my other ear and hold it up with my shoulder so I can wash my hands before I start cooking. "How are you?"

"We're good. Your dad and I are good. How are you?"

"I'm..." I bite my lip, looking down at my hands and the towel I'm using to dry them. "Hanging in there."

"Brynn? Are you sure?" Worry creeps into her voice.

She's always worried, especially since what happened, but never enough to come home. They came right after the accident, but eventually they had to go back to Mexico. Their livelihood is there. When the press coverage became brutal, I was happy they were gone and didn't have to see what I saw, but I wouldn't mind a hug from my mom, or my dad ruffling my hair.

After that last letter, it's imperative they stay gone.

"Mom, I promise, everything is good. I found a job and I'm saving my money. Everything is going according to plan." When I first told her what I was going to do, she agreed I needed to find a new path. I guess that's the bright side of having adventurous parents.

"A job? That's great, honey. Where?"

I laugh softly. "You'll never believe it, but I'm working with a handyman."

She snorts disbelievingly.

"I know. It's not quite what I'm trained for, but it pays cash."

"Enough said." She laughs. "It's probably not the worst thing in the world for you to learn how to take care of things around a house. How is your boss?"

Connor... He's a lot of things. Handsome, for starters. He's better-looking than any of the men I met in clubs, and I've met more than my fair share. Connor doesn't have to try, and I think that's what makes him even more attractive. He has gentle eyes that crinkle when he's trying to hear everything I'm not saying. I know how he holds back, how he tries to ask questions that aren't intrusive, but will tell him something about me. Like I'm an orange that has already been emptied of juice, but maybe he can squeeze a bit harder for the last few drops.

"He's okay," I manage to say through all my thoughts. "Sometimes it's hard not to say too much, you know?"

"I'm sure it is, especially for someone as personable and outgoing as you."

I bark a bitter laugh. "You're talking about someone who doesn't exist anymore."

"Hidden, maybe, but I bet she still exists."

"Survival changes a person, Mom." So does character assassination.

"Honey," Mom breathes the word, her voice full of emotion.

The pain of it sweeps through me, thickening the base of my throat and filling my eyes. "Can we stop talking about this, please? Tell me about you and Dad."

Swallowing, I will myself to calm down while my mom talks about their days fishing. She's telling me a funny story about a woman who tried to wear wedges on their last tour, and how she refused to take them off when they told her the shoes wouldn't be good for being on a boat.

"I think she was picturing cruising on a yacht, and she really should've listened, because she wasn't too happy when she fell and got her white pants dirty."

I laugh along with my mother, grateful for the distraction. My dad calls for her, his deep voice saying something about the next charter, and she tells me she needs to go. As much as I don't want to, I tell her I love her and say goodbye.

I miss her more than ever right now, but I'm happy she and my dad are far away. I didn't tell her about the last letter. In the beginning, when the first letter arrived, she begged me to tell the police what Eric Prince was doing. I refused. He'd already been through so much, how could I put him through more? He needed time to get over his suffocating anger.

The last letter was the push I needed to do what I should've done right after the accident and I was cleared of wrongdoing. *Get the hell out of that place.* In a handful of months, I'll disappear, and Eric Prince will hopefully find his peace.

In the meantime, I'm going to learn how to make sour beef and dumplings, despite what Connor might have to say about it.

WHEN I'M DONE COOKING, I MAKE MY WAY OVER TO WALT'S.

I'm only halfway up his front walk when he opens his front door. He's wearing a gray newsboy cap and a frown.

"What do you want, Bryan?"

I stop in my tracks and point at him. "No sour beef for you." Pivoting, I march through his yard. I'm not serious, but it won't hurt for him to sweat.

"Wait, wait," he calls after me.

I turn back around and raise one eyebrow at him. "You want to try that again?"

He releases a short, exasperated breath, but does what I've asked. "Hi, Brynn." He says my name like he's a teenager being forced to greet an old aunt who insists on kissing you right on the mouth.

I grin. "Much better. Come on." I wave him my way. "I'm having you over for dinner."

Walt fishes his keys from his pocket and locks his front door. Although he's slow down the stairs, he's still in good shape, both mentally and physically. It appears, anyway. What Connor told me earlier has been nagging at me. There has to be some truth to what he said, even if it was probably turned backward and inside out by the time he heard it. Similar to my case.

The truth: I ran over a mother and her infant in my car and killed them.

The lies: I was drunk and the mother wasn't committing suicide.

Cassidy steps outside as we walk up.

"Brynn? Walt?"

Her astonishment is as plain as the color of dirt.

I wave. "Yep. Hi."

She looks at Walt, her eyes growing wider, then back at me. I see her unease. I've seen it in myself enough times to recognize it in others.

"Everything okay?" she calls out, her hand finding the porch railing. She leans on it and keeps her gaze on us.

Walt rolls his eyes and makes an annoyed grunting sound.

"Everything is fine, Cassidy. Thanks for checking." I send her a goodbye wave, and open the door for Walt. The aroma of vinegar, beef, and ginger wafts out.

He shuffles in and stops. "Sorry about that," he says, turning back to me.

"It's okay." I shut the door and lock it. "But you do have some explaining to do." I walk past him to the kitchen.

Walt follows. "It sure smells good in here."

Opening the fridge, I pull out a pitcher of tea and set it on the counter. "No dodging, Walt. If we're going to be friends, I need to know why people are wary of you."

He leans a forearm on my kitchen counter and watches me move around. I take two plates from a cabinet, along with forks and knives, and set them at the small table against the wall. He tries to help me with the pitcher of tea, but I shoo him away. When everything is ready, I motion for him to sit down, and take the one opposite him, where the second setting is. Without a word, I fill his plate with his favorite food.

Loading his fork, he takes a bite, and I see his eyes close

in pleasure as he begins to chew. "It's just like Daisy used to make it."

My eyes feel hot at the corners, and I have to blink back the sudden urge to cry. I take a bite too, finding it's actually pretty good. The name doesn't do the dish justice.

"How long were you and Daisy married?" I ask cautiously.

He takes another bite and wipes his mouth with a napkin from the stack at the center of the table. "Forty-six years," he answers, taking a sip of his iced tea. "Daisy was a good woman. We'd only been married a year when I was called to Vietnam. She wrote me, and I wrote her. It wasn't easy, you know? But we managed." He shrugs and falls quiet. Maybe he thinks I don't want to hear more about it, but I do.

"What else?" I ask. "Did you have kids?"

"Daisy became pregnant soon after I came back from the war, but she miscarried." He shakes his head, remembering. "She was devastated. After what happened, they told her she couldn't have children. It changed things between us for a while. She became withdrawn, and I was angry." He looks up at me, eyes squinting. "Why am I telling you all this?"

I don't think he's trying to be rude, but his voice takes on that familiar growl.

"Because I asked, Walt, and I'm interested, but you don't have to keep going if you don't want to."

Lifting his cap, Walt brushes his hands over his matted, sparse hair, and sets it back down. "Sorry," he grumbles. "I don't know why I do that." He coughs, and I stay silent, waiting. "We had a hard time of it for a while. She even left me once, but I went and found her. She was at her sister's house. She came home with me, and we were never apart again. Until she got sick, that is. After that, it was swift. Stage four, and all that."

His eyes grow shiny, and I don't ask anything more. I take his plate, which I'm certain is cold by now, and place it in the microwave.

"I'm sure you've heard from your boyfriend about what happened with that young girl," he says while the food is heating. His gaze goes to his hands, folded on the table in front of him.

Behind me the microwave hums. "Connor is not my boyfriend, and yes, he told me about the girl, but I'd rather hear about it from you."

He looks at me gratefully. "I don't know what came over me that day. It was only a month since Daisy had died, but that's no excuse. I could blame it on the war too. That kind of training never really leaves a person, but that would be an excuse also. The truth is, I just flipped a switch that day. She pulled up too close to me at a red light, and I stopped thinking and started acting."

"Did you really say...those words to her?" The microwave beeps, penetrating the thickness in the air.

I take a few extra moments retrieving his food, but really I'm giving him the chance to answer without having my eyes on him. By now I know what he's going to say, he doesn't need me to watch him say it.

"I wish I could tell you no, but that wouldn't be the truth."

I take the steaming hot food to him. He thanks me as I place it in front of him.

"Everyone makes mistakes, Walt." I gesture to the plate. "Eat."

He takes a bite. "You're awfully young to be so wise."

"I'm not wise, not by a long shot. I do know that I'm not

saying another word until you eat your favorite food while it's hot."

He obliges. When he finishes, we take our glasses and pitcher to Ginger's outdoor table. Unlike Walt, Ginger's table is in the yard, not on the porch. Each seat has throw pillows and the table has built-in cup holders.

When we get settled, he turns his shrewd eyes on me. "Are you ever going to tell me why you're hiding?"

I look away, up to the tallest nearby pine, where a squirrel runs up the length of the trunk. "Who said I'm hiding?"

"It takes one to know one."

I bring my knees into my chest and rest my chin on the crevice they form. "Walt, I had a good life, or what I thought was a good life. I see now that it was empty. Full of meaningless nights and friends, and then something happened." I falter, my throat thickening as soon as the thought enters my brain. "Something really, really bad, and even though it wasn't my fault, it felt like my fault. Then things got even worse. My whole life was torn apart, examined, and conclusions were drawn. I withstood it far longer than I should have. Finally I decided to leave it all behind."

Walt is quiet, watching me. Could he possibly understand?

"So you came here?" he asks.

"For the time being."

He nods once. "This is a stop along the way?"

"Um hmm."

"Does your boyfriend know that?"

I look at him, irritated, and he gives the look right back to me. "I already told you, Connor is not my boyfriend. He can hardly stand me." I know this to be untrue, but it's important I tell myself this lie. It helps me keep him at arm's length.

"Have you ever met a boss who picks up his employee for work, and takes them home at the end of the day?"

I shake my head, my lips moving into a small smile. "Do you spy every day, all day?"

Walt, for the first time since I met him, laughs. "There isn't much for an old man to do."

We chat for a little while longer, but not about heavy things. He tells me about Connor's dad before he got sick, and I tell him about my parents' business. He asks a lot of questions about deep sea fishing, most of which I cannot answer.

When his eyes begin to droop, I wrap up leftovers for him and walk him home.

Back at my place, I clean up the kitchen, get ready for bed, and double check the door alarms on both the front and back doors. I climb into bed, thinking of tonight and wish I'd thought to take Walt's picture while he was here.

When I leave, I want to remember him.

8

CONNOR

"Anthony, turn that shit off." I reach over and swipe the volume on his phone. "You have terrible taste in music."

Anthony stands in front of an open tool locker, picking out what he needs to pull the dent from my fender. He pauses what he's doing just long enough to flip me the bird, then goes back to choosing tools.

"Don't act bad because you think you beat me yesterday." His voice bounces off the metal and floats back to me. I'm sitting on a stool beside my truck. I'd offer to help, but I know nothing about cars.

"I did beat you yesterday," I argue, watching him scratch the back of his head. He reaches in for one more item, then pulls away and nudges the closet door closed with a booted foot.

"Next time will be different," he warns, dumping the contents of his arms on a bench. I wince at the loud sounds of metal clanging together. He picks through it, grabbing what he needs first, and points the tool at me. "Next week you might not have a reason to spar."

"Something tells me I will," I grumble, shifting on the uncomfortable wooden stool.

"Is Brynn really that bad?"

"Yes."

"I think you're just that affected by her."

I shoot him my death glare and he holds up his hands. "Hey, man, I'm just calling it how I see it. You haven't been this upset by someone since *you know who*."

I look off to the other end of the shop, where one guy has the hood of a car lifted and he's bent over the engine. Another guy rolls around under a truck.

"Don't be pissed," Anthony says, right before he plugs in a machine and applies it to the dent.

"I'm not." Not at Anthony, anyway, for pointing out what I already know. I'm pissed off at myself for even caring about Brynn in the first place. She has given me no indication I should be developing feelings for her. I've been alone for a while, and I miss being with a woman. In walks a gorgeous, mysterious girl and I want her. It's pretty simple to understand, almost like a fucking equation.

Anthony looks at me from his seat in front of my truck. "Go get lunch for us. I'm hungry, and you're paying." It's a fair trade, considering he's not charging me to do this work.

Reaching into his pocket, he tosses me his keys. I leave the shop and find his car in the small parking lot. Anthony is shorter than me, so I have to adjust the seat and mirrors. That should make him really happy.

I'm craving Chinese food. When I get there, I place an order for takeout and sit on a red leather chair near the hostess stand, waiting. The big front window looks out onto an intersection. While I wait, I alternate between reading an article on my phone and looking out the window. The fourth time I look up, I see light blonde hair across the street. Shoulder-length. A tank top I've never seen before hugs every inch of her chest, but it's too far away to read the lettering on the front. As I watch, Brynn chooses a table and smiles at a server when they come over. She places an order without taking the menu being held out to her. When the server walks away, Brynn pulls a book from her purse and opens it.

"How much longer?" I ask the hostess, who I'm pretty sure is also the owner.

"Ten minutes," she answers, wiping down a menu and inserting it into the cubby connected to the side of the hostess stand.

"I'll be back," I mutter, getting up and pushing open the door. The little bell rings behind me.

The Walk sign says Do Not Walk, but there aren't any cars coming, so I cross anyway and jump up the curb onto the sidewalk. Brynn's back is to me. She tucks a stray hair behind her ear and turns a page.

"Hi," I say, touching her shoulder.

She shrieks. Snatches my hand. Her nails dig in, and hot pain flashes across the top of my hand. She looks up at me and lets go.

"Fucking hell," she whispers angrily. Fury fills her eyes, her jaw flexes.

But I saw it.

Before she was angry, she was terrified.

"Brynn, I... Fuck, I'm sorry." Cautiously, I step around the table and grip the top of the blue wrought-iron chair.

Her eyes are on the table, so I dip my head, trying to get her to lift her gaze. She won't. Instead, she places an open palm on her chest and takes deep, even breaths. She finishes, and only then does she meet my eyes.

"I'm sorry, Connor. I overreacted." She looks shaky, but I think she means it.

Reaching down, I pick up the book she dropped when she grabbed me, and hand it back to her. She stows it in her bag without a word. The server comes back, drops off her tea and sandwich, and leaves again. Brynn pours cream into the hot tea, and one sugar. I've never seen anybody have tea like that.

Reaching for the spoon, she stirs the swirling brown and white mixture. "I went to London when I was fourteen." A faint smile dusts her lips. The spoon clinks the side of the cup. "My mother is impetuous, and my father is a sucker for her whims. So, off to London we went. I saw a woman having tea this way, and I tried it too." She lifts the cup to her lips. "Since then, I've never had it any other way."

"Can I sit?" I ask, hoping she won't shut me down.

She motions to the empty seat, and I restrain myself from leaping into it. It'd be great if I could show some self-control around this girl.

"What are you up to? Just out and about on a Sunday afternoon?" Brynn takes a bite of her sandwich and waits for my answer.

"Grabbing lunch. My best friend, Anthony, is fixing my fender. He's not charging me," I add when I see her concerned look. "Save your pennies. Honestly."

She evaluates me with those penetrating eyes, then I guess she decides I'm telling the truth, because she sits back and takes another bite.

"Did you make sour beef yesterday?"

She nods.

"And? How was it?"

"Not as bad as you'd think from the name of it. Actually, it was pretty good." She smiles, a grin that reaches her ears.

She's stunning. I've never seen anybody like her.

"Walt loved it. He said it tasted just like his wife used to make it."

I bristle at the mention of Walt but keep my mouth shut. I don't want a repeat of yesterday.

"So, you have a nice time with Walt?" I keep my tone light.

Brynn knows what I'm doing. She smirks. "Yes. He only threatened me once. Wait, no." She touches the pad of her pointer finger to her chin and pretends to think. "Two times. Yes, two times. I almost forgot that second one."

My eyes narrow, and she snickers.

A waving hand across the street gets my attention. It's the woman from the Chinese food place. She's holding our lunch in one hand and pointing to it with the other.

I get up from the table and tell Brynn I have to go.

"I'll pick you up in the morning. Unless you've suddenly obtained a car."

Her eyes flicker down to her lap. "Uh, no."

Lucky me.

"Brynn, I'm curious about something."

She shakes her head, exasperated. "What?" Her attitude is back.

I nod to her chest. "I want to know what your shirt says, but the lettering is kind of at an awkward position."

She looks down at herself. "It says 'Sorry I'm late, I didn't want to come.'"

"Very funny." I'm trying to look anywhere but at her chest. It's a feat of gargantuan proportions. Her breasts are big, full, and round, and I'm trying desperately to forget the cleavage she has when she leans forward.

"Connor?"

I swing my gaze to her. "Yeah."

She points across the street. "Your lunch?"

"Right." I step away. "Tomorrow morning."

"Tomorrow morning," she echoes.

This time the crosswalk has a Walk sign, so I hurry across it and into the restaurant.

"Sorry, sorry," I say to the woman up front. She hands me a plastic bag filled with take-out boxes and knotted at the top.

"It's okay. Food can wait when there's a pretty girl." She winks at me.

I take the bag and hand her my credit card, grunting my agreement. I can't make small talk right now. I keep seeing Brynn's eyes when she was scared, and I'm trying to commit it to memory. The storm was back. Desire to paint slams into me.

It has been months since I felt this rush, this all-consuming need to be home and in my living room, paint-brush in hand.

Moments like this must be seized.

Anthony will just have to deal with his hunger for a little while longer.

YES.

This is what I've been waiting months for.

Just when I thought my talent had dried up, leaving my soul desiccated, inspiration struck.

Taking a step back from my canvas, I study my work. It's not finished, but it's close. Close enough to make me want to run through the streets wearing these paint-spotted jeans. No shirt, no shoes, just as I am now.

Someone knocks on my front door. I answer it, knowing damn well who it's going to be.

Anthony strides in, flashing me an irritated look. He tosses my keys at my chest. "Hey, asshat. Good thing I had a banana stashed behind the counter in the shop."

I tuck my keys into my pocket and ignore him. Taking a step back, I point at the painting.

He walks to the canvas and stands in front of it. Anthony whistles, low and slow. "You got your mojo back."

I stand beside him and take it in. "For an afternoon, at least."

He steps closer, running his finger in an arc just an inch off the canvas. "You should call it Eye of the Storm."

He's right. I've painted an eye, and within the eye are waves and dark sky. The skies are shades of gray, from medium to dark, and the waves are a mix of color. Lines of yellow, light blue, and forest green run alongside the blue of her eyes. *Brynn blue.*

"What are you going to do with the center?" Anthony looks at me.

I go to the kitchen and grab two beers. Handing him one, I confess I have no clue yet. The idea came to me only eighty percent finished. The problem is that I don't know what the center is. What is the iris? What is Brynn's fear? I have an urge to paint it white, or maybe outline it in black. The painting represents Brynn's fear, but when I picture it, I keep seeing the innocent color, the absence of dark.

Anthony points to the painting with the mouth of his bottle. "Did Brynn inspire this?"

"Yeah. That's what her eyes look like when she's angry." *And fearful.* But I don't want to say that. Fear seems personal.

"How do you already know what she looks like when she's angry?"

"What does that mean?"

"Just seems to me that anger isn't something that comes out this early. Aren't people on their best behavior right after they meet? And even more when that person is an employee?" He shrugs. "I don't know, man. She's either nuts, or you hooked her."

"She's not a fish, dipshit."

"Obviously, but you get my point, right?"

What Anthony is trying to say is something I can't wrap my mind around. There's no way Brynn likes me. When I'm not probing her for information, I'm insulting her new friend, or scaring the daylights out of her. I'm sure she's counting the minutes until I provoke and exasperate her again.

"I understand your words, Anthony, I just don't agree with them."

"Alright, fine. You say she doesn't like you. You say she has an attitude that's mostly aimed at you—"

"She befriended Walt Jenkins! Of all people." I blow out a disgusted breath. "Can you imagine how hard that must've been?"

"Pretty fucking hard, all things considered, but here's what that tells me: She's capable of kindness, just not toward you. And why not?"

I open my mouth to respond, but Anthony continues. I don't think he wanted an answer in the first place. "She's not nice to you because you frighten her. Not like *Boo!*"—he holds up his hands and yells the word—"but more like you agitate her. She doesn't like what she feels when she's around you, and it makes her mad at herself." Anthony taps my chest in time with his next words. "Not. At. You."

"Do you have any more of what you've been smoking? It must be pretty good."

"Actually, yes, I do have some good shit, but I'm not sharing." Anthony tips up his beer and drains it, then hands me the empty bottle. "Here's what you're going to do. Tomorrow, when you spend the entire day working around her, read her body language. Does she turn toward you? Does she lean in when you talk? Touch her once, in a non-sexual way, and watch how she reacts."

Anthony grabs his keys from the coffee table, stuffs them into the pocket of his jeans, and walks to the kitchen. "You better not have eaten all that food you went out for," he says on his way in.

The sounds of a refrigerator door opening and closing reach me from the kitchen. A cabinet slamming. Plates moving around, then finally the dull, clunky sound of a microwave door shutting.

I sit back on the arm of the couch and look at the painting. Anthony thinks I should spend more time watching Brynn's non-verbal cues. This whole time I've been trying to get her to be more verbal, but maybe she doesn't communicate that way. All my questions, direct and indirect, the thinly veiled probes for information met with icy responses, may have been for nothing. I wonder if she's been talking all along?

Light pink.

I sit up quickly and hurry to the shelf where I store all the paint.

Brynn's iris is a soft, sweet, innocent light pink.

9

BRYNN

THINGS HAVE BEEN WEIRD.

Connor has been different.

He hasn't been asking me questions, for one. This worries me. Did he search for me online? Did he find Elizabeth Montgomery? It has been months since I typed my name into a search engine. I learned my lesson the hard way. *Never look for something you can't handle finding.*

If he knows, wouldn't he have said something by now? Maybe not. Maybe the sight of me sickens him. Maybe he can't believe he has been spending his days with someone whose face appears next to cringe-worthy headlines.

Baby Killer!

In Our Hearts, She's Guilty.

Could She Have Stopped?

I'm sickened by the thought of Connor reading these things about me. Today is day four of Connor being quiet. What will it bring? I'm so sick to my stomach I nearly text him and tell him not to pick me up this morning. If it weren't for the money, my intense desire to get the hell away from society and hole up somewhere, I'd do it. But, no. I have to stand even when I want to fall. My future peace depends on me.

Connor picks me up with his usual greeting. "Hey, Brynn."

"Hello," I say, stiff.

Last week he peppered me with questions the second I had my ass in his passenger seat. *How was your night? What did you do?* Today, like the past three days, he says *nothing*. Not even about my shirt, which I chose because I thought it might make him laugh.

He must know.

We get to the first house on his list. We're cleaning gutters, which really sucks. Connor takes two ladders from the truck, one by one, and sets them side-by-side along the front of the house. He climbs up the first, I go up the second one, and he tells me to pick out the biggest debris. We work for forty-five minutes, switching ladders when one of us is done with our section, and it's silent. Horribly, terribly silent.

When I'm finished with my section, I climb down, but you know what happens when you're upset? You get sloppy. On the last rung, I'm sloppy. Instead of stepping down, my foot catches on the side of the ladder. I fall, luckily not far, right onto my ass. At least it was onto soft grass and not the pavers three inches away.

Mortification consumes me. For almost an hour I've been picking large twigs from a gutter while vomit-inducing headlines float through my brain, and now I'm on the ground. I'd love to stand up, laugh at myself and keep going, but I can't. It's too much, all of it. My heart is heavy and it hurts, and the horror floating through my mind has weakened me.

I squeeze my eyes closed and will the burning heat in

them to go away.

"Brynn?"

More heat. A warm hand rests on my shoulder.

I look up to see Connor, his knees bent, level with me. His eyes hold concern, but more than that, they hold emotions I didn't expect to see from him. Dismay and anguish, care and uncertainty.

It fucking wrecks me.

I hate the tears, the way they are big and fat and roll down my cheeks, the next one coming right after the last. Everything inside me needs this cry, but every ounce of self-preservation screams at me to stop.

Connor wraps his arm around my shoulder and pulls me in. His hand brushes the top of my head, running through my hair and tucking it behind my ear.

The front of his shirt smells like body wash and salty sweat, and I have to stop myself from clinging to it. I want his warmth, his touch, his voice. I want someone to love me despite the tragedy that now defines me. These are all things I can't afford to have, much less want, but in this moment that doesn't matter.

"Connor," I say through my tears.

"Shh, Brynn." His thick, deep voice floats down to me. "It's okay. You don't have to explain. I don't need to know anything."

"Thank you," I whisper.

When I'm down to only sniffles, Connor stands and helps me up. I'm embarrassed, and I don't want to look him in the eyes, but after all that, I feel like I should. I force my gaze to his and find him smiling.

"What?" I ask tentatively.

"Surely not everybody was kung fu fighting."

Laughter bubbles up. I glance down. Using two fingers, I

pull the T-shirt away from my body and read it upside down. "I thought you might find this one funny." The admittance makes me feel bashful.

"You wore that for me?"

Shit. "I... No. I mean..." Where are my words? Why can't I talk? Why can't I turn on my ice queen defense and leave this conversation frozen in a glacier?

Connor takes a step backward and turns, climbing two feet up his ladder. He stops and looks back at me. "Remind me to tell Anthony he was right."

I cover my eyes from the sun and look up at him. My eyes still hurt from crying. "Right about what?"

"Things people say when they aren't talking."

I'm not sure what he means, but I know I need to discourage him. One day I'll leave. End of story.

"I didn't wear this shirt for you, you know. Not really, anyway." Even to my own ears, my rebuttal sounds weak.

"Come on up here," Connor calls. He's nearly to the top of the ladder by now. "There's somewhere I want to take you. Help me finish this so we can go."

So I do. We flush the gutter opposite the downspout. Connor double-checks it has proper flow, and I bag the debris and tie off the opening. Thank goodness for thick gloves.

When we're finished, Connor tosses the bag into his truck bed, along with our gloves.

"Do we need to stop for lunch?" I ask when were settled in his truck.

Connor leans over, reaching into the backseat. He stretches out, his chest brushing my upper arm. The hair on my neck stands straight up. A spot near my heart twists. I want to touch Connor, run my fingers through his light-brown hair, sweep my lips across the small, flesh-colored scar on his neck.

My desire, my want, my *need* is strong, and with Herculean strength, I abstain. Tucking balled fists in between my knees is the only way I can stop myself.

Connor rights his body, pulling a little ice chest from the backseat. He plunks it down between us.

"Are you okay?" he asks. His eyes glint like he's happy or amused. "Your cheeks are pink."

"I'm fine," I snap, instantly feeling bad. "What's that?" I ask, my voice much nicer. I point to the cooler.

"This"—Connor says, opening the lid and peering inside—"is lunch, courtesy of my mother."

The smell of bacon wafts up. "Are you saying you're sharing?"

"Maybe, but you better be careful. If you're not nice, I'll share with someone else."

"Who?" I ask. I didn't even think about there being someone else in Connor's life. How stupid of me. He's... Well, he's everything. One day, someone will be very happy with him.

Heat rips through me at just the mere thought of this person, whoever she is. It's not fair or right, but when is anything? I can't have Connor, so instead I'll hold onto the envy I feel. In ten years I'll think of him, and I know in ten years I'm going to be as jealous as I am today.

"I'm teasing, Brynn. Of course this is for you and me. Unless you want me to share it with Walt."

"The way to Walt's heart is definitely through his stomach." I laugh. "He calls me Bryan sometimes, and he hates my shirts. He also told me my spaghetti tastes terrible, and he was only being nice when I took it over to him and he said it wasn't awful. He was kidding though."

Connor replaces the lid on top of the cooler and buckles his seat belt. "He sounds like a real treat," he mutters, looking in his mirror before pulling out onto the road.

I grab the cooler and place it on the floor next to my feet. "He's like one of those sour candies. Once the first layer wears off, what's below is actually sweet."

Connor looks at me. "Sounds like someone else I know."

"I'm sour all the way through," I joke.

"I bet you taste pretty sweet on the inside," Connor says, then loses all his cool. He blushes and stammers. "I didn't mean it like that. Not that you're not sweet or anything, because I actually think you are, but the way it sounded, it was just, um, not how I meant to say it and—"

I laugh. Embarrassment is adorable on Connor.

"Chill." I touch his shoulder. "It's fine. I know how you meant it."

I take back my hand and set it right where it should be. On my lap. My lap is a safe place.

Maddeningly, Connor falls silent. Like my fall and subsequent tears never happened, like he isn't taking me someplace and sharing lunch with me, like embarrassing words didn't just fall from his mouth like rocks in a landslide.

I slump into my seat and try not to think about Connor, which is impossible because we're sharing the same oxygen at the moment.

Closing my eyes, I lean my head against the window, watching the trees go by.

"WHAT DO YOU THINK?" CONNOR ASKS, LIFTING TWO sandwiches from the cooler. He hands me one.

We're sitting on a brown wooden bench, the food between us. In the distance are rolling hills, and though they look small from here, I know how massive they really are. In between the hills and us are trees that fade into scrubby brush, and beyond that lies desert. To the southwest of us are the red rocks of Sedona.

"It looks like a new box of crayons, but the crayons in the middle are red and orange and pink, and the ones surrounding it are shades of brown and green."

Connor stares at me.

"What?" I ask, conscientiously wiping my mouth, even though I haven't taken a bite of food yet.

"Would you mind if I painted that? The crayon box like you described?" He bites into his sandwich.

I do too, and then I moan, in this utterly embarrassing way, but Connor only laughs. I take another bite and raise my eyes to the sky.

"She uses jalapeño bacon and avocado." He eats a quarter of the sandwich in one bite.

"Holy crap," I say, swallowing. "Please tell your mom how amazing this is."

"You can tell her yourself." He reaches into the cooler and pulls out two small bags of chips. "I told her you'd come over tomorrow after we finish. My parents would like to meet you."

"Okay, yeah. Sure, that makes sense." And it does. It makes perfect sense to a sensible person, but I'm me, and in me there is now sheer terror. It's mixing with the jalapeño bacon to create something that feels foul in my stomach.

"My mom will be happy. She has been on my case since the day I told her I hired you."

Let's just hope she doesn't watch the news and have a great memory. She can have one of those things, but both is bad news for me.

I reach into my bag and grab a handful of chips. Opening my sandwich, I toss them inside and close it up. I take a big, amazing, crunchy bite, and notice Connor staring at me.

"What?" I ask, around my mouthful.

"Did you just put chips in your sandwich?"

I finish chewing and swallow. "Have you never seen anybody do that?"

"No. Does it taste good?"

I roll my eyes. "Tastes like ass. That's why I do it."

Connor smirks. "Because you love the taste of ass?"

I laugh and reach over the cooler to shove him. "You're crude."

He grins. "You're rude."

I nod. "Very true."

"The sky is blue."

"Nope. No way." I shake my head. "I'm not playing a rhyming game with you."

"Come on," Connor says, standing. He slides the cooler over on the bench to where he was sitting and settles down in its place. He faces me. I sigh, lifting my left foot and setting it on the bench. I turn to him and hug my knee into my chest. The toe of my right foot dangles in the dirt below us.

"Finish your bite," he says pointing at the small square I have left.

"I'll try with all my might." I smirk and pop it into my mouth.

"Quit putting up a fight."

I swallow. "You better shut your mouth, unless you want a smite."

Connor slaps his knee and laughs silently. "Sometimes you're so cold, I think I'll get frostbite."

My mouth drops open, and my shoulders shake with laughter. I lean in, playfully shaking my head. "I think you have a hero complex, the way you play white knight."

He grins, leaning in too, and he's closer than he has ever been to me. My heart hammers, my breath is shallow yet somehow still deep enough to burn my throat.

"I bet right now you wish you could take flight," he says, in a quiet, ragged voice.

I can only manage a whispered response. "All I wish for now is that this fire won't ignite."

I think it's my admittance of the fire's existence that brings Connor in closer. He rubs the tip of his nose against mine, and my chest splinters.

"Red light?" he murmurs, his question softly hitting my lips.

My whole body feels like it's rising on tiptoe, wanting his touch so badly it hurts. I just want, for one fucking second, to feel good.

"Green light," I say, and I move my mouth to his.

He kisses me back, in a way I've never been kissed. He takes his time, runs his hand over my cheek, pushes my hair behind my ear and trails his fingers back down along my jaw. He tastes like I know I do, spice and salt, mixed with the wetness of tongues and skin.

I'm overwhelmed by him, by his touch, by how much I missed being wanted by someone.

We both pull back, sucking in air. Our eyes stay locked, my chest heaves in time with his.

"Brynn—"

"Stop." I put out a hand. "Don't say anything. Please just do that again, and again, and again, and again." I lower my knee so it's no longer between us and clutch my hands to my chest as I say it.

Connor doesn't say another word. He pulls me in, and this time I'm flush with his chest. He kisses me like I asked, and then his lips move to my jaw, my neck, and back up to my lips.

When his lips are on me, everything that hurts floats away.

I am Elizabeth Brynn Montgomery. I'm not a baby-killer, and I'm not running away. I'm a twenty-four-year-old woman who's letting a man use his hands and lips to make her feel good.

I'm normal again.

10

CONNOR

THINGS I'VE LEARNED ABOUT BRYNN SINCE I WOKE UP
yesterday:

1. She's a pretty crier. She doesn't scrunch her face like
most girls do.

2. She's amazing at the rhyming game.

3. Her lips taste even better than I thought they would.

I DON'T KNOW WHAT SHE'S GOING TO BE LIKE TODAY, BUT I'M
excited. Yesterday, after our intense thirty-minute make-out
session on the bench, we still had to work together all afternoon. We didn't kiss again, but things were a one-eighty
compared to earlier in the week. She smiled at me and playfully bumped into me, and I touched her waist when I
needed to step around her.

I'm in such a good mood, I even wave at Walt as I pass
his place. He scowls, but that's to be expected. I'm early to
get Brynn, and when I left my house, I texted her and told
her I was coming early. She told me she was finishing up
some exercise. Maybe it's that barre thing she mentioned

before? I'm not sure how someone does that in their home.

I park in her driveway and walk up. She pulls open the door for me before I can knock on it.

"Hey," she says, her lips curving into a small smile as she bites her bottom lip.

From the living room comes a woman's voice. "What's that?" I ask, confused.

"That would be the exercise I mentioned. It's a yoga channel I found on YouTube. I just love this woman." Brynn leads the way to where her laptop sits open. She presses a button and the voice stops. I peer around her at the screen.

My eyes pop and my mouth hangs open. "That looks like it hurts." The woman on the screen is bent at an angle and has her arms intertwined beneath her. "Is she pregnant?" Her stomach is round and big, and she looks pregnant, but it's a gamble to ask the question.

"Yep. She looks amazing." Brynn picks up the computer and closes it. "Sometimes her husband will do a video with her. He's funny. I think he used to play professional soccer. She mentioned it once, in an older video."

"Her hair is very red."

She grabs a piece of her hair and tugs. "I thought about dying my hair like hers once." When she says it she gets that faraway look I've come to recognize.

"I like your blonde hair." I reach for her, but she steps away.

"I need to take a quick shower. I'll be right out." She hurries down the little hallway and into a room, quickly shutting the door behind her.

My frustrated sigh fills the room as I let some of my excitement go. I should've prepared for this. Why would Brynn fall into me so easily? Did I really expect her to completely change her behavior, just because we kissed? I sit down on the couch to wait for her. A paperback book lies on the side table, probably the same one she dropped when I scared her last weekend. I grab it and look it over.

The cover shows a girl carrying a shopping bag in a city scene. She wears big sunglasses and has red lips. It doesn't look like Brynn's style. Maybe it's Ginger's, though I can't imagine her reading this either. I open it and see a note written on the inside flap.

Elizabeth, you really know how to throw a party. This is the book I told you about. Shots are on me next weekend.

Ginger must have picked this one up at a rummage sale. I chuckle and flip to chapter one.

"What are you doing with that?" Brynn's voice is hard.

I look up. She's standing at the opening to the hallway, wearing a white tank top and bright yellow shorts. If I'd only heard her voice, I would've thought she was angry, but seeing her face, I know what she really feels is panic.

"Nothing." I toss the book on the table with too much force, and it skids off like a rock skipping across water.

Why does Brynn look like that? Is this her book? Why is it addressed to Elizabeth?

She grabs the book from the floor, fingers curling around the spine. She grips it so hard her nail beds become white.

"Ginger is a funny lady. Yard sales are her favorite." I stand and point to the book. "She probably picked that up from someone who had a daughter home from college."

"Right," Brynn says, her voice shaking.

"Are you ready?" I ask, trying hard to sound normal.

"Umm hmm." Brynn walks into the kitchen and grabs her purse. When she comes back, the book is gone.

"Plain white shirt?" I ask, trying to thin out the thick air.

"I wasn't sure what to wear to meet your parents. Most of my shirts have something snarky or a cuss word."

"An accurate reflection of your personality," I say, teasing her. Brynn offers a stiff, perfunctory smile.

"Hey." I reach for her. She lets me pull her closer, but even against my chest, she's rigid. "What's wrong? Is this about yesterday?"

She shakes her head. "No. Maybe." A strangled sound comes from her. "I don't know. I shouldn't have done that yesterday. We can't do that again. It's going to mess things up."

"What is there to mess up?"

Brynn steps back from me. Her face is sad. "Can we stop talking about this, please? I can't handle it right now."

"Yeah, I guess." I turn, leading the way to the front door and opening it. Brynn locks the door, and I climb into my truck. Cassidy is out front, putting Brooklyn in the car. We exchange a wave, and I see her say hello to Brynn.

Brynn's response is lukewarm. A halfhearted wave, a poor excuse for a smile. Cassidy is the nicest, most trusting person I've ever met, and I bet she wants nothing more than to be friends with Brynn.

Join the club, Cassidy.

We work the rest of the day in awkward quiet. If unspoken thoughts were pieces of furniture, they'd be lying haphazardly between us, and I'd trip over every single one. What's more annoying is that things were fine this morning, until she saw me with that book. Whatever sent Brynn into a tailspin has to do with that.

Or maybe it's this mystery person.

Elizabeth.

I'M NOT SURE HOW SHE'S GOING TO ACT THIS EVENING.

She's been tense all day. She dropped a wrench two inches from my toe. She helped me install a garbage disposal, if helping really means sticking your head under a sink and barely moving.

We've finished up at the last house, and we're headed to my parents' place. Her nails click a rhythm as she drums her fingers on the armrest of the door.

"Doing okay over there?" I throw out the question because *oh my god* it's weird in here. It's killing me.

The worst part is that now I know a different side of her and I can't stop thinking about that. She makes little pleased sounds in the back of her throat when I kiss the soft skin just behind her earlobe, and I'd give anything to hear that again. She tastes like rays of sunshine and cherries and peppermint, and basically everything I've ever tasted and liked.

She's so beautiful, and she wears her hurt right out in front of her. I want to assemble the hurt into a ball and throw it off a cliff, but I can't do any of that because she won't let me into her space. Not literally, and definitely not figuratively.

"I'm fine," she says, curt.

Truth be told, I'm starting to get pissed. Why can't she just say what's on her mind? It's a good thing my parents' house is around the corner, because I'm two seconds from pulling a Brynn and letting her know just how pissed off I am.

We pull into the driveway, and Brynn does the weirdest

thing. She leans forward, peers out the windshield, and smiles at the house.

"This is adorable. I love the river rocks and wood beams. It's like a cabin, but...not. I don't know."

She gets out and meets me at the front of my truck, next to the garage.

"That would be my dad's work." I reach out and smack the smooth surface of a stone. "He created this facade. It took forever, arranging it all so it fit together nicely."

"Did you help?"

I eye her. It's the nicest tone she's had with me since I picked up that book. In my head, I've been referring to it as Pandora's box. "Yes. That was years ago, when I was in high school. I was less than thrilled to be helping him."

My mom had guilt-tripped me into staying home from camping with Anthony's family and helping my dad. If I'd known only eight years later my dad would be sick, I wouldn't have made her talk me into it. If only I could go back in time and say yes every time he asked me to do something with him.

"You want to go in?" Brynn has walked a few feet away, closer to the front door. She waits for me to catch up. I stride past her and lead her inside.

"Mom? Dad? Brynn and I are here."

"Connor, we're out back," my mom shouts, her voice sailing through the house.

"Come on," I say, grabbing Brynn by the hand as I go. If she's having a reaction to me touching her, I can't tell.

The sliding glass door is wide open. We walk through and out onto the screened-in porch. Mom sits with a magazine in her lap, and Dad is in the chair beside her.

"Well, Brynn. We finally get to meet you." Mom sets down her magazine and stands. She's smiling at Brynn and holds open her arms. I'm not sure what Brynn's going to do. I think she's made it perfectly clear she's not one for invasion of personal space or strangers touching her, but of course Brynn doesn't do what I think she'll do. She steps into my mom's open arms and gives her a squeeze. My mom rubs her back a couple times. Dad's eyes meet mine and I shrug.

Brynn lets my mom go and when she pulls back, she lets out an embarrassed chuckle.

Mom grins. "You needed a hug, didn't you?"

Brynn nods.

I can't help the irritated stream of air that escapes my lips. I've been around her all day and very available for a hug. What the fuck?

Mom puts her hands just below Brynn's shoulders. "It's nice to meet you, Brynn. Connor has stayed very tight-lipped about our new employee." She gives me a pointed look. "I'm going to grab the peach iced tea I made this afternoon."

She leaves, and I introduce Brynn to my dad. He tries to smile at her, but it's more of a bare-teeth growl as he attempts to make his facial muscles work.

Brynn doesn't miss a beat. She smiles happily at him, bending at the waist and taking his hand. "It's lovely to meet you, Mr. Vale. Your handiwork on the front of your house is stunning. It took my breath away when Connor pulled in. Thank you for hiring me. I needed this job very, very much."

Tears prick my eyes and I have to look away. Fucking stupid. Why would watching Brynn show such kindness to my dad make me emotional? I'm probably just shocked she's capable of kindness. Yep. That's what it is.

He responds slowly, telling her thank you. "Connor needed help. I'm glad he found you." It's my dad's voice, but the words don't sound like his words. They are thick, like his tongue is too big for his mouth.

Brynn winks at him. "I'll try to keep him in line. It's hard though. He nearly broke my toe today when he dropped a wrench next to it."

My mouth falls open.

Brynn laughs. "Okay, maaaybe it was me who dropped the wrench next to Connor's toe." She makes a funny face and my dad laughs. The asinine tears return, pricking the backs of my eyes. *Dad hasn't laughed in a while.* Why don't we make him laugh more? Mom is preoccupied with his care, and I'm running the family business, but that's no excuse.

Mom returns then, carrying a glass pitcher and four blue plastic cups nestled inside one another.

"What's so funny out here?"

"Brynn," Dad says.

"She's funny and a good hugger. Sounds like a keeper." She gives me one of her looks over the pouring of the first glass of tea. I roll my eyes and reach forward, taking the glass and handing it to Brynn.

"Tell me more about the business," Brynn says, sipping her tea.

The sun dips lower and sneaks across the porch, bursting through Brynn's golden hair and making it shine. Her throat bobs as she swallows and I have an urge to press my nose to her neck, taking in her sweet scent. I've never responded to a kiss the way I did to Brynn's yesterday. This girl has something I didn't even know I was missing because I've never had it before.

Mom launches into the story of Vale Handyman Services. "There I was, pregnant with Connor, when David came home and said he'd been let go. He told me not to worry, that he had a plan. And he did. It started out with just a few houses, and then I made flyers and attached them to every public surface I could find. Business was booming after that, and it hasn't stopped since."

"That's great." Brynn nods and smiles. "American spirit and ingenuity."

Mom leans forward, and places bent elbows on the table. "What about you? How did you end up in Brighton?"

I lean forward too. Am I finally going to learn something about Brynn?

"Just looking to get out of Phoenix. Summers are hot, and I wanted some cooler temps." She shrugs one shoulder. "That's about it."

Liar.

My mom knows Brynn isn't telling the truth. I can tell by the way her mouth twitches, but she leaves it alone. She's the one who suggested Brynn is afraid of something, and she probably knows not to push the subject with her.

"Like most people," Mom says, going along with her story. "I swear this town shrinks by half in the wintertime." She gets up from the table and looks at Brynn. "I hope you're staying for dinner. I didn't confirm with Connor, but I made enough for four."

Brynn gazes at me. I can't tell from her look if she wants to stay or run.

"Sure," she says, switching her eyes back to my mom. "Can I help you?"

Mom says yes, and Brynn gets up.

"Hey Brynn," I say, before she disappears into the house. "Why don't you tell my mom all about your sour beef and dumplings."

She looks back at me, shooting daggers with her eyes. I laugh, knowing I've just forced her to tell my mom about her friendship with Walt.

"Quit pestering that girl," my dad says, when my mom and Brynn are gone. "She likes you, you know."

I snort. "It doesn't feel like it." I take a drink and set down my cup.

"She does. She looks at you when you're not looking at her."

Huh.

"I've never noticed," I murmur, swiping my thumb across the drops of iced tea sliding down the outside of the cup.

"That's because you aren't looking." Dad grunts a laugh. His face muscles strain, trying to assemble into the right formation to show laughter, but they only manage a partial expression.

I bite my lip and try not to show any sadness.

Mom comes out a few minutes later, Brynn behind her. They set food and plates down on the table.

Brynn is happy and calm, breezy and chatty. She asks my mom questions and makes my dad laugh three more times.

I have no idea who this girl is, but I know I like her.

The question is, who will she be once we leave?

11

BRYNN

I SHOULDN'T HAVE DONE THAT.

Being myself was the worst thing I could've done.

Someone who's savvy, who remembers her endgame, would've declined dinner. She wouldn't have let the familial warmth cloud her judgment the way I did, but it felt so good to be hugged by Connor's mom. Watching a smile struggle onto his dad's face felt like the best gift in the world.

I wasn't always this frightened, anxious person. I used to be vivacious. That's what my old boss called me. I had moxie, and I was fun. I created a scene inside the club that made people want to be there, having what I was having because if they had what I was having, they could be as happy as me.

For a little while tonight, I was me again.

We're in Connor's truck now, on the way back to my place. We pass through the bigger streets, come to life with the collective exuberance only a Friday night can create. Crowds of people hang out on the stadium-style concrete seats of the amphitheater. Teenagers laugh and playfully shove each other. Families push strollers, and couples hold hands.

Connor must notice me taking it all in, because he says, "We could stop if you want."

"No," I say quickly. I've been too happy tonight, too carefree. I'm way past the limit of happiness I'm allowed in one day.

"Okay," Connor says, and I can tell he's trying to cover the hurt in his voice.

"It's not you, Connor." My voice is low. I feel awful.

"Right," he says, but the word is empty.

We arrive at my house, but I don't get out right away. There's so much I want to say and so much I cannot say. I'm searching, trying to find a spot somewhere in the middle where I can land safely. Trouble is, I don't think that exists.

I turn to look at Connor and find him watching me. His eyes flicker over my face and down to my neck.

"Can I paint you?"

I jump at the sound of his voice. "Why...why would you want to do that?"

He lifts his chin and closes his eyes. "For me to paint, I need to feel certain things. Emotions. I use my hands to communicate those emotions, and when I'm around you, I have enough emotions to carry me through three paintings."

He opens his eyes and looks at me.

"I guess what I just told you isn't *why*. That was my need to paint. I want to paint you because you're beautiful. I want to make sense of you, and I don't know how else to do it. You're a mystery. A question mark in human form."

"You can paint me." The words tumble from me, and as I say them, I see how this is the perfect solution to my problem. I can't tell Connor specifics, but if this will make him

happy, help him make sense of me, then I'm a willing partic-
ipant. I want to be understood.

Connor licks his lips and bobs his head. "I'll pick you up
tomorrow afternoon. Is that okay? Do you have plans?"

I give him a derisive look and he chuckles. "I don't know,
maybe you have plans with Walt."

"Actually, I do. I'm taking him lunch and then I'm going
to help him with his backyard."

Conner's eyebrows pull together in confusion.

"He has junk everywhere," I explain. "I can be ready by
five."

"Then I'll be here at five."

Small butterflies take flight in my stomach. *Connor is
going to paint me.*

I reach for the door handle. "So I'll see you tomorrow?"

Connor's eyes me tentatively. "Can I kiss you
goodnight?"

Another thing that's a bad idea. "Yes," I answer, ignoring
the internal chiding happening in my brain. Will it really
hurt anything? Just one more kiss?

I let go of the handle and move over, so I'm closer to the
center. Connor takes my face in his hands. Just when I think
he's going to kiss me, he starts talking.

"Don't attack my mouth like you did before. That was so
embarrassing. For you, I mean. Not me. I was the victim—"

I squeal and smack his arm, and then he kisses me. His
lips are soft and strong, giving me what I need and taking
just as much. I don't want to stop. Not at all. It's Connor who
pulls back first.

"Brynn, what did I say about attacking me? I swear, it's
like you didn't hear a thing I said." He grins playfully.

I narrow my eyes, my breath still coming in pants. "Do

you want to paint your big toe tomorrow? Because you might have to. Turns out I might be busy after all."

Connor snaps his fingers. "That's it. I'll paint my toe with your face as the nail."

My top lip curls. "Ew. Connor, that's gross."

He laughs. "Five o'clock, Brynn. Be ready."

A thought pops into my head. "How should I 'be ready' for you to paint me?"

"Just be yourself. Wear a shirt that tells everyone you have an attitude long before you open your mouth and prove it."

"That's it. I'm getting out." This time I not only grab the handle, I actually open the door. "Bye, Connor."

"Bye, Brynn."

He waits for me to get inside before he leaves. I laugh to myself as I set my stuff down and plug my phone into the charger. It isn't until I'm in the shower that I realize what I forgot.

I climb out, cautious. Now that I've remembered, the danger feels real. Reaching for a towel, I wrap it around myself, ignoring the drops of water from my wet hair that slide down my bare upper back. I creep down the short hallway and to the front door. Using my foot, I slide the door alarm into place. Next, I go to the back door and double check that one is still in place, and then, for good measure, I look under the bed and check the closet.

My towel loosens, falling down my torso as I sit on the end of the bed and take a deep breath.

One day, I won't look under beds. I won't use door alarms. I won't fear a monster in the distance.

"WHAT THE HELL IS THAT?"

Walt wrinkles his nose and looks at the package with disdain.

I shake it. "What does it look like?"

He turns his face away from me. "I don't need those."

"Yes you do, and badly, too. I can see the hair from here, even though you've turned away. They reach out, like tentacles. One day I fear they might be so long they'll poke my cheek."

Walt grumbles and takes the nose hair trimmers from my outstretched hand. "Am I supposed to thank you?"

I grin, happy he has accepted them. It was a gamble buying them for him. "I'll be the one thanking you when you put them to use."

Walt tosses the plastic container on his kitchen counter. "Are you here to help me or nag me?"

I get up from his small table and go to the door leading to the backyard. "Come on. Did you get those heavy-duty garbage bags?" I dropped by two days ago to give Walt a small shopping list for today's project.

"I got everything you asked for, and a couple more items." He points to the side of the house. Containers of brightly colored flowers sit in a row, and beside them are two bags of soil and mulch.

"Flowers?"

"Don't go getting misty-eyed. I'm still a grumpy old man."

I roll my eyes. "Yeah, you can totally be a grump while sitting on your porch and staring at pretty flowers. Let me know how that goes for you."

The work in Walt's backyard isn't easy. He has years of junk piled everywhere. Wooden pallets, plastic five-gallon buckets, various tools strewn about, coils of chicken wire, an abandoned clothesline, and other things for which I have no name.

We're an hour into sorting when I ask him why he has all this stuff.

"I had plans for it all, I guess. Sometimes, things don't go the way you think they will. I'm sure you know that by now, but there's a difference between knowing that, and being on the other side of those unfulfilled plans." He pokes a foot at the short end of a wooden plank. "This is all just unfulfilled plans."

"Do you ever think of fulfilling any of these plans?"

He laughs, a harsh and disbelieving sound. "No, Brynn. Not anymore."

I focus my efforts on filling a bag with wood chips, rusted screws, and other random crap.

"Why don't you tell me what you're running from?"

My hand freezes inside the bag. Slowly I unfurl my fist and listen to the items clatter as they join the contents. We've talked about this briefly once before, but he's asking again. I can't blame him. I'd be curious about me too.

"You don't drive, you don't go anywhere except the few stores that are a couple streets over. You haven't made friends except the Vale boy. Who I saw you kiss last night, in case you're wondering." He gives me a pointed look. "No, I wasn't spying. I happen to have a front window and eyes. That's all."

Despite my upset, I chuckle.

"You're doing a job that doesn't suit you. No offense, and it's not that you're not a hard worker, but you're charismatic. That job doesn't exactly require personality, which you have in spades."

"You're more observant than I gave you credit for." Walt

is more than observant. He takes his observations and turns them into conclusions.

He lifts his shoulders and drops them right back down. "I just call it like I see it, and right now, I see you're dodging my question."

"It's hard to explain." I stand up, dropping the big bag and letting it fall slack against my ankles.

"I've found there isn't much that's hard to explain. You add one word to another and soon you have a sentence. The hard part is everything the sentence doesn't say." Walt slips his hands into his pockets and continues. "When Daisy died, it was easy to think *She had cancer and she died.* The difficult part was saying the words out loud, for my own ears to hear, because it meant a lot more than those six words. It meant I was alone. That my love was gone. That my reason for waking up had closed her eyes for the last time."

My heart lurches. I think I would've loved Daisy.

Wiping my forehead with the inside of my forearm, I look up at Walt. "We've talked about this once already. Something bad happened in Phoenix, and I had a hard time." I shake my head, thinking of just how hard a time I had. "It became clear I needed to get away for a while. Maybe for forever, and here I am."

"Are you in trouble?"

I shrug. Possibly yes. Possibly no. I don't know for certain. The threat of trouble is present, that I know for sure.

"Are you safe?"

"As safe as the next person," I say, trying to turn it into a joke. In my head, I see Eric Prince's angry letters, his blunt, capitalized words.

"Alright, I'll mind my own business. Just let me know if you ever need something."

I draw in a sudden breath, feigning shock. "Walt, do not tell me I've managed to wriggle my way into your heart."

He flicks out a hand like he's shooing my words. "Bah. No way. You're cheap labor and you keep me from having to eat so much cereal."

"I think you mean I'm free labor," I tell him, winking.

He laughs, and we work together for another hour. It's more me working, and Walt arguing about why he needs to hold on to things he can't remember why he bought.

I leave at four, take a shower, let my hair air-dry, and send an email to Darby, my property manager. Walt's questions this afternoon made me want to check in with her.

Connor told me to wear my attitude on my chest, so I pick out a shirt that should make him roll his eyes. I wonder if he'll paint it into the picture. Actually, I wonder what this night will be like at all.

12

CONNOR

THAT FUCKING SHIRT. OF COURSE SHE WOULD PICK OUT A shirt that would say that.

"We're not going straight to my house," I tell her after I read the shirt. *'I can't be held responsible for what my face does when you talk.'* It's funny, actually, but Brynn might not want to wear that shirt to meet Anthony and his new girlfriend, Julia.

She sets suspicious eyes on me. "Where are we going first?"

"I told Anthony we would meet him at Riley's Tavern. I'm hungry and I thought maybe you would be too."

Brynn looks down at herself. "Crap. Okay. I'll be right back."

She comes back out a few minutes later and my heart picks up speed at the sight of her. She's wearing a white sundress, the kind that looks sweet and innocent but the longer you look at it you realize it's deceptively sexy. The red cowgirl boots make it even sexier.

Brynn stops a few feet from the truck and turns in a circle. "Better?"

"Yep," I cough. What the fuck is wrong with me? I've seen a woman before. It's the cowgirl boots. Holy fucking shit.

Brynn hops in and looks at me, wary. "You okay?"

"Um hmm. Just fine. How was your day?"

Brynn squints like she's trying to figure me out, but she lets it go and tells me about helping Walt.

"Is he still being nice?" I ask.

She blows out an irritated breath and lets me have it. "Maybe you should take some time to get to know him. He's a sweet old man and he'd probably be a lot nicer to everybody if they'd just be kinder to him. How you all can continue to castigate a man who's clearly just *lonely* is beyond me."

She falls quiet, and I feel awful. Especially because I'm certain she's talking from her own experience.

"You're right," I say, starting up the truck and driving away. "I'll make an effort. He goes to the diner for lunch on Tuesdays. The next time I see him, I'll make conversation."

Brynn beams. Rays of blinding sun could be shining right from her, that's how happy she looks. "Thank you."

Anything, if you promise to look at me like that again.

"Tell me about Anthony," she says, relaxing into her seat. "What's his story?"

"He's been my friend since seventh grade. Went to college on a football scholarship but was injured and never played again. He came back and started the auto body shop I found myself needing after a gorgeous blonde wandered into the road and I had to swerve to miss her."

She smacks her forehead and groans. "Oh no. Anthony is the friend who fixed your truck? Great. I bet he thinks I'm a lunatic."

"Brynn." I reach over, putting my hand on her leg. Her

dress has ridden up since she climbed in and my hand falls onto the warm, smooth skin of her thigh.

She looks down at my hand and back up to me. Her eyes are watchful, and her chest rises with a big gulp of air.

"Red light," she says, pointing.

At first I think she's talking about my hand on her, but then I look up and realize she means it literally. "Sorry," I mutter, braking harder than I'd like to avoid rear-ending the car in front of me.

When I've regained my composure, I tell her Anthony has been looking forward to meeting her.

"He's on a date tonight, and he asked me if I'd bring you around. He has been seeing Julia for a month and I haven't met her yet."

Brynn tucks her hair behind her ears and nods. "Sounds good."

"Plus you can have a drink and loosen up a little bit. You seem nervous. The painting will be fine, I promise."

Brynn looks out her window. "I don't drink."

"Like, ever?"

She shakes her head. "Nope."

"Sparkling water it is," I say, but my brain is turning this over. She doesn't drink, or drive. Is that why she acts the way she does sometimes? Did something happen related to drinking and driving, something bad enough to make her swear them both off?

She asks me about my day, and I prattle on about what I did. I set up the workspace for tonight, I drove to a place twenty-five minutes away to get some new paint, and then I went to the boxing gym. She's happy to listen, interrupting to ask me questions about the gym.

We get to the tavern and park. Inside it's packed, but Anthony has a booth along the back wall.

"Hey," I call out above the music.

His arm is around Julia's shoulders, but when he hears me, he scoots out of the booth. Julia gets up too, and everyone does that awkward *hello, nice to meet you* thing. Anthony asks me to go with him to grab drinks from the bar. After we place an order, he looks back at the booth. Julia and Brynn have sat down, and now they both lean forward against the edge of the table, talking.

"You didn't say she looked like she stepped out of the pages of Sports Illustrated." Anthony punches my shoulder. "I prefer brunettes, but Brynn must have the men falling all over her."

Just as he says it, two guys approach the table. Brynn shakes her head at them and they turn around, dejected.

"See, what did I tell you?" He laughs. "Did you do what I said to do?"

The bartender passes our beers and Brynn's sparkling water over the bar top. Anthony thanks me when I throw down a twenty and turn away, two bottles in one hand and Brynn's drink in the other.

"You were right. She says a lot more than I thought."

Anthony can't keep back his shit-eating grin. "You're welcome. Next time I'll charge."

We get to the table and hand out drinks. Anthony slides in and puts his face in Julia's neck.

"What did those guys want?" I ask Brynn.

She sips her water. "They wanted to know if you guys are single," she says around the straw still in her mouth.

I bark a laugh and grab her thigh under the table, squeezing. She squeals and squirms, giggling. One hand falls to my chest as the other pushes against my arm, trying to push it off her leg.

"Stop," she pants, laughing still.

I keep my hand there but release the teasing grip. She smiles and leans into me. Across the booth, Anthony raises his eyebrows.

"So, Julia," I start, and ask her a question. I follow that up with another one, and then one more after that. Soon she and Brynn are talking a mile a minute about something called contouring, and which shows they've seen in Vegas.

While they talk, I plan out my process tonight, thinking about lighting and positioning and what paints will work best for her skin tone.

At one point she glances at me and grins, reaching over to rest her hand on my knee. She turns back to Julia, her sentence never faltering.

The hot robot who made me dent my fender can also charm the pants off a complete stranger. I shouldn't be surprised. The grumpiest guy in town is her new best friend.

"YOUR PLACE IS NICE." BRYNN CIRCLES THE KITCHEN, touching the cabinet pulls I installed last year. She runs her fingers over the forest green agate, her index finger bumping along the irregularities in the rock.

She seems nervous. She keeps touching things. If it's not the countertops or the agate, it's her fingers drumming on her thighs. I'm nervous too. Grabbing the pitcher from the fridge, I pour two glasses of water.

"Are you ready?" I ask, handing her one.

She rests her lips on it, but she doesn't take a drink right away. "I guess so. I'm not sure what it entails, but I'm game." She sips from the glass and watches me.

"Come on," I say, taking her by the hand and leading her to the living room. We both ditched our shoes as soon as we walked into my house, and the drop cloth is rough against my bare feet. I love that feeling because it means I'm creating.

I walk with her to the stool I've set up two feet from my canvas. "This is where you'll be. For now, just sit down. I'm going to think for a moment about how I want you."

Brynn listens, lowering herself gracefully onto the seat. I stand back, watching her. She points to the picture of the eye, *her eye*, and asks about it. I would tell her all about the painting, how she was the inspiration, but I'm not sure she'll be happy about it. Instead, I give her a blasé response. I'm busy watching her talk, thinking about angles.

"It's captivating," she says, her voice warm and appreciative. "It has depth. All the colors, everything about it, it's incredible."

Watching her talk has given me an idea. As much as I love her face, I think I want to paint her profile.

"Turn to your left about forty-five degrees," I instruct. She does as I ask, but it's still not quite right. "Turn the same direction, but half that distance."

Again, she listens, but now she's facing away from me. I step closer, reaching for her shoulders and twisting her upper half.

"Can you manage this? Twisting this way? I'd really like to get your profile, but like you're looking out over your shoulder."

She listens well, dipping her right shoulder toward me and looking away.

"Perfect. Yes, just like that." I hurry to the canvas, pre-drawing as fast as I can. "Brynn, you're stunning."

"I'm sure you say that to all the women you paint."

I pause, my pencil poised. "I've never done this before."

"Okay." She doesn't say more, but I can tell it pleases her.

The longer she sits, the more her body relaxes. The white strap of her sundress slips from its place, falling to her upper arm and dangling there. She reaches to fix it, but I stop her.

"Wait," I say, studying her bare shoulder. It's soft and womanly, her skin creamy. "Would you mind if we kept it off?"

Her eyes meet mine. "The strap?"

I nod. She watches me, and in her eyes I see her making a decision. "Would it be better if I lost the top half of the dress? I'm not facing you. It's just a suggestion, I'm not the artist here, but—"

"Yes," I blurt out. "It would make the painting more sensual, with your bare back."

"I like that idea," she says, her eyelashes fluttering as she looks down.

"Me too." My voice is low, and I need to get a grip. I'm a professional. I can see Brynn's bare back and survive.

I turn to the canvas, busying myself with absolutely nothing. Really I'm pretending to run my pencil over the lines I've already drawn. Brynn is in my peripheral vision, struggling with the zipper.

"Do you want help with that?"

"Yes," she says, her voice small.

Swallowing my desire, I grab the zipper that is only a quarter of the way down and tug. Down it goes, revealing her smooth, pretty skin inch by inch. I want to run my fingers over it, find out if it feels as silky as it looks. I keep my hands to myself though, and when I'm finished, I step away. I need to put distance between us.

"Thank you," Brynn murmurs. She slides the straps down her arms, pushing at the front of the dress until it bunches at her waist. "There," she says, swiveling back into position. She moves too far forward, and the underside of her breast is visible between the inside of her upper arm and ribcage.

"Uh, Brynn, not that I have a problem with it, but a bit of your breast is visible," I motion to the spot, and she quickly brings her arm into her side. The underside of her breast disappears, but now there's whole new problem.

My eyes meet the ceiling and I squeeze them. *I will never be able to unsee that.* Brynn's breasts are big and round, with exquisite rose pink nipples. I know this because trying to cover the underside of her breast makes the top of it visible in front of her arm. Her profile, with the incredible looking mound and pert, pebbled nipple will haunt me until the end of time.

"What's wrong now?" There's hurt in her voice. "Maybe you can position me? I'm sure I'm doing it wrong."

I know better than to do what I want to do to her. Treading lightly is mandatory around Brynn. I don't trust myself to speak right now, but I don't want to hurt her feelings either.

I take a big, quiet breath and attempt to calm myself down. The front of my pants has grown incredibly tight in the last minute, and I hope she doesn't notice.

Slipping on a mask of cool professionalism, I walk to her and stand behind her. I keep my eyes trained straight ahead, desperately trying not to see anything that will crumble my resolve.

With the palm of one hand, I press lightly on her shoulder, lowering it a fraction. Grasping her chin with two fingers, I move her jaw a couple inches closer to me and then push it down slightly. "Grip the side of the stool with one hand and let your elbow bend along your side body."

She does as I ask, and I step back to the canvas. My

insides celebrate, throwing confetti everywhere. I managed not to be swept under.

"Why won't you look at me?" Brynn's voice is thick. My eyes fly to her face, and in them, I see unshed tears.

I run my hands through my hair, grabbing fistfuls in my frustration.

"I can't, Brynn. I fucking *can't*."

"Why? Am I that terrible? Am I that awful? Do I look horrific on canvas?" She dashes tears away from her cheek with the back of her hand.

I shake my head, not knowing what to do or say. How did I get into this mess with her? I'm attracted to her, and I'm not sure if I'm allowed to be. It's driving me insane, trying to figure her out.

"You drive me crazy," I yell, dropping the pencil. "I don't know what to do with you. One day you're wearing a shirt that says 'Fuck Off,' and then you're kissing me like you need air and my mouth is oxygen. What am I supposed to do? How am I supposed to read you?"

Her lips tremble. She crosses her arm over her chest and rises. She turns around, facing me, and I see she has one breast clutched in a palm, and the other pressed against her forearm. In both cases, neither has enough surface area to properly cover her. Below her chest is a toned stomach and a cute-as-fuck belly button.

"You should drive me home," she says, her face cold. If there weren't still tears pouring from her eyes, I'd say she were made of stone.

"Are you going to run away from me, Brynn? From this?"

"What should I do? Continue to sit there and watch you not look at me? You're supposed to be painting me and you can't stand to look in my direction."

"Fuck, Brynn. I think you might be a few bricks shy of a

load." My hands ball into fists. "Of course I can't look at you. How can I? I never know where I am with you. You're sitting there on that stool, and I can see your breasts, Brynn. They're incredible, and you look even more incredible with your hair falling onto your shoulders. I can see your nipple peeking out from behind your arm, and of course it has to be the most delicious looking nipple I've ever seen in my life, and I have no idea if I can have it." I'm nearly out of breath, but I manage to add, "So there. That's why I can't look at you."

Brynn watches me, her lips parting enough to leave a space in the center of them. Her chest rises and falls, her chin tips up slightly. She licks her upper lip and moves the arm that covers her.

The air rushes from my lungs. If I ever thought I knew beauty before this moment, I was wrong. Beauty is Brynn right now, opening up her heart and her body.

"Touch me, Connor."

She doesn't have to ask me more than once. In seconds I'm in her space, grabbing her face and moving over her mouth. I want all of her, every moan and every whispered request, every flicker of her tongue and every taste.

I lift her, and her legs encircle my waist. I carry her down the hall, breaking our kiss, and replacing her tongue in my mouth with what started all this. She gasps and her thigh muscles tense.

"Connor," she groans against the side of my head.

I take her through my bedroom door and straight to the bed. We fall on it together and she laughs, a carefree and happy sound.

Brynn is a present, wrapped in bows, and I want to untie her slowly, but it's hard to go slow when I learn how much I like to hear her call out my name. Before I'm inside her, I've made her call my name three times. She smiles each time she comes down from the high, and her glossy eyes are sated.

When I slide into her, she sighs and looks up at me.

Brynn's eyes are a gateway to her feelings, and now I know what her eyes look like when I'm inside her.

I LOVE THE CURVE OF BRYNN'S LOWER BACK. IT'S SEXY AND womanly, a dip before the beautiful curve of her ass begins. I can't help but admire that part of her anatomy also. She's on her stomach, her arms stretched out above her and disappearing under a pillow.

If it weren't for waking up to her this morning, I might need someone to tell me that last night happened. Unbelievable. There is no better feeling than being inside Brynn. Her body was made for mine, I'm certain of it. I've had sex enough to know that it doesn't usually feel that way. Sure, it felt good enough to get the job done, but not like that. Like there's a special place inside her only I can fill. Not just physically, either. I swear I'm the right person for her heart, too.

I need breakfast. She will also, once she wakes up. I'm not sure when that will be. We were up again at two in the morning. Brynn reached for me, climbing on top, and ten minutes later we were both satisfied and on our way to dreamland.

I get out of bed, trying to be as quiet as I can. Pulling on sweats, I head to the kitchen and start the coffee. I'm at the stove, flipping pancakes, when Brynn walks in.

"Good morning," she says.

I turn around to say hi, but the greeting dies on my lips.

Brynn is naked, gloriously naked, and standing in my kitchen in full sunlight.

"I was afraid you'd be embarrassed or shy this morning," I manage to say.

She tips her head to the side and smirks, walking closer. Her breasts bounce with the steps. "And why would I be?"

"Uh, well," I look to the pan, at the golden pancakes that soon will be burned. Grabbing the handle, I quickly dump them onto the plate next to the stove. Brynn reaches around me, grabs a perfect, fluffy pancake, and tears off a piece. She brings it to her lips, blows gently, and pops it into her mouth. *Lucky pancake.*

"We did some things last night that you might not want to talk about in the light of day. I thought you might wake up and regret them."

Brynn bites her lower lip, tosses down the pancake, and lifts herself onto the kitchen counter. She grabs me by the neck, pulling me so I'm standing in between her legs. "That's where you're wrong, Connor. All those things we did last night, I also want to do in the light of day. Right now, actually."

She reaches down, slipping a hand into my sweats. She grins. "I think you want to do those things too."

Fuck yes I do.

Sorry, pancakes. Cover your eyes and close your ears.

13

BRYNN

I WENT OVER TO CONNOR'S HOUSE LAST NIGHT EXPECTING A painting.

I don't want to analyze it. I don't want to think about it at all, but, of course, that's not going to be possible. I could say things I don't mean. Telling him that last night and this morning was an isolated incident would be the smartest thing I could do.

Or I could do what I really want to do, which is jump him right now. That would be unsafe, obviously. He's operating a vehicle. Now that I've done it once—okay, three times—I want it constantly. Blame it on me being parched, in the proverbial sense. Before last night I hadn't had any *water* in a very long time. Connor's *water* is everything *water* should be. Refreshing, delicious, and satisfying.

Watching him drive is a chance to study him. He has strong forearms. Hands that knew exactly what to do with me. Biceps that bunched and hardened when he lifted me and carried me to his room. He'd buried his face in my breasts while he walked, and I thought I was going to die right there on the spot.

I didn't know last night was going to happen. Honest. When Connor refused to look at me as I sat there, exposed, my emotions boiled over. I realized how starving I was for the touch of a man. And not just any man. I wanted Connor.

Thinking about him this way makes me want to have sex with him again. And again. And again, and again, and again. Placing two fingers upright on the console, I walk them over in a sneaky but obvious way. Connor looks down at my fingers and laughs, watching them as they get closer to him. The red light turns green, and he looks up to drive. I don't have to pay attention to the road, so I can continue my quest.

My fingers walk up his thigh and to their destination. Connor's eyes flick to me when I brush against him. "Brynn," he says, his voice low. "What are you doing?"

"What does it look like I'm doing?"

He glances down, where my fingers brush back and forth across the front of the same sweats I found him in this morning, then back up. "You're insatiable."

"For you, I am."

He turns onto my street. "It's a good thing we're here, then."

I rub harder, for good measure. He groans softly. I grin. "In case you're wondering, that was my invitation for you to come inside."

He pulls up to my house and throws the truck in park. "You better believe I plan on coming inside."

He laughs an evil little laugh as my mouth drops open. "Don't do it too quickly, or I might be horrified." I'm getting good at this rhyming game.

He shifts in his seat. I can tell he's thinking of a retort, but I'm making it difficult.

After a moment, he says, "We better get out, before I fuck you curbside."

"Yes!" I yell, clapping my hands. "You win. Let's go inside, so we can both win."

We're halfway up the front walk, our feet pounding the pavement, when someone calls our names. "Brynn! Connor! Thank God."

Cassidy rushes across the small length of grass that separates our driveways. "My sitter called in sick and I have nobody to watch Brooklyn. I knocked on your door twice, but nobody answered, and I thought that seemed weird because you're always home—" Cassidy's lips press together. Her eyes grow in size as she looks from Connor to me. Is it obvious I'm wearing yesterday's dress? Maybe not. It's just a sundress. "Anyway," she fumbles, trying to get back on track. "Please say you'll watch Brooklyn for me. I can't call in for my shift."

Panic swiftly replaces desire. Me, watch a child? A *small* child. Um, no. No no no no no.

"Sure," Connor answers.

Instantly a thousand erratic, panicked butterflies zoom around my stomach. I want to bend over right there on the cracked sidewalk and be sick. Everyone is oblivious to the pandemonium in my stomach. Connor makes some kind of joke that I don't register, and Cassidy presses her hands together like she's praying.

"Thank you. I appreciate it. The next time you come in" —she points back at herself—"your Cuban is on me."

"Sounds good," Connor says, smiling down at me. I scowl at him.

"I'll bring her over in twenty minutes." Cassidy turns toward her house, but looks back over her shoulder. "Thank you, Brynn. Seriously." She is genuine and sweet, and has no clue the turmoil I'm in.

I grunt a response and watch her hurry to her house. She dashes up the three stairs to the porch and rushes inside, the screen door smacking shut behind her.

"Are you fucking kidding me?" I hiss, stomping to my front door. I pull keys from my purse and unlock it. Connor follows me inside, closing the door behind him.

"What's your problem? I mean, I know we had other plans, but Cassidy needed help. I probably should've asked first, but I didn't think it was a big deal. Brooklyn is a sweet kid."

"You definitely should've asked first," I yell. The butterflies have transformed into crazed ants, running headfirst into one another as they spin out of control. "You don't know me, Connor. You don't understand."

"Then tell me more about you, Brynn. Because you're right, I know next to nothing."

My desire to tell him everything is strong, even when I know it's not smart. I want to be known. To be understood. Even so, I know better. It's better to keep people at arm's distance for now. My personal baggage is a special type of fucked-up shit. It comes with media, mass hatred, and an irate person who might still want to punish me.

Connor throws up his hands at my silence. "Continue to tell me nothing. I'll continue to not know you. I'll pretend like your responses to situations are normal, like you're not harboring something heavy, and you keep being an ice queen." He walks back to the front door and turns the handle.

"Wait," I shout. "Where are you going?"

"Home, Brynn. I think we need to cool off."

"Uh, no. You're not going home." I point through the

walls, to Cassidy's house. "I cannot watch that child by myself."

"Have you seriously never babysat a kid? It's not hard."

I picture Brooklyn's face. In my head, I hear her little voice yelling and talking, the way she does every day in her backyard. Maybe it's not hard to take care of a kid, but there is no way in hell I'm doing it alone. My hands begin to shake. I curl them into fists to hide them from Connor.

"Please," I whisper, my voice pleading. "Don't go. I need you."

The fight leaves me. My shoulders slump as the panic retreats to hidden spots within me.

Connor crosses the room, arms folding me into his strong, solid chest. "Brynn," he whispers against my hair. "What the hell happened to you?" His question isn't a request for information but a statement of wonder. He knows I won't answer. "I won't go, okay? I'm here. As long as you need me."

I cry into his chest, and I have no way to explain why. I'm living on borrowed time. At some point, I'll have to be honest with him, and with myself.

"SEE?" CONNOR INCLINES HIS HEAD MY WAY. "IT'S NOT HARD."

We're sitting on the couch. Below us, Brooklyn sits cross-legged on the ground. Her backpack lies on the coffee table and she's digging through it. Cassidy sent her with plenty to keep her occupied. She has coloring books and crayons, picture books and Play-Doh. Apparently none of that interests her. She sets it all off to the side and reaches in again. This time she pulls out a plastic square with teeth on all four sides, like a comb. She reaches into the bag once more and out comes a plastic baggy filled with colorful bands.

"A loom!" I sit up, looking closer.

Brooklyn looks back at me. "Yes, but it's too hard for me. I get it wrong."

I reach forward, grabbing a band from the bag and holding it up. I stretch it out a couple times. "I had these. I loved playing with it."

Connor nudges my legs and nods at Brooklyn.

Right. That's what a normal person would do.

"Brooklyn, do you mind if I help you?"

She doesn't respond, but she scoots aside. I lower myself from the couch to the floor below and stick my legs out under the coffee table, trying not to let her proximity send me over the edge into hysteria. I loop the band I'm holding around one peg on each end and reach for another. "I had a trick for making this work. Like this..."

Soon we're working together. Brooklyn gets it wrong a handful of times, weaving the wrong section or forgetting some entirely, but she's happy and pleased with the outcome.

After that's over, we have a snack and go outside to water Ginger's flowers. Connor is good with her. They seem like they know each other, and when I ask about that, he tells me he knew Cassidy back when she first got pregnant. When Brooklyn is across the yard, he tells me what happened with the dad. I feel bad. Here is Cassidy, this single mom trying to be nice to her new neighbor, and I shut her out.

Cassidy arrives mid-afternoon with food in take-out boxes. "It's the Sunday Special," she says, setting it on my kitchen counter. "I hope you like turkey breast and mashed potatoes. Kind of like Thanksgiving in June."

She gathers Brooklyn's things and hurries her out the

door, thanking Connor and me again. "You guys are cute together, by the way."

I glance at Connor. He's standing at the door, poised to close it. "Bye, Cassidy."

Her laughter floats through before the door shuts.

Connor turns to me, his eyes dark and carnal. "Since you climbed out of my bed this morning, I have been waiting to get you back into one." He stalks toward me.

I shriek and run to the hallway. He chases me down, catching me at the foot of the bed.

"Right where I want you." He pushes aside my hair and kisses my shoulder. He bites the skin, the tiniest bit of pain mixed with so much pleasure.

"Mmmm," I moan, my voice thick.

Connor drags his lips across my skin, to the hollow of my neck. His tongue darts out, tasting, and his hand slips down to the front of the shorts I changed into before Brooklyn arrived. I groan again, my knees weakening, and cling to his arms to keep me upright.

"Turnabout is fair play." His voice vibrates over my skin. He pushes me back gently until I'm lying on the bed. In minutes I'm reaching for a pillow to cover my face. The homes on the street are close together, the walls are thin, and Connor makes me loud. We figured that out last night.

Tomorrow, I'll tell him everything. He deserves to know why I am the way I am. For tonight, I want to pretend to be normal.

14

CONNOR

"I'm Elizabeth."

Brynn's back is to me, and that's probably a good thing. I don't know which reaction is on my face right now. I know which one is in my head. It's a little *What the fuck* mixed with *At least I know something about you.*

"Okay." The word slides slowly from my lips. I don't know what to say next. Besides, I think Brynn is the person who needs to keep talking.

"Do you want to know why I'm going by my middle name?"

More relief. At least the name I've known her by is in her real name at all. I think Brynn suits her better anyway.

"Why?"

Brynn turns over. Her eyes are frightened, wide and round, but they're on my face. She lays her head on her pillow and continues talking. "Until I decided to come here, I was Elizabeth Brynn Montgomery. Technically, I still am. It's not officially changed. Nobody ever really called me Elizabeth, anyway. Liz, mostly. Lizzie, to my closest friends, and then my name was in the media, and they referred to me as

Elizabeth. Kind of like your mother calling you by your full name when you're in trouble. That's what I was in. A whole lot of trouble." Her eyes fill with tears. "I'd been reckless for a while, but never anything too terrible. On the morning it all happened, I wasn't doing anything wrong. I wasn't speeding, I wasn't texting, I hadn't been drinking."

The puzzle pieces aren't fitting yet, but they are shifting.

"A new mom jumped in front of my car. With her stroller." Brynn chokes on the word *stroller*. She squeezes her eyes shut.

This is so much worse than what I thought it was. I don't know what I thought, but it was never this. "Brynn, you don't have to tell me all this. I see how upsetting it is."

She takes a deep breath and opens her eyes. Now they are shiny but less frightened. "I do, Connor. Keeping the truth from everybody is a terrible burden. If I can tell at least one person, it makes me feel just a little bit lighter."

I take her hand and wrap it in my own. "I'm listening."

"They died instantly. It was a major road, and she just..." Her voice trails off, her head shaking rapidly. "I still feel it sometimes. The awful bumps. You've never heard or felt a sound like this, Connor. Never. There's no way to describe it, but it will never leave me. I can't un-feel it or un-hear it."

Tears trickle out of her eyes and run sideways into the pillow, but she doesn't stop talking.

"The media didn't care that I was innocent. They didn't care what the police told them. They cared only that their headlines got clicks. I was turned from a club-promoter to a raging, selfish party girl overnight. They dragged up every person I ever came into contact with, even people I don't remember having a conversation with. A couple years before I'd been pulled over, and cited for drinking and driving. They used that in their smear campaign, of course."

Her eyes are haunted, the ghosts of what she's been through floating through her mind. It wrecks me to see her in so much pain.

"Nobody needed to read the story and see the date. All they needed to make a judgment was the headline. *Driver who struck and killed mother and baby cited for DUI* sounded a hell of a lot like the DUI went hand-in-hand with the accident. I was a victim of what that woman did, but in the court of public opinion, I was the executioner. I was fired from my job. Nobody wanted my name associated with their business, my so-called friends were history, and I pushed away any real friends I had."

"So you came here to get away from it?"

"Sort of. I'd recently begun to get letters from the husband of the woman who jumped in front of me. They were," she pauses, her lips twisting, "not nice, I guess you could say."

"How not nice?"

Getting up from the bed, she walks to the dresser and opens the top drawer, coming back with a stack of envelopes.

"Here," she says, climbing back into bed and setting them between us. Instead of lying back down she sits cross-legged. I sit up, doing the same, and reach for the first envelope.

By the time I'm through them all, I can barely see straight. Fury clouds my vision. This man is delusional. Brynn isn't safe. No wonder she was so mean when she met me. Anybody in her position would protect themselves the way she did.

"Brynn, do the police know about this?" I hold up the last letter, the worst of them all.

She shakes her head.

"They need to."

She shrugs, defeated. "I can't. I just can't bring myself to report him. I already took his family, whether I'm innocent or not. It happened. *My car.* Am I supposed to hurt him further?"

"If he's going to hurt you, then yes, you need to nail that fucker to the wall."

"He's not going to hurt me," she says, but it's without conviction. She wants to believe he won't, but deep down she's not certain.

"He doesn't know where I went. And"—her eyes are timid, but she forges ahead—"Brighton is only a stop along the way. I needed a safe place, a job, and anonymity."

Her revelation hits me like a bullet, piercing my flesh and ripping through my insides. "You're not staying in Brighton." The words leave me hollow.

She shakes her head. "The plan has always been to make as much as I can until my parents can help me. They have their fishing business, and the high season starts now."

"And then?"

"My end destination is Brazil. On a beach, renting out lounge chairs to vacationers." She takes the last letter from my hand and stacks it with the other ones. "Somewhere I can fade into the background, and watch everyone around me live."

I hear what she's not saying, and I wonder if she hears it too. She's not just running from the crazy husband and father who wants to hurt her. This is some sort of penance. I have no idea what it feels like to be involved in the death of someone else, especially an innocent baby. Or to have my name smeared in the media. It sounds like she should be suing them for slander.

"You weren't part of my plan, Connor." She runs her fingers down the length of my arm. Her lips twist.

I nod, trying desperately to recover from the proverbial kick in the nuts she just delivered to me. "You're still planning to leave?"

She nods, but it's so small, so imperceptible, it makes me think she doesn't want to go through with it. "Every day takes me a little farther from what happened. One step closer to a semblance of normalcy. I want a life where I don't need to use door alarms anymore. Where I don't have to fear recognition. For that, I need distance."

I wish she weren't right. I wish I didn't understand. I wish I had it in me to guilt trip, manipulate, and coerce her into staying.

I slip a curled finger under her chin and tip it up. "Promise me something?"

"I can try."

"Don't leave without telling me."

Her eyebrows pinch. "Wouldn't it be easier if one day I was gone? If neither of us had to go through the heartache of a goodbye?"

"I don't think so."

She sighs and looks at me. The pain in her eyes hurts me too.

She doesn't mention the promise again. Neither do I. We're different. I want to put myself through the experience. She wants to avoid it altogether.

I stay with her that night. It's not only that I want to protect her. Now there's an invisible clock, ticking away every second we have together. I want to bury my head in the sand and forget about it, want to bury myself in her and pretend her problems don't exist. I settle for curling my body behind hers and slipping into her in a luxurious and unhurried pace.

At the crack of dawn, I leave to go home and change. I take a shower, dress, and go to my parents' house.

Typical Monday. Yet my life is now anything but typical.

15

BRYNN

SUPPOSEDLY THE TRUTH WILL SET YOU FREE, BUT I DIDN'T know it could also open up a well in your soul, allowing you to go deeper and feel more.

I'm walking a tightrope of emotions. Too far to one side and I'll never get to experience Connor the way I want to. Too far to the other and I'll abandon my plans to some unknown detriment.

I've been thinking about that almost constantly for the past two weeks. Probably since the moment I woke up in Connor's bed that first morning.

This far removed from my old life, it's too easy to think maybe there isn't that much danger after all. Distance was what I needed. Maybe it's what Eric Prince needed too. If I'm not there to threaten, he'll give up. Can't terrorize a person who's no longer available.

Every day that passes, the line becomes more and more blurred.

I'm pretty sure it's all Connor's fault. Why does he have to be so easy to like? Why does he have to have a crooked grin that I only see on his face when he's inside me? If I'd never let my guard down and allowed that to happen, his crooked grin would be a secret. A secret sex smile. That's what he has, and just knowing that I know that about him makes my chest do this warm, tingly thing.

This is why each day is getting more difficult. How am I supposed to stay the course when Connor is now on it too? It's like I'm trying to drive the getaway car and he has tossed tacks on the road, like some kind of cartoon. Which is obviously a terrible analogy, considering I no longer drive.

Connor will be here soon to pick me up for our double-date with Anthony and Julia. Dinner at some bar and grill place. Bowling. Things normal people do on a Saturday night. I'm not kidding myself though. I'm still not normal. Normal people's hearts don't race when they drive over speed bumps.

But I'm trying. Connor is patient with me. He doesn't challenge the quiet that takes me over at times. When I go off in my own mind, he doesn't try to bring me back. I know he wants to, and I also know he's not sure if he should try. The problem is, I'm not sure if he should try either.

I'm ready early, so I go visit Walt.

Usually he opens his door before I have a chance to knock, but tonight I have to bang on it twice.

My fist is raised for a third and much more insistent knock when he shouts from inside, "I'm coming, I'm coming. Keep your pants on."

He opens the door. There is blood on his forehead, and I can't tell how big the wound is because the blood is smeared. It's darker around the edges, like it has begun to dry. "Walt, what happened?" I reach out but curl my fingers back in.

He opens the door all the way and retreats into his

home. Stepping in, I shut the door with my foot and follow Walt to the kitchen.

He stands at the open fridge, pulling out different items. Bags of deli meat, cheese, a loaf of bread, and lettuce. He tosses each one by one on the counter, and leans back down to search for something. After a moment he grabs a jar of pickles and stands, shutting the refrigerator door.

"Want a sandwich?" he asks, shuffling over to the counter.

"No thanks. Are you going to tell me what happened to your forehead?"

He ignores me, attempting to open the jar of pickles. When it doesn't open he sets it down too hard on the counter and growls. It's a gravelly, bearish sound. I hear the frustration behind it.

"Walt?" I come up to stand beside him at the counter and gently elbow him out of the way. "Let me do it."

"I'm not helpless, you know." Still, he walks away and sits in a chair at his little kitchen table.

"I never said you were." The lid twists away from the pickle jar with a *pop*. "Although you are kind of being an asshole today."

"Sorry, sorry," he mutters.

"Do you want tomato on your sandwich?"

"Yes." After a moment he adds, "please."

I assemble the sandwich and place it in front of him, then go back to the fridge and take out a cold can of beer.

"Do you want this? Might be refreshing."

He nods, his mouth full, and I crack the top. I slide it over to him and take a seat across from him.

"Now will you tell me what happened?"

He nods, looking at the table top. I follow his gaze to a screwdriver with a black and yellow handle. "I'm a grown man. I've been a grown man for a long time. I was tightening the screws in my TV stand. It's old but it's fine, just needs some attention now and then. The damn screwdriver wouldn't work."

I give him a look.

"My hand works just fine, thank you very much. Not my fault the damn thing flew up and hit me." He takes another bite and chews angrily.

"I think you're lucky you were working with a flathead and not a Phillips."

His bushy eyebrows lift, and I grin. I'm proud of myself.

"Well, look who knows her screwdrivers."

"I've picked up a few things from Connor."

"Try not to pick up an STD. Or that other one, what's it called? Gonorrhea."

I exhale and cross my arms. "Walt, you are beyond words."

"What? I'm just saying. I've noticed his truck over at your place an awful lot during late hours." He sets down his sandwich. "Do you know what you're doing with that boy?"

I think back to last night and try not to let the smile I'm feeling show on my lips. After dinner at his parents and a banana split at that cute shop in town, we were so ready to be alone that we couldn't make it to either of our houses in time. He'd pulled into the farthest parking spot at a deserted park and I climbed on top of him. Thank goodness for tinted windows.

I push down the memory and turn my attention back to Walt. "What do you mean?"

Walt swallows the last bite of his sandwich and drinks the remainder of his beer. He places the empty can sideways on the plate. "I mean, does the boy know this place is only a stop for you?"

"I've told him."

"What does he say about that?" He sits back, his stomach pushing against his plaid button-up. The white fabric of his undershirt peeks through a button he has missed.

"He doesn't say much. He hasn't asked me to stay, if that's what you're getting at."

"I'm not getting at anything. It was just a question. But the boy must have some opinion on the matter. Most men would."

"He asked that I say goodbye first. That was all he said."

Walt folds his arms. The frown on his face looks more at home than his infrequent smiles.

"What?" I ask, agitation in my voice.

"Do I get a goodbye too?"

I look down to my empty hands in my lap. "I didn't agree to say goodbye."

"Did you say no?"

My head shakes, the small hoop earrings I'm wearing gently bump my skin.

"Then don't say no to me either."

I cough, hoping the sting of tears I feel behind my eyes will stay back there.

Leaving becomes harder each day that I stay.

"DID YOU GUYS KNOW BRYNN HAS ANOTHER SPECIAL MAN IN her life?" Connor leans back in his seat and looks from Anthony to Julia, then back to me. We've just placed our order for dinner.

"Who said you're special?" I ask, my lips smiling around

the straw in my mouth. I sip my grapefruit juice and soda water.

Julia laughs and Anthony snorts.

"Who's the *other man*?" Julia asks me.

I roll my eyes. "His name is Walt, and he's eighty-two years old. He's kind of like a prickly pear cactus. His needles hurt, but he grows sweet fruit."

Three bewildered faces turn to me.

"Come on!" My hands fly through the air in front of my face. "Don't tell me you have no idea what a flipping prickly pear cactus is."

"Coming up empty, Brynn." Julia's trying not to laugh.

"Ugh." I cross my arms. "You higher elevation snots."

Connor laughs into a fisted hand, his shoulders shaking. "We're snots? You're the one from *Snotts*dale."

"Correction." I hold up one finger. "I had a Phoenix zip code." Maybe another time I'll tell him I grew up in Scottsdale, a suburb of Phoenix, and the nickname is totally undeserved. Mostly, anyway. Well, maybe it is a little. Ok, fine, it's deserved.

I jostle my shoulder against Connor's. "How did that nickname make it's way all the way up to the pines?"

"It took a left at the prickly pear cactus and went due north." Anthony is laughing so hard while he's talking the words barely come out. Everybody understands him anyhow, and Julia laughs until she has tears rolling down her cheeks.

"Anyway," I say loudly, reaching my hand into the bowl of pretzels and tossing some at Anthony. They bounce off his forearms and onto the floor.

Connor and Anthony start talking about the car he's repairing this week. Julia is kind, funny, and easy to be around. Despite this, I'm wary. I can talk to her all day about basic subjects, pop culture, and common knowledge, but I'm not sure how to go past that. I've been burned at the stake by people I considered friends.

"So," Julia begins. "What brought you to Brighton?"

"Change of scenery," I say, gesturing outside. "Summer is better up here."

"Will you go back to Phoenix for winter?"

I steal a glance at Connor. He's talking fast and punching the air. I guess they've moved on from the car repair. Turning back to Julia, I say, "Probably not."

She winks. "He's quite a catch, right? Snatch him up now. I know a lot of ladies in my office who would love to know how this guy hasn't been on their radar."

"Tell me about your work," I say. *Good Lord, I want to change the subject.*

"I work in the mayor's office. Right now I'm in charge of planning the first annual Independence Day Parade."

This is something that should be exciting, but Julia isn't smiling.

"Uh huh. Okay." I nod my head, encouraging her to say more. She doesn't say anything, so I ask, "What's the problem?"

"I don't think anybody even knows the parade is happening. I've been working on it for months, planning and getting communities, programs, and businesses signed up to make floats. But when I ask people around town if they're coming to the parade, they look like they've never heard of it." She sighs, and it's such a crestfallen sound it's like I can hear her spirit sinking.

"This event is for everyone, yes?"

Her eyes are interested and confused. "Yes."

"And your goal is to increase attendance?"

She shrugs. "I guess so."

"What have you done to market it?"

"It's on the home screen of the city's webpage. Next week we'll hang a banner from the street lights where Main Street begins."

"How will you inform and entice all the people who haven't recently visited your website or driven through that light?"

She shrugs. "I don't know."

Taking a pen from my purse, I grab a paper napkin from the container at the end of the booth.

"Here's what you're going to do." I uncap the pen and start writing. When I'm finished, I slide it across the table to her.

"This is"—Julia glances up to me and back down to the napkin—"incredible. How do you know about all this?"

I wave my hand in the air. "A past life. It's not hard. Honestly. You identify your product, and who wants it. Then you take it to the places where they put their eyes." I recap my pen and slide it into my purse. "Easy peasy."

Julia reads over my notes. "The grocery store idea. I mean, duh. So perfect." She looks up at me. "Thank you. I've been stressing about this like crazy. You have no idea."

Our server interrupts Julia to drop off our food. Connor and Anthony remember their dates and ask us what we've been discussing.

"Oh my gosh," Julia says, stuffing an onion ring into her mouth and chewing. "Brynn basically just snapped her fingers and solved all my problems with the parade. I was so stressed but now"—she makes a show of taking a deep breath—"I can chill."

"Are you chill enough to try that thing I want to try?"

"Anthony," Connor complains. "Are you for real?" He

balls up a napkin and throws it on the table. "We do not want to hear about your requests in the bedroom."

Julia reddens. "That's not what he was talking about."

I ignore them and eat my sandwich. Fried chicken. With pickles. I mean, really? Has anything ever been this delicious? I hear them again when Connor says *body shot*.

"No, I've never done one, dipshit. I just want to know what they're like." Anthony holds up his hands. "Sue me."

"They're not that exciting," I say, retrieving a pickle from my plate and popping it into my mouth. "You either take the shot and then lick the salt off someone, or you drink the liquor out of someone's belly button. It's not that great. Unless you're talking about the ones that happen at house parties or frat parties, and those can get crazy." I meet the eyes of three surprised people. They're more surprised than they were about my prickly pear cactus comment.

"Not that I would know," I add. "I've never done one, but I've seen them a lot."

Connor kisses my temple. "What else is in this beautiful head of yours?" he murmurs against me. His breath tickles the baby hairs at my hairline.

"Many, many things. Like types of screwdrivers and how to line up brackets to hang pocket-rod curtains." Our job yesterday was installing and hanging curtains in a living room with eight windows. I had no idea how much math went into a job like that. It was a great reminder that I'm still terrible at math, as though I could've forgotten.

"Connor, have you painted anything recently?" Julia asks.

"Umm...well..." Connor stammers. An outline of my half-naked form doesn't count as a painting.

"He painted an eye," I answer for him. "It's really cool. It has all these colors inside it, kind of like a storm or something, right, Connor? But it's like the sky is painted typical storm colors." I'm using my hands to describe it. "The water is colorful. It's fascinating."

"You like it, huh?" Anthony says. His lips are pinched like he's holding back a smile.

"Yes. Of course I like it. Why?" I squint, trying to figure out why he's asking before he can tell me.

"No reason." He looks at Connor and then signals to our server. "Another round, please," he says when the server stops by.

Julia leans forward. "Connor, there's an empty space downtown. We've been talking about trying to introduce more culture into the area. If I'm able to get my boss to agree to an art exhibit, would you put some of your pieces on display?"

"Of course!" I blurt out, then cover my mouth with my hand. "Sorry. I got excited. I'll let him answer."

Connor chuckles and winds his arm around my waist, pulling me into his side. "I'd like that," he says to Julia.

She claps her hands together twice. "I've solved two work problems in one evening. We should double-date more often."

Anthony gives her a hungry look. "Does this mean I get to take a body shot off you?"

She rolls her eyes and looks exasperated, but I can see her interest. "I guess."

When our server delivers their second round, I order two shots of tequila and limes.

Once everything is set up, I begin my instruction. Julia and I are both wearing short sleeves, so I show her how to rub a lime on her shoulder, right beside the curve of her neck.

"Now, pour on the salt. The lime juice helps it stick."

I do it too, and a few salt granules slide down my tank top.

"You two," I point at Connor and Anthony. "Take the shot. Then lick the salt off us, and bite into your lime wedge."

Both guys do as I say. Connor nips my skin after he licks the salt, keeping his eyes trained on me when he bites his lime. My fingertips press into the spot he bit and licked. He wiggles his eyebrows.

"Now what?" Anthony asks. His cheeks are already flushed from the tequila shot.

"Bowling?" Julia says.

"Do they have tequila?" Anthony asks, eying Julia's shoulder. He pushes her hair aside and brushes a kiss onto the spot he just licked.

"They have a bar. Let's go." Connor stands, pulling his wallet from his back pocket.

He and Anthony settle the bill and finish their beers. Julia looks at me and shakes her head. "Is this going to be a long night?"

Anthony pretends to deliver a punch to Connor's stomach and Conner jabs back.

"You might want to lay off so you can drive later," I say, looking back at Julia.

"Good call. I'd say the same to you, but you aren't drinking tonight. Why not?" She hooks an elbow around my arm as we walk out.

"I don't drink at all. I don't enjoy the feeling." It's the best answer I can give her. It's honest. Partially, anyway. Drinking the way I used to gave everyone ammunition. Maybe one day I'll have a drink, but it's not happening any time soon.

"I like you, Brynn. You seem like good people."

I grin at her, but the happy feeling is dampened by

knowing I'm going to leave her too. Walt, Julia, Connor. I came to this town to blend in, not make friends and start the foundation of a life here. Every second we spend together is only going to make it harder when the time comes for me to leave. What am I thinking, allowing this to continue? I need to be stronger, better, say no to everyone and become a hermit until my parents deposit that money. I could protect them all if I would just—

"Stop thinking about whatever it is your pretty little head is overthinking." Connor's voice is low, a rumble in my ear.

"I'll drive," Julia offers, pointing at her silver sedan.

"Am I that obvious?" I say to Connor.

"Yes. Now stop. Be here, in this moment, with me. With us. We'll worry about tomorrow later." Then he delivers a swift smack on my ass, the kind that crackles in the air.

16

CONNOR

UGH. I HATE MYSELF.

Why did I do that? Stupid. Is there cotton in my mouth? My tongue snakes its way around my palette and over my teeth. It doesn't help, because my tongue is like sandpaper.

"Hey, you. I thought maybe you'd sleep all day." Brynn's voice filters through my head like a ray of sunlight in my dust-filled brain. "I have something for you to drink, and medicine. I'm assuming you need it."

I open one eye. My jeans and T-shirt are folded and laying on top of Brynn's dresser. On top of the stack is my coiled brown leather belt.

Brynn sits on the edge of the bed, sideways in my vision. "Last night was a bad idea," I grumble.

"I don't know about that. Here, sit up," she says, trying to lift my shoulders. I sit up and take the medicine she's holding out. "You had a great time licking me."

"Best sentence ever," I mumble, then swallow the pills with a mouthful of water. I drain the rest of the glass and hand it back to her. "How many pills did I just swallow?"

"Four. Two Tylenol, two activated charcoal. The charcoal works wonders. I promise."

The authoritative tone of her voice reminds me what she used to do for a living, how much experience she probably has with hangovers, and of who is really at fault for the bricks clashing in my head.

"You made this happen." I point to my head and fall back down on the pillow.

"Nope. I won't be taking credit for that. You did it to yourself. I merely gave you the information. You used it."

She climbs onto the bed and sits beside me, her legs crossed. I read her shirt and laugh, immediately regretting the laughter. It makes my head pound.

"Your shirt is ridiculous."

She looks down at herself. "I know. It's not suitable for public viewing. I only wear it to sleep in."

The shirt reads, 'Live. Laugh. Love.' The three words are crossed out, and below that it reads, 'Don't be a twat.'

"When is your birthday? Maybe I can get you a shirt that doesn't have a cuss word on it."

"I don't have a birthday."

"Everyone has a birthday."

"Not me."

"When is Elizabeth Montgomery's birthday?"

"July 2nd ."

"That's in two weeks. You were going to spend the day around me and not tell me it was your birthday?"

"I guess so."

I shake my head. "That's ridiculous."

"How are you feeling?" she asks, changing the subject in the most unsubtle way.

I reach for Brynn, my arms encircling her waist. She scoots forward when I tug.

"I need help feeling better. Do you know what will work?"

"More medicine?"

I shake my head.

"Breakfast?"

"No."

"Another nap?"

I'm done with words. I pull Brynn down on top of me and bite the same spot I nibbled on last night. She exhales and relaxes into me.

"FEELING BETTER?"

Brynn's sitting on a chair in her backyard, her feet curled beneath her. She looks peaceful and happy.

I'm in the doorway with a towel wrapped around my waist. I feel a hundred times better than I did when I first woke up. A shower and a nap were what I needed. And Brynn. She's the best medicine.

"I'm starving. Any chance you have some sour beef hidden somewhere?"

Brynn smiles at me. "No chance. I don't have much for groceries either. I guess I could've walked to the store while you were sleeping."

Oh. Right. My truck. We left it at the bowling alley.

Brynn's phone sits on the table beside a glass of water. "Can you order an Uber for me? I need to get my truck back and get us some food."

She picks up the phone, presses a few buttons, and sets it back down. "It'll be here in fifteen." She looks back out at the tree line, her fingers running over her neck and lightly pinching the skin at the base of her throat.

"What's wrong?" I come out of the house, holding the towel in place with one hand, and sit down opposite her.

"Just thinking about Walt." Her head tips to one side and she looks at me. "He lives alone. What if something happened to him?"

"He has a phone."

"I know." Her voice is thick with worry. "Yesterday when I went over there he had a gash on his forehead. He told me it was from tightening screws on his rickety TV stand. The screwdriver slipped and cut him. He has so much junk over there. What if something really bad happens?"

I like Brynn's concern. Beneath the sarcasm and playfulness is a massive heart. It's giving me an idea.

"My ride will arrive soon and I'm naked beneath this towel." I stand and lean over, kissing the top of her head. "Let me get my truck and pick up some food, then we can talk more about how to help Walt. Deal?"

She nods, looking less worried than she did a moment ago.

I change back into last night's clothes and step out front, just in time to see my ride pulling up.

The driver says three words the entire drive. Fine by me. I'm not interested in small talk at the moment. Once I'm in my truck, I make a snap decision and stop at a home store. I have one specific thing in mind.

When I'm finished loading it, I hop back in my truck and go to the grocery store. Supermarket Sweep contests have nothing on me. I race through the place and pay, tossing the groceries into the backseat. Brynn is going to love what I have in my truck bed.

I'm so excited that I try to stride right into her house and get shut down by a locked front door. My forward momentum nearly takes my nose right into the door.

"Brynn," I call out, knocking.

She turns the lock a moment later. "Hi," she says, opening it all the way. She looks down at my empty hands and frowns. "Did you forget about your hunger?"

"Come on out here. I want to show you something." Turning, I lead the way to my truck. When Brynn is beside me at the tailgate, I lower it and show her the boxes.

She leans over, her hips pressing into the world's luckiest tailgate, and peers at the picture.

"A TV stand?" Confused eyes meet mine.

"For Walt," I clarify.

"Oh," she says softly, her hand resting on her chest. "This is just so...so...kind. He'll never accept it, but the gesture is lovely."

I frown. "Why won't he accept it?"

She shrugs. "I know him, and I know he won't accept generosity like this. Unless..." Her lips twist while she thinks. "Unless we put it together here and tell him you took it from someone's front lawn. Say that it was meant for bulk trash."

"You think he will accept something that was on its way to the landfill?"

"You haven't seen his backyard. Before I helped him clean it up, it could've been mistaken for a landfill."

"Alright. We'll set it up here and carry it over there." I reach for the first box and drag it toward me. Brynn's arms shoot out to stop me.

"You can't. He's super nosy and watches this street like a hawk. He's going to see us carrying these boxes."

"Seriously? What are we supposed to do?"

Brynn glances down the street and back to her place. "Back into my driveway at a bit of an angle. Not a super obvious one though. We'll carry the boxes into the backyard through the side gate."

"Not a bad idea."

Brynn beams. "I'll meet you in a second. I need to find the key that unlocks the gate." Brynn hurries inside.

I take the keys from my pocket and start for the front of the truck.

Working together, Brynn and I get the boxes to her backyard. The basic tools we need and box cutter are in my small toolbox. I carry that back with me and we get to work. We are practiced at working together, and assembling is no different. Brynn has the pieces sorted into what I will need at every step. While I work, she puts away groceries and makes a late lunch.

"Here ya go," she announces, stepping outside with two plates in her hands. "A Brynn sandwich."

I set down what I'm working on and meet her at her outdoor table. "What makes this sandwich worthy of a name like that?"

"Just try it."

I take a bite and *crunch*. "Chips." I grin around my bite. Brynn leans over and pecks my lips with a mouth as full as mine. She pulls away, munching happily.

My heart wants to dance and also fucking shatter. How did I get so lucky and unlucky at the very same time?

"HI," BRYNN CHIRPS WHEN WALT OPENS THE DOOR.

He looks beyond her, glaring at me. *What is it Brynn likes about this guy? He looks like a lion that has his balls caught in a vise.*

"Sir." I reach around Brynn and extend a hand. My

mother would smack me with a ruler if she learned I was anything less than courteous, especially to an old man. Even if it is Walt.

Walt's gaze flickers down to my outstretched hand and back up to my face. I take back my hand and clear my throat.

"Knock it off, Walt." Brynn steps inside and motions for me to come too. I follow cautiously. I'm stepping into the angry lion's den. The TV stand is lucky it's hidden around the other side of the garage, out of Walt's sight.

Brynn turns abruptly, so the three of us form a triangle. She looks at Walt and points to me. "Walt, this is Connor. You may no longer refer to him as *the boy*." She turns to me. "Connor, this is Walt."

"Hello, sir." I try again with an outstretched hand. This time he takes it and grunts a hello.

I'll take it. Beggars, choosers, yada yada yada.

"We brought you something," Brynn sing-songs.

Walt's bushy eyebrows draw together. "I saw you two carrying something."

Brynn noisily blows out a breath. "It's impossible to surprise you. Do you know how annoying that is?" She pivots and marches outside. "Come on," she yells to both of us.

We follow and find Brynn trying to lift the damn thing on her own.

"Stop, stop," I tell her, putting my hand on her shoulder.

"Then help me," she grunts, still holding up her end.

I rush to the other side and lift. Walt trails behind as we carry the piece of furniture inside.

Brynn sets it down next to a threadbare brown woven recliner. She points at Walt. "You're cooking tonight."

"Grilled cheese?"

Brynn crosses her arms and looks at him. "Add bacon and tomato?"

What's with this girl and adding to a sandwich's status quo?

I don't see Walt as an eye-rolling guy, but if he was one, he'd be doing it right now. "Well, yes. Of course."

Wait, am I missing something? Have the Cuban's and Monte Cristo's blinded me to all manner of sandwich possibilities?

Walt sinks into his recliner. It creaks as he settles. "What the hell is that?" he asks, looking at the stand.

"That"—Brynn states, jabbing a nail in the direction of the piece—"is your new TV stand."

"Now you listen here, missy—"

"Now you listen here, missy," Brynn repeats, using an old person voice. If this exchange wasn't so bizarre, I'd be laughing right now. It's like Brynn is an annoyed and concerned daughter, and Walt is her obstinate geriatric father.

Walt glares at Brynn, and she lifts an eyebrow. Walt breaks first. There's a tiny grin on his face, and it looks all wrong. Maybe it's because I've never seen him look like that. Whenever I see him around town, he looks like he's ready to smack people with a cane. Granted, he doesn't use one, but still.

"Don't worry, it came from a garbage heap," I say, cringing. That was awkward as hell.

Brynn's lips twist because she's trying not to laugh. "What Connor means is that we rescued it from imminent death. Someone was going to subject it to a slow, painful demise in a landfill. Connor passed it today and, remembering what I said about your TV stand, stopped and tossed it into his truck bed." She hardens her gaze, as if willing him to comply. "Nice, right?"

Walt looks at me for two seconds and then back at Brynn. "He's just trying to get in your pants."

"Too late. I've done all manner of dirty things with him," Brynn says cheerfully, while I'm busy almost choking on my tongue.

"Brynn," I manage to say, chastising her word choice.

She comes closer and pats my back. "Don't worry. Walt won't respect you unless you give it back to him. How do you think I slingshotted my way past his defenses?"

She's looking up at me, grinning, and if it weren't for Walt, I'd lay my lips down on hers right now. This girl's infectious personality sends me spinning in the best way. She's funny and bold, sassy and big-hearted. How am I ever going to let her go?

"If you say it's used and free, then I'll take it." Walt's voice brings my heart back down to earth. It's probably best, considering it was hammering and threatening to jump right from my chest.

"Check, check." Brynn grins at me. "Put those muscles to use, Connor." She walks to the outdated TV and pats the top, then frowns, looking at her open palm, and drags it across the side of her jean shorts.

Walt watches us switch out his TV stands, barking out orders, while Brynn threatens to put him in a home. When we're done, Brynn steps back to admire our work.

"Hey, Bryan?"

I can't help my snicker. Brynn sends me a dirty look and glances back to Walt. "What?"

"What is a"—Walt squints at her midsection—"twat?"

Brynn's eyes grow big as they lower to her shirt. In her

excitement about the surprise, she must've forgotten what she was wearing. "I'll tell you another time," she sputters.

I hang my head and shake it. I have no words.

Walt says he's going to make grilled cheese and starts for the kitchen, but Brynn hurries ahead of him. "I'll do it," she says.

"Knew the whole time she'd do that if I pretended I was going to do it," he says, shuffling over to his chair.

I settle into the couch across from him, and Walt turns on the Diamondbacks game. The sound and smell of sizzling bacon wafts into the room.

"Brynn's a special girl," he says, after one at bat of silence. His eyes are trained on the TV, but he keeps talking. "I don't know what happened in Phoenix, but it hurt her very badly. Wounded birds need time to heal before they can fly. I'm worried you're going to clip her wing."

For a man who carefully navigates his front steps and has more dust than hair, he's alarmingly astute. He's also wrong.

"I'm not planning on clipping her wing." My eyes stay on the TV too. The volume gets louder as the pitcher strikes someone out at first base. "If she wants to fly, she can. I won't hold her back."

Now Walt looks at me. "Do you know what she's running from?"

I nod.

"Is it as bad as she seems to think?"

I consider the letters she has hidden away in a drawer. Hate drips from every word. This man believes Brynn ruined his life. "Yeah."

"Might be best to let her go then."

I nod, looking back at the screen. He's only saying things I've already told myself.

"World's best sandwiches," Brynn shouts from the kitchen. "Slap yo' mama delicious." She comes into the room holding three plates. She passes one to Walt and sits beside me with the other two. I'm not hungry, but something tells me I shouldn't decline.

"What's wrong?" she asks, passing a plate to me.

"Nothing," I say, lying through my damn teeth.

"You look sad," she says, biting into her sandwich and pulling it away. A string of cheese stays attached to her teeth, dropping limply as she bites through it.

"No," I say, shaking my head. I wind an arm around her shoulders and pull her in close. "Everything is fine."

17

BRYNN

I probably shouldn't have done that just now, and by probably, I mean definitely.

It was irresponsible. It will put me back months if my parents don't get a big catch this season.

But...

But...

But...

Connor will be happy.

He was melancholy when he left last night. *He left.* It's the first time in weeks that we haven't stayed together overnight. On the walk home from Walt's, I asked him what was wrong. He told me he had a lot on his mind and then he kissed me goodnight and climbed in his truck.

He should be here any minute to drive us to the first job, and the truth is I missed him last night. Ten toes are half the amount I want in my bed. I'm already used to rolling over and reaching for his warm shoulder. This morning when I first woke up I forgot he wasn't there, I reached for him and found only air.

Carefully I walk out front with my full cup of hot coffee

and wait for him. Streams of sunlight drench the front porch in warmth. My coffee is only half gone when I see Conner's truck rolling down the street. My heartbeats speed up, and I can't blame the caffeine.

"Hey," I say, hopping into the passenger seat.

"Guess what?" Connor's eyes are bright.

"What?"

He drums a beat on his steering wheel for a few seconds. "I sold a painting this morning." His grin is big and bright.

"Wow! Congrats. That's amazing." My loud claps bounce off the interior of the truck cab.

"Thanks." He eases off the brake and drives away. "I checked my email just before I left my parents' place." He shakes his head, a slow grin easing onto his face. "I was beginning to think I might never sell another painting."

"You're too good for that." It's true, too. If I still had my connections in Phoenix, he'd be selling every last one of his pieces. I saw them all this morning on his website. Thank goodness he has a way to purchase straight from there, otherwise I wouldn't have been able to pull it off. I used an old, nondescript email address on the order form. Bada-bing, bada-boom.

Across the console, he offers me his hand, and I slip my fingers through his. "We're done after Old Lady Linton's house this afternoon. Want to take a drive somewhere and celebrate?"

"What do you have in mind?"

"Does your agreement dependent upon how good my idea is?"

"My agreement should be assumed, and all I care about is the quality of the company."

"Do you like blueberry muffins?"

"Who doesn't?"

"Then it's settled." Connor nods happily.

Happiness emanates from him as he drives, and I can feel it the same way tension makes air feel thick, but this air is better. It's fluffy like a cloud, like possibilities floating around, and I could pick one from hundreds. Buying that painting was the right thing to do.

"You're going to love Old Lady Linton." He grins at me. "She's something else."

"Why do you call her that?"

His lips move as he thinks. "I'm not sure. It has always been her name. She'll bring you homemade lemonade. It tastes awful. Drink it anyway."

"Got it," I nod. "Old people are my specialty, remember. I'll do just fine."

"Maybe you could get Walt some kind of new smell for his house." His nose wrinkles. "It's not awful, but it's not pleasant."

"Just be happy he used the nose hair trimmers I gave him."

Connor barks a laugh as he stops at a red light. He leans over and kisses the breath out of me. He pulls away, laughing again. "I love you." His eyes open wide. The expression on his face belongs on a guy in a horror movie when he discovers the killer is behind him. "I don't love you. I mean," he blows out a loud breath. "I don't *not* love you, but I don't *love you* love you."

"I wish I had popcorn," I say, straight-faced. "This is really fun to watch."

The light turns green and Connor starts forward. His jaw flexes every few seconds, and his eyes stay trained on the road.

"Connor, it's not a big deal. Slip of the tongue, right?"

"Right." His expression now is less *the killer is behind me,* and more *the killer has murdered everyone else and I'm determined to live.*

"You sold a painting today." My tone is extra cheerful and his jaw relaxes a little. "And you're about to have delicious lemonade. If you're lucky, I'll stick my finger in it and sweeten it up for you." Finally, his lips part, the teensiest smile moving them.

"Are you saying you're sweet?"

"Are you saying I'm not?"

He pretends to think. "You're more sour than sweet. At least you used to be."

"I hope you enjoy your awful lemonade today."

Connor slows to stop in front of a medium-sized home. A late-model sedan is parked in the driveway and the garage door is open.

He points out my window. "See that garage?"

I look. Boxes upon boxes are stacked everywhere. A fake Christmas tree stands in the corner, which is really depressing. Nothing kills the magic of Christmas like seeing a fake and undecorated tree lying against a wall.

"That's our job today. Mrs. Linton needs us to move all that out of the garage and repaint the walls."

"It's not my idea of a good time, but okay." I'm in no position to argue, especially since my bank account took a dip after I woke up today. Maybe I can find another way to make money. I hear inmates pay top dollar for used underwear. I gag on the thought.

Apparently I gagged for real, because Connor eyes me with concern and asks if I'm okay.

"A bug flew into my mouth." Yep. A bug has been in the car with us this whole time and we didn't know it until it careened into my mouth. I can tell he's not buying it, but I said it and now I'm committed.

He makes a face before lowering his mouth to sip coffee from his forest green thermos. When he's finished, he nods toward the house. "Let's go. She's probably waiting for us to get out."

I slap on a smile and get ready to work. I need the money now more than ever.

MRS. LINTON STANDS ON HER FRONT PORCH, WAVING GOODBYE. I wave back, mustering an exhausted smile, and climb into Connor's truck.

"I thought the mountains were supposed to be cooler in the summertime." The inside of Connor's truck is sweltering, the stagnant air more like a fog. "I think I sweat through my shirt at least two hundred and seventy-two times today."

Connor starts the truck and turns a couple knobs. Air blasts me, but it's not cold yet.

"It's a heat wave." Pulling his blue T-shirt over his head, his eyes focus on mine as he tosses it in the backseat. "You don't watch the news?"

I shake my head slowly. If he doesn't have another shirt to put on, it's going to be hard for me not to jump him while he's driving. He leans across into the backseat. His ab muscles flex as his core holds him in place. Moving boxes and painting all day really sucked, but this display might be making it worth it.

Sitting up, Connor pulls a white T-shirt over his head. Why is he looking at me like that? Oh, right, he asked me a question.

"No, I don't watch the news. Too many bad things on there." That, and the fact that at one point, *I* was the bad thing on the news.

Connor doesn't pick up on that, so I don't share it. No need to put a damper on our time.

He drives away from Mrs. Linton's house with a final wave at her. I watch in the side mirror as the sweet old woman walks back into her house. "I know I said we'd get blueberry muffins, but I need a shower first. You?"

He sniffs the air. "You really do need a shower."

I smack his arm. "Not funny."

"Want to save water? We can shower together." He grins.

I tap the center of my lower lip with the pad of my finger. "I think I've seen that on a T-shirt somewhere." He laughs like I'm kidding, but actually, I'm certain I have.

"What do you say?" He snatches my hand and holds it up, kissing the top.

"Drive faster to whoever's house is closer."

THERE'S SOMETHING TO BE SAID FOR SHOWER SEX. IT'S slippery and fun, but with Connor, everything is fun. Even dragging a limp Christmas tree across a garage.

We're on our way to a small town east of Brighton. *Sugar Creek.* The name itself makes me want to go there.

I reach back, lifting the hair off the nape of my neck. I gather it into a small ponytail and attempt to twist it around my finger like I did a million times before I cut my hair. Sighing silently, I drop the hair. How long will it be before I can twist my hair into a bun that doesn't have short pieces of hair sticking out like shards of broken glass?

"Birth control time," Connor says when the alarm on my phone goes off in my purse. "You're definitely going to need to take that pill today."

Memories of what was happening half an hour ago flood

my mind. I grab my purse and pull my little wheel of pills from the pocket. I pop the next one into my mouth and take a drink from my water.

"All set." I toss my purse back down on the floor. "Ready for your next load."

Connor lets out a surprised laugh and shakes his head. "You have the most incredible mouth."

"That's the second time today you've said that."

"Hah," he says loudly, his shoulders shaking.

I watch him laugh. He tips his head back every time he laughs. It's only a little, his chin lifts just a few degrees, but it's adorable, and when he laughs, he does it without reservation. So many of the guys I dated and spent time around concealed their laughter or happiness because they thought it made them look weak or less attractive. In my industry, attractiveness was paramount. If you acted like a happy-go-lucky, nice guy, you probably weren't going to be admitted into the club. Girls like the challenge a brooding, reserved man offers, and the club wants the girls, because the guys want the girls. So many times I'd imagined tossing a wrench into the spinning gears and watching them grind to a halt. What would happen if everyone acted like themselves for a night?

"Lost in thought over there?" Connor's voice filters through my memories of pulsing lights and manic music.

"Thinking about my past life, I guess."

"Anything you want to share?"

I finger the ends of my hair. "I used to have long hair. I chopped off ten inches before I left. I almost dyed it, but I couldn't bring myself to do it."

Connor grabs a strand and lets it slip through his fingers. "I like your hair this length."

"Thanks," I murmur, running a hand over the back of my head.

"What else do you miss about your old life?"

I look out the window, the trees flying past us, and bite on the end of a nail. After a moment to think, I drop my hands into my lap, squeezing them between my knees. "I miss the work I did. It was fun meeting people, talking to them, getting them excited and wanting to party. I'm sure to you that sounds empty, but I was a social person. I could talk to anyone. I used to walk around the clubs I worked for and introduce people, get them hyped, and make them want a table and bottle service. I miss being capable of something. It wasn't about giving them something they didn't want. I was showing them what was available to them, when they didn't know it was there."

"So you're an educator."

My head tips as I think. "Yeah, I suppose, in a non-traditional way."

"You educated me."

"How so?" I ask.

Connor pulls off the interstate and turns right. "I wanted someone to spend time with, I just didn't know you existed."

I smile at him. "Connor—"

He waves a hand between us. "I know, I know. I shouldn't say things like that." He flashes me a smile. "It's my turn to educate you on blueberry muffins. I'm about to ruin you for all others." He pulls into an open spot and gestures out the front windshield.

In front of us is a quaint storefront. It's red brick, attached on both sides to other stores. Looking down the street, I realize it's all brick storefronts and up front parking. It's adorable, like something from a movie.

"I've been to a lot of places, but this might be the cutest."

I climb out and walk to the front of the truck. Connor slips his hand over mine and points to a window painted with a cup of coffee with steam swirling up from it and a muffin.

"That's Lady J bakery. Kiss all other muffin memories goodbye."

He leads me over and holds the door open. Stepping inside is like stepping into someone's grandmother's kitchen. My mother never baked, or even cooked. She called herself an *assembler*. One bag of salad with one container of pre-cooked chicken and dinner was served. My grandmother was a different story. She baked every Sunday, and her kitchen smelled like this bakery—warm spices and sticky sugar.

A bell chimes overhead, announcing our arrival. It's late in the afternoon, and there are only a few other customers. Connor steps right up to the counter and orders.

"Two blueberry muffins, please, and two coffees."

"Sure thing," chirps the friendly girl at the register. She gets everything together and sets it on the counter between us. Connor pays while I grab the two coffees and paper bag and find an empty table.

"Thanks," I tell him when he sits down across from me.

"You can thank me later," he winks.

"You're insatiable," I say, but the muscles in my thighs tighten at his suggestion.

Taking the muffins from the bag, I set them in front of us and choose one. They smell too amazing to waste time removing the wrapper. I sink my teeth into the top of what is the most delectable thing ever to be created in the history of everything.

"Ohhhh," I moan, taking a second bite even though I haven't swallowed the first.

"I know," Connor says, doing the same.

"I don't know whether to thank you or be furious you've stolen all future muffin joy."

He uses a napkin to brush crumbs from the corner of his mouth, and sits back, watching me. "Would you rather have something exceptional once, or something basic all the time?"

I stretch my legs out so they reach between his under the table, and lean back against the chair. "I know what you're asking, and you should know my answer."

"When we get back to your place tonight, I'm going to exceptionally—"

Riiing.

Connor's mouth closes as he reaches for his phone, and looks at it. "It's my mom. I should take this. My dad had a doctor's appointment this afternoon."

I retract my legs so he can get up. "Of course."

He stands and strides out of the bakery. From the window, I can see him put the phone to his ear and say hello.

"Are you enjoying yourself?" A pleasant voice chimes behind me. I turn back from the window. A strikingly beautiful woman smiles at me. Her dark hair is gathered into a high bun and her expression is open and kind. She's wearing an apron with Lady J Bakery printed on the front.

"Immensely," I say, "I'm sure you're aware these are the best muffins on the face of the planet."

Her lips curve into a knowing smile. "I've heard that once or twice before."

"Are you Lady J?" I ask.

"Jane," she says, extending a hand.

I stand to shake it. "I'm Brynn."

"Would you mind if I sit?" She gestures to Connor's vacant seat. "I've been on my feet all day."

"Please," I say quickly, grabbing Connor's empty muffin wrapper and putting it in the bag.

She sits down, exhaling softly. "I love this place, but by the end of the day I'm exhausted."

Last year a statement like that would've meant something obscure to me, but after working with Connor, I empathize. I understand the feeling of exhaustion felt everywhere, even in your fingertips, after using your body all day long. Glancing out the window to Connor, I tell her I understand that feeling.

"Is he your boyfriend?"

I look back to Jane and see she's looking at Connor too.

"Uh, no." I shift in my seat, crossing one ankle over the other. "He's a... friend."

She chuckles softly. "Sounds complicated."

"I wasn't expecting to meet him." The admittance feels good. "I had other plans."

Something flits across her face, an emotion I can't see long enough to name. One slender finger rubs the base of her empty ring finger on her left hand. It looks like an absent-minded action, something the body does when the mind recalls a specific memory.

"That's the way it goes sometimes." She drags her gaze away from Connor and back to me. "Are you from here?"

I shake my head. "Phoenix. I'm staying in Brighton currently."

That look comes onto her face again, but this time it stays. *Nostalgia. Remembrance. Regret.* All wrapped up in one tormented expression. Before I can ask her if she's okay, she opens her mouth. "Brynn, I don't have anybody to give advice to, so I'm going to give it to you. Is that okay?"

"Sure."

"Don't let your plan limit you. Plans can make you shortsighted. They don't take into account the wonderful, beautiful, messy parts of life, and you'll end up missing them. Blind devotion to a plan can lead to regret, and regret can choke the life out of you."

"You're speaking from experience."

Jane swallows and averts her eyes. "Some regrets are forgotten over time. Others, well, they last a whole lifetime." The bell chimes and Jane looks up. "Your friend is back." She stands and smiles at Connor, but it's a shaky smile. Nothing like the warmth she exuded when she first approached me. "Hello," she says to him and walks behind the counter.

He responds to Jane and sits down. Worry creases his forehead.

"Everything okay?" I ask.

"My dad's appointment was fine. Nothing new. But"— Connor pauses, the corners of his lips turning down—"my mom told me someone stopped by a few minutes ago, looking for me. I wasn't at home, so she went to find me at my parents' house."

"She?" My voice is cool, even though my insides feel hot. Connor isn't mine. I'm his employee, and we're fucking. I have no business feeling territorial.

"Desiree. My ex."

Cue the fake smile. False happy head nod. "She probably realized what a mistake she made. I certainly would if I was your ex."

Pushing back from the table, I stand and gather my trash. "Ready?" I ask, locating a trash can and depositing the empty coffee and muffin wrapper.

I don't want to talk any more about Desiree. Jane might be right, some plans are limiting, but not this one. If

Connor's ex wants him back, I should bow out. Maybe this is a sign I need to hop back onto my path.

Connor tosses his containers in the trash and strides over to where I stand beside the door. His mouth is set in an unhappy line. The drive home will be a lot less fun than the drive here.

"Brynn?" Jane calls from behind the counter, making Connor and I both look over. "You said you're from Phoenix. I know this is a long shot, but you wouldn't happen to know someone named Aubrey Reynolds, would you?"

"No." I shake my head.

I did know an Aubrey Cordova. She wrote the insurance policy for my parents' fishing business. I handled it for them because they were out of the country. She was professional and jaw-droppingly gorgeous. At the time I thought she would've made a great club promoter if she weren't so buttoned-up, although I wouldn't recommend that job to anybody now.

"Sorry," I add when I see my answer has disappointed Jane. That name must have something to do with her advice to me.

"It's okay. Good luck," she waves.

"You're very different from the person I thought you were when we first met," Connor says quietly on our walk back to his truck. He opens the door for me and I climb in, sitting sideways and letting my feet dangle.

"Maybe you should be open to Desiree, Connor."

His jaw flexes, tense again. "And why is that?"

"My basket is flimsy. Don't put your heart into it."

"I thought that saying was about eggs."

"Whatever the content of the basket, it has the same ending. Splat." My hands slice sideways through the air.

He reaches up, gripping the top of the doorframe, and

leans in so we're less than a foot apart. I can't help but stare at him as his shirt rides up, his arms and muscles flexing with the grip of his fingers. "Sometimes, with you, it's like I'm in combat."

Despite the seriousness of our conversation, I grin. "Be careful, I fight with a baseball bat."

"Until I have you on your back, and then you mewl like a cat." Connor winks. "I'm done rhyming. Kiss me and don't tell me to be open to anyone else again."

"Connor..."

"Do as I say for once, Brynn."

Fuck it. For now, anyway.

I reach up. His cheeks are rough with tiny, stiff hairs, and I love the tingle it puts on my palms. I know I shouldn't let Connor have his way, but I can't help it. His lips are soft against mine, and he gives just as much as he takes. I thought the blueberry muffins were the best taste in the world, but I was wrong.

The sweetness of their aftertaste on Connor's tongue is even better.

18

CONNOR

THE OLD MAN'S WORDS SIT IN THE BACK OF MY MIND EVERY damn day. Ignoring them is nearly impossible. They lurk like a creepy shadow, hovering over every thought.

Might be best to let her go then.

I can't think of Brynn or the future without the approaching darkness of his words.

Walt wants to protect Brynn, I get that, but I want to protect her too. I don't want her to make a choice that will haunt us. Somehow, someway, I'm going to find a way out of this for her.

The thing is, I'm not the only person Brynn is getting close to. Walt is attached to her. She turned his human equivalent of a growl into a whisper. Before Brynn's arrival, I would've filed the chances of that ever happening under *No Fucking Way*.

Julia likes her too. Brynn has a natural ability to make people happy. She's likable, she relates to people on their level. She's not the ice queen I thought she was. She's still hot, but she's definitely not a robot.

Brynn's with Julia now, helping her execute the plan to make the Fourth of July parade a big deal. This afternoon I have my meeting with Candace, the person in charge of taking the empty space on Main and making it into an art gallery. She's coming to my house to see my work, and I've been trying to set up everything the way I want her to see it. When Brynn left this morning, she suggested the big windows in my detached garage might make for good lighting, and when I looked out there, I saw what she meant. Big windows run down both sides of the walls, making for a bright space. I spent most of the morning cleaning up the room, and I've just finished moving in all the paintings.

It's warm today, despite the heat wave breaking, and my sweat has soaked through my shirt. The garage door is open while I arrange everything. Old country music filters through my work area. My mom has a thing for Patsy Cline, and although I refuse to admit it out loud, so do I. "Crazy" plays loudly from my open laptop as I stand back and survey the painting I hung a moment ago.

Hands snake around my waist, startling me, but the feeling goes away quickly. "That was fast," I say, turning around to kiss Brynn.

But it's not Brynn.

"What the hell?" I shout into Desiree's face. Everything in her expression looks smug. The set of her mouth, the shine in her eyes, the rise of her cheekbones.

"Surprise," she says, her voice seductive. There was a time when that voice could melt me, but that time is long gone. And dead.

Her arms tighten, as though she's going to pull me closer. I put my hands around hers and push them off my hips, taking a step back. "What do you want?"

She pouts. "You're not happy to see me?"

I say nothing. There is no part of me that wants this person to be here.

"Aw, come on, Connor." She steps closer and traces her fingertips over my stomach. "Do you like my hair? I grew it out, just like you wanted me to."

"I think you need to find a dictionary and look up what the term *broken up* means." I swat her hand away. I'm curious to know why she's back, but I don't want to ask. More than anything, I'd like to know when she's leaving again. Maybe I can buy her a one-way ticket.

"Don't be mad at me, Connor. I've missed you." She blinks up at me, trying her best to look innocent. "Maybe I can make it up to you?"

Behind Desiree, a car pulls into my driveway. *Shit.*

Julia and Brynn peer through the windshield, the same confused look on their faces. Julia knows Candace, so she knows this isn't her. She says something to Brynn, and Brynn nods slowly. Desiree turns around, glaring at the car, and then the worst thing happens. Julia starts to back out.

Hurrying around Desiree, I jog out to where the car was parked and wave my arms. "Stop," I say, but Julia ignores me, and Brynn? She smiles. *She fucking smiles.* It's a disappointed, reluctant grin, and I hear the words hidden underneath. *Be open to Desiree. It's okay. This was temporary, right?*

The car moves farther down the street, then turns and disappears.

"Fuck," I yell, my hands fisted at my sides. "You." I point at the she-devil still standing in my garage. "Leave. Now."

Desiree stalks out in her tall heels and tight skirt. Her dumb clothes only make me want Brynn's snarky T-shirts more. She stops when she gets close to me. "If she wanted you, she would've stayed to fight for you. Keep that in mind."

"Fuck off, Desiree. Don't come back here."

She strides down the driveway and to her car, pausing at her open car door. "Ball's in your court. You know where to find me."

Hurrying inside, I grab my phone and call Brynn. It goes to voicemail. No surprise there. Candace will be here soon, so I can't go after her, but the second Candace is gone, I'm out of here like my ass is on fire. Brynn doesn't need any more nudging in the direction of that beach in South America, and Desiree may have just given her the shove she needed to skip town.

THERE AREN'T TOO MANY PLACES SHE COULD BE. SHE DOESN'T have a car. I've already tried her house. Wherever she is has to be within walking distance, unless Julia took her somewhere. Anthony could help me figure that out, but I'd rather not bring him into my drama.

"Come on, Brynn," I mutter, circling the same route for what feels like the hundredth time. She's not downtown, that I can tell. I parked and walked all through the busiest areas, looking for her. I went into the places I know she likes to eat, I walked through the grocery store, I checked the library. Nothing. That leaves me with one more choice.

I slow to a stop and get out. I wouldn't be doing this if it wasn't my last option.

I climb the steps and knock on the door, remembering what Brynn said about how he watches everything from his front window. If that's true, it means he has noticed each passing of my truck, and he knows I'm here right now.

Finally, he answers the door. "What do you want?" he growls. Any progress I made with him last weekend is gone, but that tells me Brynn is here now, or was here at some point.

"Is Brynn here?"

"No," he says, curt. "Anything else?"

"When was she here?"

"She left twenty minutes ago, after the last time we saw your truck pass."

"Which direction did she go?"

"I'm not telling you that."

I squeeze my eyes and try not to give in to my desire to say something rude.

"I guess I should thank you, boy. You reminded her that she needs to put her well-being first. You were holding her back, and now she can focus on what she came here to do."

I'm over this conversation. Arguing with this loon isn't getting me anywhere closer to finding Brynn. Without saying anything else, I walk back to my truck. It's late and the sun is setting. Brynn wouldn't go anywhere at night. She's too afraid.

Turning the truck around, I drive down the street and into Brynn's driveway. I know Walt is watching from his post at the window, so I send a one-fingered wave his direction. My mom would try to put me over her knee for that, but right now I don't care. Walt doesn't have the market cornered on asshole behavior.

"Brynn," I shout, knocking on her door. "I know you're there, so don't act like you're not."

The door opens. She looks at me like she's perfectly fine. There are no tears, no wavering lips. The waters of her eyes are calm.

"What's up?" she asks. Her voice is fine too. Chirpy, even.

"I've been blowing up your phone. Why aren't you answering?"

"I put it on silent when I left your house."

"Listen, I'm sorry about that. Nothing was going on and—"

"Connor, I know nothing was going on. You were standing in your open garage."

"Then why are you upset?"

"I'm not upset."

"What are you then? I was just at Walt's looking for you, and the way he acted made it seem like you were out for my blood."

She rolls her eyes. "He's melodramatic, in case you haven't noticed."

"Can I come in? Can we talk?" My weight shifts forward automatically, like my request will be accepted.

"I don't think so. Seeing you with her was good for me. I needed to remember why I came here. You don't need to be caught up in my mess."

"I want to be in your mess." Leaning my palm on the door frame, I settle in for a fight.

"Don't say that. Nobody wants to be in my mess."

"That's what people who care about each other do. They sit in the muck together, until they can stand and get out of it."

"No, Connor. I'm sorry. You and I can't go any further. I got caught up and shouldn't have allowed it in the first place. Please accept this as my immediate and official resignation. Personally, and professionally."

Her hands clasp together in front of her and her face is passive. No expression whatsoever. On my face, there is a lot of expression. I feel the opening of my mouth, the shock of my pulled-together eyebrows.

"Brynn, you can't be serious. Do you remember last night? You slept in my arms."

She nods. "That was nice. Thank you for giving me companionship."

"But... but..." I hate how I sound. I hate how I look. How can I salvage this? It doesn't help that the longer I stand here, the angrier I feel. "Companionship? That's what this was?" I'm working to keep my voice down, but it's tough. "No, Brynn. No. You're lying right now. To yourself. Your eyes have been telling a different story since our first kiss."

Finally, *fucking finally*, her facade breaks down. She steps back into her house and I follow her in. She slams the door shut and turns to me, her finger pointing my direction. "You weren't supposed to happen."

"I'm not going to apologize for that. I didn't expect someone to step in front of my truck *while it was moving*, but guess what? Someone did."

"Stop. Just stop. Let it go." Her hands move to her heart. "Let *me* go."

"No, Brynn. You're not deciding this for the both of us."

"My mom emailed me this morning. They're depositing money into my account next Friday. I can go away, Connor." She looks sad, so sad. Her hand is at her heart, as if she's holding it in. "You can move on. We always knew this was coming."

I slam a fist into my open palm, the loud smacking sound bouncing through the tiny entryway. "Fight, Brynn. Fight for us. Fight against *him*. Don't let him win."

"This isn't about only that." Her voice wavers.

"You're punishing yourself and you don't need to. You. Weren't. At. Fault."

"I am at fault!" Brynn screams, tears pouring from her eyes.

"Brynn, no."

"Yes, Connor. Yes. I saw her that day. Amy Prince. I was in a bookstore that morning, and she was there too. I didn't speak to her, but I saw her. She was fearful and agitated. She needed help. Her baby cried, and she stared at it like it was this unbelievable thing. It cried and cried. She did nothing to help it."

Brynn hands run through her hair, pulling it up in handfuls, then she drops it.

"I saw someone who needed help, and I didn't give it. *I walked away.*" She wipes away tears with the back of her hand. "I got a cup of coffee and picked out two books, bought them, and left. She was standing on the sidewalk, and I had no idea she was going to step in front of my car, but the first time I saw her, I knew she needed help. If I made the right choice the first time, Amy Prince and her baby could still be alive."

My heart twists. For Brynn's pain, her guilt, and her shame. What happened was not her fault, and yet she can't escape the feeling that it was. It's utterly heartbreaking, but I see it now. I see her need to run. Eric Prince isn't the only demon chasing her. Even worse, I don't think I can help her.

"Come here." I grab her shaking hands, but she stiffens, not allowing me to pull her in.

"Don't make this harder than it has to be," she whispers, looking down at the floor.

Tucking a finger under her chin, I nudge until she gives up and meets my eyes. "I wasn't supposed to happen. I get it, but how the hell are we to know what's supposed to happen? One second you were driving in your car, the next second two lives ceased to exist. I don't know how it can be that one second can change the course of our lives, I only know that it can. Amy Prince stepped in front of your car and changed your life forever. You stepped in front of mine, and my heart will never be the same."

"Connor, please, I'm doing this for you. For us."

"Bullshit. You're doing this because you're scared. Under all the guilt and fear, you're scared of me. Of what I represent. My heart makes your heart want to run and hide, and you're listening to it."

She stays silent, but her face is strained.

"You have nothing to say?" I'm so frustrated I could tear my hair out.

She shakes her head, her gaze going left, down to the ground.

A short, irritated breath surges from me. "Are you leaving next Friday?"

"Possibly." Her voice is tiny.

"The art exhibit opens next Friday night. Will you stay long enough to come to that?"

"Yes."

"Did you mean it? Are you quitting?"

She finally meets my eyes. "I have to, Connor. I just...have to."

"No, you don't. You could—"

Brynn moves for the door. "I think it's time you go."

I stride past her, stopping when I'm in line with her. My gaze locks on hers. "Over and over I tell myself to let you go, that it's best for you. What if it's not? How do you know? How do I know?" I continue on out the door.

"We're still friends," she says, her voice soft behind me. "I'll be there Friday night."

I keep going.

Down the stairs.

Across the yard.

Into my truck.

I drive away, ignoring every part of me that's fighting to turn around. Nobody said love would be easy. In fact, all the poems and songs make it clear just how fucking relentlessly difficult it would be.

I shouldn't be surprised.

19

BRYNN

I HAD A SERIOUS BOYFRIEND IN HIGH SCHOOL. WHEN HE BROKE up with me, I learned the meaning of the term *heartbroken*.

What I'm feeling right now takes that experience and makes it look insignificant. The pain of that heartbreak stayed in my chest. This pain? Systemic.

My fingertips feel the absence of Connor's warm skin.

My body yearns for his proximity.

My heart aches to see emotions in his eyes.

My lips crave his kiss.

All of me hungers for all of him.

This is what the great poets meant when they wrote about life-altering love.

"Ugh," I shriek, frustrated beyond words.

Another crumpled piece of paper joins the small pile on the floor beside me. My legs stretch out under the coffee table. A small stack of white printer paper and a pen are on its surface, and I'm attempting to keep myself together when all I want to do is fall apart.

It's just a letter. I've told myself that so many times it could be considered my mantra for this Sunday morning.

All I want is to write Connor a letter that will capture what he meant to me during this time. The problem? I keep writing in present tense. *You mean so much to me* should read *You meant so much to me.*

My heart wants Connor in the present. It doesn't want him placed in the category of *past.* Usually the brain overrides the heart, but this morning, on my seventh attempt to write him a letter, my heart takes control of my brain. What I feel for him leaks out of my chest, travels my veins, coloring my insides so they're no longer blood-red but now shades of Connor. The colors leave my fingers as words, and the words don't say goodbye. They say things I can't tell him. An admission of love, a brave declaration that I'll take Eric Prince head-on and fight him like I should.

I can't say any of that.

Sinking down, I tip my head back and lower it onto the couch cushion behind me. I close my eyes, letting a deep breath fill my chest. This is harder than I knew it would be. I didn't promise Connor a goodbye, but he deserves one. I straighten and pick up the pen. Maybe my eighth try will be successful.

My phone rings from the kitchen counter.

Connor?

I stand quickly, bumping my knee on the table in my haste. "Ow," I grumble, rubbing the throbbing bone as I hurry to the kitchen and grab the phone.

My heart sinks when I see the screen. "Darby, hi. How are things?" It's the same way I greet her every time she calls to update me on my condo. I'm expecting Darby to respond the way she always does, which is basically along the lines of *the property looks great, no changes, blah blah blah*, but not today.

"Brynn, you seem to have an enemy." Her voice shakes as she speaks.

Fear sets into my limbs. I know perfectly well I have an enemy. That wasn't something I shared with my property manager when I hired her, and now the fear that had retreated to arm's distance is up close again. "What happened?"

"I'm standing at your front door. There's a big hole in it. It looks like it was kicked in." She clears her throat. "There was a note in the hole."

"Read it to me, please." My voice trembles.

Darby hesitates. She's breathing into the phone, making a crackling sound. "It's nasty, Brynn. Are you sure you want me to read it?"

"I need to know what it says, Darby. Please." My voice is strained in my effort to stay calm.

Over the line, I hear the sound of paper unfolding. "It says, *Innocents don't run. Only fucking whores. I'm going to find you, and when I do, you'll wish it was dead.*"

My limbs, once full of bone and muscle, feel like they've been hollowed out with a serving spoon. The acidic taste of bile swirls at the base of my throat.

"Brynn?" Darby sounds afraid. Of me? When I hired her, I didn't tell her why I was going away. If she recognized me, she didn't mention it. I was so relieved to be talking face-to-face with someone who didn't look at me with fear or pity.

"I will take care of this, Darby," I say, summoning all the strength I have left. "Have you called anybody about the door?"

"Like the police? Because that's who should be called." Her voice is high-pitched now. Not quite hysterical but damn near close.

She's right. My guilt, my shame, my remorse, and regret,

can't be an excuse for allowing an unhinged man to function in society. "Darby, please keep that note. Leave my door alone. I'm going to handle this. You'll probably receive a call from Detective Wilkes."

"Brynn, what's going on?"

"Type my full name in your internet search bar. Just remember that no matter what it says, there's a reason I'm not in jail, and that I left town. Bye."

I end the call. Filling my lungs with a deep, shaky breath, I search my contacts. When I added him to my new phone, I hoped to never need him. While the phone rings, my gaze lands on the alarm sitting tucked under the back door. Walking over, I press on it with my big toe until it sounds, then stop. Just checking.

"Hello?"

Tears sting my eyes without warning. Memories of that day flood me. The bright light of the interrogation room, the smell of stale coffee, the eyes of someone who thought maybe I'd hit and killed two people on purpose.

"Hello?" he repeats. It's a voice I never wanted to hear again.

"Detective Wilkes, this is Elizabeth Montgomery. I need help."

I DIDN'T WANT TO DO IT. I REALLY, REALLY DIDN'T WANT TO.

My flight is booked. I did it. I closed my eyes and pressed the final button on my computer. A second later my email dinged with my confirmation.

Wiping the one millionth tear from my cheek, I pick up the phone. She answers on the fourth ring.

"Mom, hi."

"Hey, hon. Hang on."

I cringe at the airy sound of wind blowing across the phone, and my mom's muffled voice. "Can you wait a second before you head out? It's my daughter. I need a moment." The windy sound disappears. "Okay, that's better. What's up?"

"Eric Prince." She doesn't have much time to talk, so I get right to the point. "He kicked a hole in the front door at my condo and left a nasty note. He threatened physical violence, and he knows I've left town."

"Did you call—"

"Yes."

"Thank God. How do you feel? Is there any way he knows where you are? What about the property manager? Does she know where you are? What if he gets ahold of her and she tells him?"

"Mom, calm down. Darby doesn't know where I went. She can't tell him something she doesn't know."

"So what's happening now? What did the letter say?"

Eric Prince's words have been playing on a loop in my mind since Darby finished reading the damn note, but I'm not interested in saying them out loud. "It was bad, I don't want to go into it. Wilkes is going to Eric's house to talk to him."

"Does your building have cameras?"

"Uhh." I think back to the hallways, trying to see the corner where a camera could be installed. "I don't know. I'm sure Wilkes is already thinking of that, though."

"I'm worried about you. I always am, but I'm *really* worried now. Let me see if I can make some arrangements and get that money to you faster. I want you out of Arizona. Ummm," she pauses, and I would bet a hundred dollars she's biting down on a pencil as she thinks. It's her thing.

"Let me talk to your dad. He's out on the boat. Maybe he'll think of something I haven't yet."

"Mom, it's okay. Don't worry about it. Friday is fine. The car I ordered can't pick me up until Saturday morning."

"I bet that wasn't cheap."

"Don't ask," I tell her.

She lets out a low whistle.

I don't want to think about the cost right now. In the grand scheme of things, it's a small price to pay. "Wilkes said he'll need my other letters, and I told him I'd give them to him before my flight on Saturday."

"I want you out of there ASAP." Her voice is stern. If there were any way I could laugh right now, I'd be cackling over her tone. Strict isn't a word that could ever be applied to my mother's parenting style. Laissez-faire? Much more accurate.

"I'm working on it."

"And Connor?"

"I thought you only had a moment to talk?"

"Just tell me so I can go."

"It's over, and that's good, because I need to leave." It hurts my heart to even say the words.

"You're okay?"

"Yep." The lie slips smoothly through my teeth, but the immediate sadness I feel gurgles around in my core.

"No you're not. I can tell."

I sigh. "You're right. I'm not okay. It hurts."

"I'm sorry sweetie."

"I knew better than to let this happen. I just," my lips purse and I see Connor's face, his grin, his messy morning hair. "I just didn't know a man like him would be here."

"I love you, babe. Everything will work out. Friday, okay? We'll get you out of there."

"Thanks, Mom. Love you. Bye."

Her voice trails through the phone as I hang up, and I know she's yelling to whoever was waiting for her. Standing by for Wilkes to call is going to drive me nuts. So are the questions running through my mind. Is he at Eric Prince's house right now? Has Eric admitted it? What if he does? Will he go to jail? Will I press charges? Do I even want to? Maybe he needs mental help, not jail. If he gets better, can I stay here? Can I be with Connor?

I grab my purse and leave the small house that has become my safe haven. I always lock the door. It's such a habit that I do it without thinking, but today I'm careful and deliberate, absorbing the reverberation against my fingers when the key slips into the lock. My ears strain to hear the satisfying *thunk* as the lock slides into place.

Today it means more.

I head for the grocery store. At first I found it depressing when the employees there learned my name, but know I think maybe it's not. Maybe it's nice. For years I went to the same grocery store in Phoenix, and nobody ever learned my name. I didn't bother to learn theirs either. There was always the perfunctory *How are you* from the cashier and my expected response *Good, thanks, how are you?* What would've it taken to learn their name? One second, maybe two? I was too busy, rushing from one event to the next, making friends and widening my circle so I could find the right people to come to the clubs and make the owners happy.

I spent all my time on people who knew nothing about me except my name and which club I could get them into, and the worst part? I didn't know a damn thing about them either. I spent my time on them, my precious, dwindling time, and it amounted to nothing. Seconds became minutes,

minutes became hours, and then suddenly it was years of empty and fake friendships.

I was so used to seeing right through people that when I saw Amy Prince and she needed help, I looked through her like she was transparent. What would've changed if I'd said hello to her? Could I have offered to soothe her baby? Bought her a croissant from the cafe in the bookstore and sat down across from her, asked her about herself and what she liked to do?

I am not guilty of involuntary manslaughter.

I am guilty of keeping my hands to myself when I saw someone falling.

Detective Wilkes calls as I stand in aisle three.

"Eric Prince says he never sent you any letters or kicked in your door." My shoulders slump, my internal debate over which cereal to buy forgotten. He continues. "I went to your property manager's office and got the note she found this morning. Brynn, I'm sorry to tell you this, but it appears to be a female's handwriting."

I sigh quietly, my gaze dropping from the boxes of cereal to the floor. "Now what?"

"I have someone looking into cameras that may have been running in the area this morning. From nearby businesses and such. I'll let you know what I turn up."

"How was he?"

"Prince? Seemed okay, I guess. A little disheveled, maybe I woke him."

I'd been picturing him as someone with a deranged glint in his eye, dirty clothes, and unkempt, too-long hair. Very different from the clean-cut guy in the family photo the news sites kept using.

"A few months ago Amy's mother found a journal. I didn't call you because I hoped you were moving on and didn't want to stir the pot, but you might as well know now." He clears his throat and continues. "We can't be certain unless we have it examined by a therapist, but it sounds like Amy was dealing with postpartum depression."

Oh. Ohhh. That makes sense. That day in the bookstore... I never told anyone I saw her before the moment she stepped off the curb. I didn't want people to know she'd ignored her crying infant. *Postpartum depression...*

"Thanks for letting me know," I say quietly. "Do you still want the letters I was sent?"

"It wouldn't hurt for me to see them," he says. "Drop them off like we discussed. If anything comes up, I'll be in touch." Wilkes hangs up.

I sigh and rub my eyes, mentally sorting through everything. I've never considered the possibility it could be anyone but Eric Prince.

If not him, then who?

20

CONNOR

"HEY MAN," ANTHONY YELLS ACROSS THE ROWS OF CHIPS AND cases of cold drinks. "You filling up?"

"Yeah," I answer, grabbing a package of sunflower seeds and the biggest bottle of water I can find. I consider buying a twenty-two of beer but decide against it. "What are you up to?" I ask, joining him. He's standing in front of the hot dogs. They roll around on the burner, glistening with grease.

"Looking for a heart attack." He shakes his head. "I can't eat this shit. I need real food." He eyes the sunflower seeds in my hand. "Looks like you could use some real food too. Want to grab dinner?"

I shake my head. "Can't. I have to go shopping."

He raises his eyebrows. "Does Brynn have you shopping with her already? You're whipped."

My heart twists at the mention of Brynn. It's been two days since I've seen her. Two days since she told me we're better off apart and stood next to her open front door, waiting for me to leave. *We're still friends*, she said as I walked away. *I'll be there Friday night.*

My gallery opening. Probably the last night I'll ever see

Brynn. Her parents will pad her bank account with as much money as she needs to get to wherever the hell she's going, and she'll skip town.

But she's not leaving without a few things from me.

Ignoring the whipped comment, I tell him I need to pick up some stuff from Sports House. The massive outdoors store on the far side of town has everything I need in one place.

Anthony walks beside me to the gas station register. He must've forgotten about the heart attack turning circles on a spit behind us.

"Good. I need to grab a few things for fishing this weekend. I lost a chatterbait to a snag and had to cut my line. Favorite one, too." Anthony shakes his head, as if this is some great loss.

I give him a look and he laughs. He knows I don't speak *angler*. "Don't you have plans with Julia?" I don't particularly want company tonight. I don't need Anthony surveying my purchases.

"Nope," he says, not getting the hint.

He whistles all the way to my truck and hops in the passenger seat. I sigh and pull the gas spout from my truck, tucking it back into the holder and tightening my gas cap. Looking around, I spot Anthony's car parked off to the side, away from the people getting gas. There goes any hope that he would need to move his car and I could ditch him.

I get in and start the truck.

"Julia is with Brynn tonight," Anthony says, as I pull away. "Parade stuff."

I tilt my head up slightly and lower it slowly. It's a lazy nod that allows me to think about what to say next. It doesn't matter though, because Anthony's moved on to something else.

He opens the small ice chest on the floor next to his feet. "Did you know you have all kinds of food in here?"

My gaze flickers over to the container of carrots, the pulled pork sandwich wrapped in tin foil, the bag of potato chips. My mother packed it for Brynn, and I didn't have the heart to tell her she didn't need to. I couldn't eat it either, even though I was starving when I finished this afternoon. Despite Brynn needing a lot of direction on the job, having a second set of hands was more helpful than I realized. I need to start looking for someone to fill her spot, but I don't want to have to tell my parents she's gone. That conversation will have to happen soon enough, delaying it a few more days isn't going to hurt anything.

Brynn's helpfulness wasn't the only thing I missed today. I missed her presence, her laughter, her chatter and the way she hummed songs without realizing it. She would've loved seeing the old photos I was hanging today as a part of a gallery wall. I didn't ask the homeowner, but I'm assuming the people in the photos were her grandparents.

It started with a black and white photo of a couple in a church and went all the way through a lifetime until a recent photo of a large family, including the now white-haired couple, and younger people surrounding them. If Brynn had been there she would've asked about the collection. She would've pointed out different parts of the pictures and commented on what she saw. The job would've taken an hour longer because she would've been making a friend while I re-configured her measurements.

"What?" I ask when I realize Anthony is staring at me.

He points down. "The food in the ice chest."

"Oh. Um. Yeah, I knew it was in there."

"You don't want it?"

Instead of answering, I use my teeth to rip open a corner

of the plastic bag and pour in a mouthful of sunflower seeds.

"More for me, then." Anthony pulls out the tin foil and unwraps it. "Yes," he hisses, grinning and taking a big bite. A little slaw falls off the sandwich and onto the spread out foil on his lap. "Your mom should sell this. Forget Vale Handyman Services."

I swallow my mouthful and take a drink of water. "Are you trying to put me out of a job?"

"You're going to be a famous painter. Brynn can run the handyman biz while you paint all day." He tilts his head and squints at me. "Maybe I'll get you a beret for your birthday. It'll look good on you. Bring out your cheekbones."

"Don't be surprised when you hook a fish wearing a beret."

"Hah," he barks and takes a huge bite of the pulled pork. "So why are you going all the way to Sports House? Can't you find what you need at the supply store in town?"

"No." I can tell he's dying to hear more, but I'm not sharing. If I tell him what I'm after, he's going to want to know why the hell I'm buying it. I'd rather not have that conversation when we're stuck in this car and I can't get away from his questions.

Anthony finishes the food meant for Brynn and tosses his trash back into the ice chest at his feet. He opens his mouth, and when I'm certain he's going to ask about Brynn, he asks if I want to hit bags tomorrow after work. I agree quickly. The tension inside me is building every minute, *every fucking second*.

When we get to Sports House, I head right for the emergency preparedness section at the back of the store. On my way, I pass a display shelf and pick up a medium-sized maroon backpack with a million little compartments. Once

I'm in the section I came here for, I grab a LifeStraw, two mylar blankets, a pocket knife, and waterproof matches. I don't know what it's like where Brynn is going, but she's going to have what she needs to survive. Water, fire, and shelter.

Anthony says nothing. He watches the items as I toss them into the cart, and when I'm finished, we walk over to the fishing section. He grabs what he needs from a massive selection. To me, it all looks the same and has the same function—catch a freaking fish. To Anthony, everything is different and meets different needs. He grabs worms from the cooler and goes to check-out.

On the drive back, when I think that perhaps, by some miracle, I've gotten away with not hearing any commentary from the peanut gallery, I'm proven wrong.

"Why didn't you know Brynn's with Julia? Why are you free tomorrow night, when you haven't been available for weeks? And for fuck's sake, why didn't she eat the lunch your mom packed for her today?"

I have some questions of my own, starting with *When did you get so observant* and *Can you go back to being unobservant?* To buy time, I scratch the back of my head with two knuckles and roll my neck around a few times. I don't want to tell Anthony for the same reason I don't want to tell my parents. Not *never,* just *not yet.*

I'm not going to get that option. I'm stuck in a small space with Anthony, and he's staring me down.

"Brynn and I aren't seeing each other anymore."

"I already knew that."

I sigh and shake my head. I should've known. Julia and Brynn have become friends. If Anthony knows about that, then he probably knows that—

"I hear Des is back in town."

"Yep."

"Does that have anything to do with you and Brynn calling it quits?" He reaches into the plastic bag on his lap as he talks and pulls out his new bait. Turning it over, he examines it through the clear packaging. I'm glad he's not staring me down right now, demanding answers with that look he gets when he's determined.

"Sort of, but not really. Des showed up at my place and tried to insert herself back into my life. Some shit about how she misses me, yada yada. I told her to beat it. Then Brynn drove up with Julia."

Brynn's expression on that day pops into my head. She wasn't mad. She wasn't threatened. Realization was dawning on her as she sat in Julia's passenger seat.

"Brynn ended things because she has other plans, Anthony. Plans I don't have any hope of interrupting." And, maybe, I don't want to. That's why I went to Sports House today. That's why I went to the hardware store when I left her place yesterday. If Brynn needs to leave to feel safe, how can I get in the way of that? I won't. Instead, I'll make her feel as secure as I possibly can.

"It doesn't make any sense to me, man. Either she wants to be with you, or she doesn't. End of story."

"It's not always black and white," I say, staring out at the dark road ahead of us. "Some stories have a lot of colors." It makes me think of the Eye of the Storm painting. I still don't know where to send it. The email said the buyer would contact me with an address.

"Whatever this story is, it must be a fucking rainbow, Connor."

The thought doesn't cheer me up. Rainbows aren't real. They're what happens when the sun shines through particles in Earth's atmosphere.

Brynn isn't the sun. She's a violent storm, an angry body of water, a churning sea spewing fear, shame, and regret. Emotions strong enough to sink an average human being, a painter masquerading as a handyman, a guy who fears he has the passion but lacks the talent. She's strong enough to sink a freighter.

Brynn is a category five gale, and I'm fucking drowning in her.

21

BRYNN

JULIA HAS TOO MANY GOOD QUALITIES TO COUNT. SHE'S caring and compassionate, funny and adventurous, and good at reading people too. Especially me. Today I'm not counting that on her good qualities list. Today I want to be overlooked. I'm tired, cranky, and seeing things that don't exist. Or might not exist. But they could exist.

When I thought Eric Prince was sending me threatening letters, I could handle that. He had an excuse, and at least I *knew* who it was, or who I thought it was, anyway, but a female? I never saw that coming. The other letters were written in all caps. I assumed it was him, because who else would write those words? There was a weird comfort in knowing who was doing it, and now that's gone. Before, I looked harder at every man who crossed my path, making certain I was safe from Eric Prince. Now I have to look harder at everyone.

Not Julia. This is the third time she has hugged me since I arrived this morning to help her with last minute parade details. I haven't told her it's my birthday. Walt drove me here, and I didn't tell him either. Julia is hugging me because she senses my feelings.

She pulls back from the hug and doesn't say anything about it. Just goes right on talking with her little clipboard and the checklist I made for her. We're both wearing the T-shirts I told her to make. I distributed them to shop owners around town, and talked Mary and Cassidy into wearing them for their shifts. The owner of the cafe let all the waitresses wear them, and they said everyone who came in was asking about the parade. Julia was ecstatic when she heard that.

She's reading off the to-do items on the list when a guy with a camera around his neck taps her on the shoulder.

"Hi, are you Julia?" With a thumb, he points behind himself to a group of people standing off to the side. "They said you're in charge."

Julia pushes back her shoulders and pulls the clipboard into her chest. "I'm Julia. Can I help you with something?"

The guy extends a hand. "I'm Craig. I work for the Arizona Times. They sent me up here to cover your parade."

Julia's eyes widen. Her fingers grip the sides of her clipboard as she struggles to maintain her cool. "The Arizona Times?"

Craig grabs the yellow lanyard from around his neck and holds it out. Dangling from the end is a laminated card with his picture and the name of the newspaper written in large letters. "There's a section for events around the state. Brighton is making the news with their first annual Fourth of July parade." He grins and shrugs. "I need some pictures if you wouldn't mind. Maybe one of you next to a float?"

"Sure," Julia says, but she stays in place.

Grabbing her arm, I lead her to the Tonolep Farms float. It's decked out with bales of hay, red and white gingham fabric bunched between the bales, and a cow statue. "Stand in front of this one. People recognize this brand. They sell their milk in all the grocery stores in Phoenix." I position her so the cow is behind her head. "Act natural. Loosen your grip on the clipboard. Maybe hold it with one hand and put the other one on your hip." She listens. I back up and let Craig work.

After he has taken a few pictures, Julia motions me over. "You helped plan it too. Without you, the Arizona Times probably wouldn't have heard about it."

Craig swings my direction, his camera still in front of his face. I lift my hands. "No no no. This is your project." Not to mention I don't need to give my location away.

Craig lowers the camera. His eyes scrunch, his head tilts. "I feel like I know you from somewhere."

I laugh, but the sound is too loud and forced. "I get that a lot," I say, trying to rein in the alarm slamming through me. "I have one of those faces."

Craig appraises me for one more second before he gives up and turns back to Julia. He asks her to lead him through some of the other floats and introduce him to other people he can interview.

They walk away, and all the frightened air leaves my body. There is nothing for me to slump against, so I settle for letting my shoulders fall and dipping my head.

Crisis averted.

"THANKS FOR ALL YOUR HELP TODAY," JULIA SAYS AS WE PULL up to my house.

Leaning over the seat, I give her a quick hug. "No problem."

She pulls back but keeps her gaze on my house. "What's that?"

I whip around, slamming my elbow on the passenger door. Lying at my front door is a dark red bag of some kind, and next to it are flowers and balloons.

"He remembered," I murmur, rubbing my elbow.

"Is it your birthday today?" Julia's tone is incredulous.

I turn back, biting my lip and eyeing her. Her mouth is hanging open and her eyebrows are raised. "Yes."

"Brynn! You let me go all day without knowing. This is not acceptable. What are you doing tonight?"

I catch myself squirming and force my hands to stay still in my lap. "Seeing Walt."

Julia lightly smacks her steering wheel. "Saturday night. You and me. Girls only."

"Sure," I say, guilt devouring me instantly. I plan to leave Saturday morning. By Saturday afternoon I'll be on a plane to Dallas, and from there I can go almost anywhere.

"Good," she nods, smiling.

I open the door and climb out, telling her I'll see her in two days at the parade. I back up and wave. She pulls away and I walk up to the house.

I was right. It is a bag, but more like a backpack. The flowers are wild, the kind I see growing all over town, and their stems are tied with red and white kitchen twine. My gaze falls on a card tucked under the backpack, just as the breeze sends the balloons bumping into the house. My name is written on the front in Connor's handwriting. At least I know that for certain.

Scooping everything up, I balance it in one arm and unlock the door with the other. I kick the door closed, glance around, and re-lock it. After dumping everything on the couch, I fill a water glass and place the flowers inside, then go back to the living room.

I start with the backpack. So many zippers, so many compartments. Am I going on a camping trip that I don't know about? Inside I find mylar blankets, something I can drink through that has a built-in water filter, a first-aid kit, waterproof matches, and a small tool kit.

I'm more confused than ever. Connor didn't strike me as a guy who needed much direction in the gift-giving department. Maybe I can drop a hint to Julia and she can—

Oh my god.

He's preparing me.

He's trying to take care of me after I leave, for as long as he can. He wants to keep me safe.

I grab the card and pull it from the envelope.

Brynn,

I tried writing you a funny rhyme, but it turns out rhyming isn't as fun when you're not thinking on your toes.

I've thought of all the ways I could make you stay. I'm not above faking a terminal illness, but then I decided I can't stop you. And I shouldn't stop you, either. Not when the stakes are so high. So, instead, I'll do what I can to get you ready to leave. No, I don't like doing it, but that's what you do when you love someone. Yeah, I said it. I wrote in pen, so unless I want to cross it out and make the card messy, I'll just have to leave it there. It's fine, because I think if you left and I didn't tell you, I'd regret it forever.

I hope wherever you end up, you find peace. I hope you forgive yourself. I hope you show life who's the boss. Me. I'm the boss, remember? Okay, enough. I'm making jokes and rambling because I'm sad, and I love you.

Two times. I said it two times.

Love,

Connor

Ugh. Knife in the chest. Turn the knife, carve out my heart. Connor loves me. I love Connor. And yet, I'm in greater danger than I knew. By extension, so is he. So is everyone here in Brighton. Connor, Walt, Julia.

I'll tell him in two days, after his show. I'll tell him I love him, and I'll tell him about the door and the note. He should know there is still a threat, that I'm leaving for a good reason.

For dinner I make chicken marsala and two cupcakes, and I take it all to Walt's. I'm not ready to tell him goodbye, so I don't. He will be my last stop on my way out of town. Walt sings to me, a gravelly rendition of Happy Birthday, and it's the best song I've ever heard. When I get home, my heart is more conflicted than ever, even though I know what I have to do.

That night, I sleep with Connor's note under my pillow.

22

BRYNN

KNOCK KNOCK KNOCK.

I jolt upright. Sunlight pours in through the blinds. What time is it? I look around, trying to get my bearings.

Knock knock knock.

Oh, right. The door. I climb from bed and go to the front door. Peering through the peephole, I see Cassidy's worried face.

Sliding the door alarm out of the way with my foot, I unlock the double locks at the same time and open the door.

"Hi, Cassidy." The bright sky makes my eyes squint.

She looks at my pajama top and boxers. To be fair, I'm wearing a shirt that says 'GFY.' I don't really mean it. It's supposed to be funny, but I'm aware *Go Fuck Yourself* is crude and that young kids can read, so it's a sleep shirt. Just like my *twat* shirt.

"Are you just now waking up?"

I shrug. "I couldn't sleep last night."

Cassidy nods empathetically. "I understand."

I really hope she doesn't understand. I pray she never

knows the nightmares that plagued me last night. They were the ones I had right after the accident, where I dream I hit Amy and Samuel on purpose.

"What's up?" I lean against the open door and wait for her to answer.

She twists her hands in front of her. Her gaze is apprehensive. "So, there's this guy I like and I've been waiting forever for him to ask me on a date. He called twenty minutes ago and asked me out for lunch. *Today*. The only problem is that I can't find a sitter on such short notice. I really, really want to go and I don't have a day off for another week." She peeks over my shoulder. "Is Connor here, by chance? I don't see his truck, but I thought maybe…"

"Connor isn't here," I say irritably. It's not her fault, and I remind myself that as I ask her why she can't take Brooklyn on the date. If the guy likes Cassidy, he better like Brooklyn too.

Cassidy gives me a look that tells me how hopeless I am. "Can you come over and play with her for an hour? Max two? You can even put on a movie." She makes prayer hands at me. "Please? She likes you."

Maybe it's the fact that I'm leaving in two days. Maybe it's my desire to do something nice for Cassidy. She greeted me on day one with a pie. Maybe that's why I say yes, even though Brooklyn still terrifies me.

"I'll be over in twenty, is that okay?" I need to change and grab something to eat.

"Yes!" Cassidy raises a fist. "Thank you. I'll make it up to you, I promise."

She turns to leave, and I shut the door.

THE INSIDE OF CASSIDY'S HOUSE LOOKS LIKE A TOY STORE projectile vomited in a small, enclosed space. Dolls and stuffed animals, crayons, building blocks, paper, and even game pieces are everywhere. In the center of it all sits Brooklyn, playing some kind of game with plastic shapes. When she sees me, she tosses the game aside, the pieces flying into the air.

"Brynn!" She runs to me and wraps her arms around my knees.

"Hi, Brooklyn." I wobble and catch myself on the doorjamb.

Cassidy laughs and shrugs. "She loves you."

I'm not sure what to say, so I tell Cassidy she looks pretty. Her white top is very low-cut for a lunch date, but who am I to judge? I let Connor paint me half-naked.

I walk farther into the small home and sit down beside Brooklyn. She's putting shoes on a doll, her previous activity forgotten. She struggles to get one of the shoes on, so I hold the doll in place for her as she works the shoe over the ridiculous and unrealistic arch of the doll's foot.

"Jeremiah's here!" Cassidy sings, pulling back her curtain. "I know I should make him come to the door, but" —she nods at Brooklyn—"I'm not ready to have that conversation with her."

"Have fun," I say as Cassidy grabs her purse and swings it over her shoulder. "See you soon."

She bends down to kiss Brooklyn's head. "Be safe and listen to Brynn." Cassidy sails out the front door just as Jeremiah is on her first porch step. His lips stretch into a smile when he sees Cassidy. The door swings shuts behind her. I'm curious about Jeremiah, almost curious enough to watch out the front window, Walt-style, but I stay planted beside Brooklyn.

When she's done playing with the doll, I have her show me where her things belong. Together we clean up the room, and then I make her a snack. Once she's finished with that, we go out back and I push Brooklyn on her swing set. She wants to go high and I tell her it's not going to happen, to which she replies that her mommy lets her do it. If Cassidy wants to send Brooklyn to the moon, that's her prerogative. I prefer a nice, safe medium-height arc.

Declaring she's going to pick a flower for her mom, Brooklyn slows to a stop and hops off the swing, walking determinedly to the vine growing along the wall. Big purple blooms compete for space down the entire length of the fence we share. Brooklyn walks back and forth, considering, before she reaches in and pulls one off.

"This one is—" Brooklyn's eyes widen, her mouth falls open. If I weren't standing in front of her, I wouldn't think such a scream could come from this small a person.

"Brooklyn, what is it?"

She grabs her throat and starts touching it. Her breath sounds shallow like she's pulling air through a mesh screen.

I scoop her into my arms and hurry into the house. I fly through the kitchen, grabbing Cassidy's car keys off a wall hook in the kitchen as I go. Going through the front door and getting into the car is a blur. All I know is that Brooklyn is buckled and she's still wheezing and crying and none of it sounds good or right. I don't know squat about first-aid, and *why did Cassidy ask me to babysit*? How could she leave Brooklyn with me? I'm the least qualified person in the world to watch a kid. I might not have reacted appropriately if she choked. I don't even know if I'm reacting appropriately now. Maybe I should have called 9-1-1.

Do I have my purse? Do I even have my driver's license? *I'm driving.*

I grip the steering wheel and try to forget about that. I knew it would have to happen eventually, but not like this. Not in a possible emergency, not when I don't have time to give in to my fear and let the road take away my ability.

I pull up to the emergency room doors and hurry from my seat. Carefully I extract Brooklyn from her car seat and thank God for even the small breath she's struggling to intake.

With Brooklyn in my arms, I run past the glass door that slides open for me, skidding to a stop at the front desk.

"I need help," I shout. The woman sitting behind the desk watches me with eyes the size of dinner plates. "She was picking a flower, then she screamed and now she's not breathing right. I need help. She needs help. Get a doctor. Right now!"

She picks up a phone and presses a button. She stares at me while she waits for someone to answer.

"Right now right now right now," I demand, fear seizing me. My ability to stay calm went out the window the second Brooklyn began to scream.

I will save this one.

23

CONNOR

I just want my trusty sandwich. That's it. The streets around the diner are a nightmare. People setting up seats along the parade route, children darting back and forth. I had to park four blocks away and walk here.

"Mary," I say, grateful for the woman behind the counter. She takes one look at me and clucks her tongue. "What?" I ask, swinging my leg over a stool and settling down with a thunk.

"You don't look so good." She sets an iced tea in front of me and leans one forearm on the counter. "Did you break that girl's heart?"

I roll my eyes. "No. Why would you think that? Maybe she broke my heart."

"She might have, but the way you two were together, there's no way her heart isn't as broken as yours."

I grunt. I don't want to talk about this anymore. I want to eat a sandwich, watch the parade from my spot at the diner counter, and get ready for the opening tonight.

"Is this a Monte Cristo kind of day?" Mary asks.

I nod and sip my tea while she goes back to the window,

hands someone my ticket, and hollers my name for my extra fries.

I'm staring at my hands, folded on the countertop, when I hear a guy from a few seats down call out Cassidy's name. She turns to look at him, eyebrows raised. "How's your little girl?" he asks loudly.

Cassidy leaves the soda station and walks to the counter, coming to a stop in front of the guy who asked her the question.

"She's good, Chris. Thanks for asking. We didn't know she's allergic to bees. She's never been stung."

"My wife said your babysitter was about to lose it."

Cassidy laughs softly and glances at me. "Brynn was a pinch hitter."

I straighten. "Brynn babysat?"

"Yeah." Cassidy is still standing beside Chris, but she's directing her words to me. "I needed a last-minute sitter. I was hoping you'd be at her place when I went to ask, honestly."

I nod and keep quiet. I'm not interested in publicly declaring our split.

"Brooklyn was stung and Brynn drove her to the emergency room. She used my car, obviously."

What the...? "Brynn drove?"

Cassidy nods. "I didn't even know she had a license. She doesn't have a car, I guess I just assumed she didn't know how to." Her face pinks, like she's embarrassed. The more she talks, the more it's obvious she doesn't know much about the person she left her child with, which is probably why she's red-faced.

Mary sets my sandwich down in front of me. The entire time I'm eating, I'm trying to picture Brynn behind the wheel of a car. The image is fuzzy in my mind, and I can barely place Brooklyn in the back. Does Brynn even know how to buckle a child into a carseat? I sure as hell don't. She must have been terrified.

I pull out my phone, bring up our text message conversation, and stare at it. My thumbs hover over the keyboard, but I can't make them type. I don't know what to say to her. How can the span of five days make us feel a world apart?

THE PARADE WAS COOL. I'LL HAVE TO THINK UP A BETTER adjective than that when I see Julia. She's going to want to hear something better than *cool*.

I'm walking back to my car when I see shoulder-length blonde hair going the opposite direction.

"Brynn," I call out before I even know what I'm doing. Where is the connection between my brain and my mouth?

She turns. Sees me. Her arms wrap around her middle. Protecting herself. Protecting her heart.

I jog to her. I can't play it cool and walk, I'm not one of those guys. Fuck my sleeve, my heart is on my forehead. It doesn't matter anyway. She's all but gone. That money should be in her account by now. It's Friday.

"Hi," she says when I get to her.

"Hey," I say back. I want to grab her and feel the outline of her body against mine. I want to run my hands through her silky hair and nibble on the corners of her lips. I want to bury myself in her and never come out. I want to run away with her.

My fucking foolish heart.

I think she wants to touch me too. Her fingers curl into her palms, which are rigid at her sides.

"Connor, I'm leaving in the morning. Something

happened this week, and I need to go. It's important I leave. For everyone."

"What happened?"

She shakes her head. "I don't want to talk about it."

"Brynn, come on. It's me."

Her eyes tear up. "I know it's you, Connor, but I still don't want to say it. I just want this nightmare to be over."

"Am I a part of your nightmare?"

"Sort of. Moving on, leaving you, that's part of the nightmare." Her lower lip trembles and the tears spill over onto her cheeks. I take a step closer and she backs up. "No. I can't handle your touch right now."

I can't hide the hurt on my face, which makes her cry harder.

"Not because I don't want you. God, no. Not at all." She swipes at her cheeks. "Because I want you too much. If I bend at all, I'm sure to break."

A car drives by us. Brynn's eyes flicker to it, scrutinizing. It turns the corner and she looks back at me.

"Aren't you already broken?" I want to hold her. That's all. Her warmth is everything I need.

She nods and takes another step away. "Will you let me drive you home?"

She says no without stopping to consider. I already knew she would do this.

"What if I promise not to talk? Then you won't have to walk."

We both smile. I didn't even mean to rhyme.

"Okay," she says softly, falling into step beside me. When we reach my truck, I open her door and she climbs in. I go around and hop in.

It's hard to breathe the same air as Brynn and stay calm. Five days without her was enough time to make her seem new again, even though I know every inch of her. The body I devoured night after night, the lips I claimed, the heart I stole, feels far away from me now.

Once I navigate out of the parade area, the drive is easy. There are only a few cars driving around us, and it's quiet for a Friday afternoon.

I make good on my promise. No talking. When I pull up to her place, she breaks the silence.

"Good luck tonight." Only one side of her mouth lifts with the smile she's trying to put on her face.

"You're coming, right?"

She nods. She looks so sad.

"You said you wouldn't leave without saying goodbye."

Her mouth immediately opens to argue. I know as well as she does that she never agreed to that, but I still put up a hand to stop her.

"I need a goodbye, Brynn. Maybe you don't, but I do."

"Okay," she whispers. She gets out of my truck and slams the door. She waves once, slowly, then turns toward the house.

Suddenly I remember something. Rolling down the window, I yell, "You drove a car."

She turns back to face me, her eyes wary. "It was an emergency."

"Maybe so, but you did it."

I roll up the window up, not giving her the chance to argue. Looking in my side mirror, I wait for a car to pass, and drive away.

24

BRYNN

UGH.

I wasn't prepared for that.

Connor's engine roars to life behind me as he pulls away from the curb. Like each of my feet is a sack of potatoes, I drag them up the front walk and to the door. By the time I step into the house, Connor is long gone.

Exhausted from two hours in the sun watching the parade, and even more drained from what seeing Connor did to my heart, I drop down onto the sofa. I tuck a throw pillow behind my head, prop my feet on the arm of the couch, and close my eyes. In the darkness of my mind, I see Connor running toward me on the street after the parade. My heart feels like it has turned inside out.

Connor is everything I want and everything I can't have.

If someone had given me a piece of paper and asked me to draw the perfect man for me, I never would've drawn Connor. Until I met him, I didn't know a scar on someone's neck could be sexy. Rhyming was a kindergarten activity until he made it exciting. I like the way he holds the steering wheel with one hand and uses his thumb to rub it absentmindedly. He scratches the back of his head with two knuckles, and I can't tell if it accomplishes the task or is just a habit, but it's adorable. I didn't know the man I would end up loving would do those things. Neither did I know my life in Phoenix would take a turn like it did and I'd end up running away from it all.

If there were ever a time for a drink, this would be it. I'd mix gin with tonic and forget the world. No. I can't be called a party girl if I don't put the stuff to my lips.

A deep breath fills my lungs. My thoughts get fuzzy around the edges, and I let sleep have me. I need to recharge before I see Connor again tonight at his opening.

25

CONNOR

"ALL SET?" CANDACE STANDS BEHIND THE MAKE-SHIFT DESK she rolled in for the opening. Her arms are crossed above her mid-section and she eyes me expectantly. I can tell she thinks I'm nervous about tonight, but she's wrong.

It's Brynn that has me walking from painting to painting, adjusting and readjusting. Will she show? She said she would, but I'm not convinced.

"I'm good," I respond, leaving the desk to walk across the small space, eying all the work.

Picasso-style abstracts in one section, landscapes in another. And then, there's me. There is no way to categorize my work except to say it's emotional. Capturing feeling is my thing. I finished the painting of Brynn, and in it, I see reluctant desire. She wanted me, but she didn't want to want me. I don't think I ever wanted to want her either. The choice wasn't mine. The decision was made by something greater, something that eclipsed thought and reason.

Eye of the Storm is here also, and underneath it is a small note that reads *Not available for sale.* I'm still waiting on the email to find out where to send it. I add that to my mental to-do list and move on. Included in my collection is an anatomically correct heart with cracks throughout, and colorful tears dripping down. Two people embracing, their faces buried in one another's necks, and the last one is two wrinkled hands grasping. It represents my parents, their marriage vows, and how now they need those vows more than ever.

"Twenty minutes to go," Candace shouts.

I meet the eyes of the other artists. One girl bites her lip and looks around. Another guy tilts his chin and crosses his arms. I disliked that arrogant prick from the moment he walked in and huffed about not being up front. Normally I'd be nice and introduce myself, but not this time. I'm too on edge about seeing Brynn again and having to say goodbye to her. I can't waste my life on that douche.

I pull my phone from my jeans and check it. No messages. I'm not sure if that's good or bad.

To pass the time, I fuck around on the internet, reading the news and playing a stupid word game.

When Candace opens the door, Julia and Anthony are the first to walk in.

Anthony claps me on the back and shakes my hand. "This is great, man. Really." He looks around at the pieces in my section. His eyes raise at the one of Brynn. "Is this a figment of your imagination? Or a real person?"

I shrug. Her profile is outlined in black. Inside she is a collection of expressions. Happy, alarmed. Pensive, coy, afraid. Different emotions wrapped up in one exquisite shell. I was careful not to include anything that would give away her identity.

"It all comes from here," I answer Anthony, tapping the side of my head.

"Connor, your work is incredible." Julia stands back

from the painting of my parents' hands. "Wow. How do I see love when I see these hands? Their wrinkles tell a story, and they aren't *old* old, because there aren't age spots yet."

"It was inspired by my parents."

Julia walks over to the painting of Brynn and studies it. Two more people, a man and a woman, walk up. Soon the place is crawling with people and I'm fielding comments and questions.

"Where do you get your inspiration?" an older woman asks, pointing to the Brynn painting.

"This is unique. Why isn't it for sale?" a young couple asks about Eye of the Storm.

A woman dressed in a long skirt and hair reaching down to her knees tells me the hands remind her of her parents when her mom was diagnosed with stage four ovarian cancer last year.

I answer everything as much as I can. My chest is swollen with pride and my body feels light, buoyant. I never expected anything like this. The number of people, the admiration of my work. It's a heady experience, a lot like being high.

My parents walk in, and the feeling gets even better. Dad makes a face, but I know it's a smile. Mom palms her chest with one hand and her eyes shine.

There's only one person I'm waiting on, and it's in the back of my mind as I continue to talk to people. Every thirty seconds my eyes find the entrance, only to be disappointed.

I wait. I answer questions. I make small talk.

I wait longer. Answer. Chat.

Brynn never comes.

26

BRYNN

A HOT STREAM OF AIR ASSAULTS MY CHEEK.

Immediately I understand, like a shark can smell blood from miles away. I haven't seen Eric Prince in a year, I was never close enough to smell him, and yet somehow I know his scent. Sharp anger, acidic desire for justice.

My worst nightmare. Except, this isn't a nightmare at all. I'm wide awake.

Terror seizes my limbs. A burning heat assails my thighs as my muscles tighten and bunch. I'm lying on my side on the couch, facing away from him. I don't know if he knows I'm awake. Surprise is my only friend right now, but I, too, am shocked. I have no way of knowing if my limbs will do as I say when I tell them to.

"Finally," he breathes the word into my ear. "You fucking bitch." His voice is too soft for such harsh words. He could be crooning a lullaby to an infant.

I have two options. I could open my eyes and try to talk some sense into him. Maybe if I could make him understand that I didn't hit them on purpose, that his wife was sick, then maybe—

Silly me.

Sense can only be talked into someone who's sensible. Eric lost his mind when he lost his family.

Second option, then.

I sit up suddenly, swinging my feet to the edge of the couch and bolting upright. Behind me is the small stone fireplace, the back of the living room. The only way out is past Eric. I lean left, prepared to skirt the coffee table and run when Eric lifts his hand. Extends it between us. My limbs freeze, my breath comes in pants. My brain screams words, so many words, and they are all the same word.

Gun.

Black. Matte. Metal. Capable of ending me before I get the chance to atone for my sins.

I really want that chance.

Eric's lips curl into a smile. It's dark and menacing, oozing like a poisonous sludge. He trains the gun on me. I don't know if it's cocked, can't remember if I heard the click. The seconds aren't passing the same way they were before. They've slowed, each one more crucial. My breath feels unnatural, thick and barbed.

And then, in a moment that feels wrong but is actually perfect, I see Amy Prince. Her gaze. Eyes that saw my car, chose it. In my imagination I hear her voice, something I never heard in real life. *Do it,* she instructs herself. *Three... Two... One...*

"Go ahead and sit down." Eric's voice grates out into the present, snapping my thoughts away from the terrible mess of that morning. He inclines his head to the chair in the corner.

"I'm not going to shoot you," he says after I'm settled in the chair. My body is ramrod. Left leg bouncing as if a jackhammer is inside it. Placing my hand on my thigh doesn't make it stop.

From his pocket, he produces two zip-ties.

I shake my head. "No no no no no." My voice cracks on each word.

He points the gun at my head. "Maybe I'll change my mind."

My whole body is rigid. I've been numbed to the sight of guns by movies and TV shows, but the reality of it is more terrifying, more paralyzing, than I ever could've guessed.

I do as he asks. I think of kicking him in the face when he bends to zip my ankles. I imagine elbowing his back when he tightens the tie on my wrists, but by the time I've gathered enough courage to do anything, it's too late.

He steps back from me. "I prefer not to shoot you right away. Too easy. It's important you understand suffering."

Bending at the waist, he sits back on the couch and keeps the gun trained on me. He is more than disheveled. The scruff on his face has grown in patchy, and on his left forearm is the bloody crust of a picked-apart scab. Holding the gun in his right hand, he lifts two fingers from his left hand and rubs them across his lower lip.

"There's comfort in imagining all the ways I can make you pay. You outsmarted the boys in blue, playing the victim like you did. Lying," he snarls when he says the word. One finger taps his temple. "But not me. I knew my Amy. She would've never done what you said. She loved Samuel. She loved *me*."

I force my breath to slow, and will my heartbeat to moderate. "She was sick, Eric." Despite the quaking of my voice, it's buttery soft. *Easy does it.* Eric doesn't need provocation. He's far past that point.

"She was not sick," he nearly screams. Flecks of saliva fly from his mouth.

Nothing I say will mollify this man. He is out for pain. My pain. He won't stop until it has been wrung from me.

The room is almost dark. The last of the day's sunlight has disappeared, running to hide behind the tall pines. Standing, Eric walks to a light switch and flips it. The floor lamp in the corner sends out a soft glow, and he hurries back to the window and pulls the curtains closed.

He's not doing a good job keeping the gun pointed at me as he moves around the room. A shred of hope lodges itself in my chest. He sits back down. Gets up. Sits down again. He seems at a loss.

"Eric," I whisper. Hate-filled eyes meet mine. "It wasn't a lie. They have footage from the traffic camera. You can see it for yourself. I know it's terrible, but—"

"Shut up," he shrieks, launching himself over the coffee table.

I shrink back and close my eyes. Cool metal grazes my forehead, slips down my temple, traces my jaw.

Dampness spreads between my legs. It's warm. *Is that...?* If I wasn't so terrified, I might feel embarrassed.

His lips are at my ear. My stomach twists at the feeling of his flesh on mine. "Don't say one more word."

He backs up, looks at me. A sick pleasure ripples over his features. He goes back to the couch and sits.

"I know you're wondering. Your mind is racing, thinking *How did he know*," he barks a dry laugh. "You make a habit of getting yourself into the paper, don't you?"

I shake my head. *No.* I declined the photo requested by the journalist.

"Oh, yes. You stupid girl. That's the thing about girls like you. You love your image so much you can't help but share it. I was buying cigarettes yesterday when the guy at the register was reading the paper. There you were, in the background of a photo, standing near some trailer. I bought the paper, almost forgot my cigarettes, and ran home."

He turns his head slowly from side to side, exhaling a short breath of disbelieving laughter.

"I watched you for so long. Almost every day. You liked brown sugar latte's from Lappert's and sushi from that place on the corner. You never went far, especially since you were usually on foot. Always alone, too."

He clucks his tongue, as though my solitude was a travesty.

"And then one day you stopped leaving. I realized it was because you weren't *there*. I looked for you, but that was one thing you did well. You left zero breadcrumbs." He pauses. Sighs. Continues. "I lost my temper a bit last weekend. I knew you hadn't sold your place. That was easy enough to check. I paid a homeless woman twenty dollars to write a note for me." He grins maniacally, proud of his subterfuge. "I didn't mean to kick a hole in your door. My anger got the best of me."

I want to scream, to run, to hurl myself at him and take away his gun. I want to save myself, but there's no way I can. I've been in danger since the day Amy Prince used me to take two lives, but this is the first time my death feels imminent.

"Your passport is on your bed. You don't have plans, do you? I wouldn't be surprised. Running away is your thing." He sits casually on the couch, crossing and uncrossing his ankles. Menacing words should be accompanied by a sneer and a growl, not spoken indifferently like we're discussing dinner options. "In case you're wondering how I got in, I punched a hole in your kitchen window and unlocked it. Your door alarms are cute though."

He sighs deeply and looks at his watch. His lips twist as he watches me.

"Detective Wilkes will know it was you." I blink twice, the sound of my own voice taking me by surprise. "I called him after you kicked in my door," I tell him.

"Detective Wilkes and I settled that. He knows it wasn't me. It was a female's handwriting, right?"

"He'll know and—"

"That's enough," Eric barks, pushing the gun into the air, closer to my head. "You sit there, shut up, and we'll wait for one of your friends to come by. Will it be the girl from the parade? Or the asshole you cried to on the street today? Connor Vale, is it?"

He watches my face twist in horror and looks pleased. "That's right. I was there, and your boyfriend had all his info plastered on his truck for the whole world to see."

Please, Connor, don't come for your goodbye. Please hate me. Go home and plan to never see me again.

Eric removes a tablet from a black bag on the floor and sets it up on the coffee table. His hold on the gun is sloppy and I'm terrified he'll misfire.

"This is something I've been wanting to show you since you hit and killed my wife and child."

Bending over, he presses the little arrow at the bottom of the screen. Amy's image springs to life. She's in a hospital bed, lying on white sheets. She wears a light blue nightgown printed with tiny flowers. Her eyes are tired but radiant. In her arms is a tiny baby, barely visible in the wrapped blankets.

"My lovely wife." Eric's loving and devoted voice charges

from the screen and into the room, bouncing around me. "Tell us what just happened."

Amy beams. Perhaps the sun was living somewhere in her chest at the moment. She looks blissful. "This is Samuel Bennett Prince," she says, her sweet voice floating from the screen, wrapping around me, making her more real than ever before.

"Oh," I cry involuntarily. I don't look up at Eric. The screen has captured me.

"He is seven pounds, four ounces of perfect." Amy keeps talking, looking directly at the screen, maybe even right into my soul. "I didn't know perfect had a weight." She grins, pulling the blanket away from the baby's face. "But it does."

Eric presses the pause button. "This is what you and I will do until someone you care about arrives." He stops to consider something for a moment. "Actually, let's make sure someone comes by tonight. What do you say?" Keeping the gun on me, he walks to the kitchen and grabs my phone off the counter.

"Let's see..." Eric presses a few buttons, swipes, and talks into the phone's microphone. "Come over. We need to talk." He presses one more button and tosses the phone back onto the counter.

"Who was that?" Fear drips into my voice.

Eric walks back over to the table where the tablet sits. "It'll be more fun if it's a surprise." He bends down, his finger hovering over the play button.

"Now we wait, and watch."

An infant's wail fills the room.

27

CONNOR

My high is gone.

Not completely, because I'm pretty damn proud of myself. As an indicator of a good night, I'm out of business cards. I sold three paintings, and I have more eyes on my work than ever before. I'm ready to paint until my hands go numb. Ideas bounce around my head but stay in bubble form. I can't make any of them into a solid when I have Brynn penetrating my thoughts.

She never promised to say goodbye.

The thought saddens me, but it also makes me angry.

I fasten a smile on my face and wave to Candace as I leave the gallery. My parents left a while ago, after my mom made sure to tell everyone within earshot that I was her son. It was embarrassing, but I loved it. My dad couldn't show his pride with his expressions, but his eyes are like windows. Through them, I saw his joy.

I hate that life took that turn for him. Capable hands turned impotent. His confident, assertive stride replaced by short, stiff steps.

Life doesn't discriminate. It took happiness away from

Brynn. One second she was driving, and the next she was driving *over* two people.

How can one second, two seconds, three seconds, be that consequential? A blip, a blink, and somehow they carry the weight of forever. How can one second differ so completely from the next? Does my dad ever think of the moments before he noticed his symptoms, before he asked my mom to make an appointment for him? How often does Brynn remember what her life was like when she was climbing into her car that morning, and compare it to what it was when she got out of the driver's seat?

I step out of the makeshift gallery into a day that is nearly night. The sun hangs low behind the trees, it's darkening light filtering through the branches and casting shadows on the road. The heat of the day has tapered off, and the humidity retreats with the sun. I don't usually pay close attention to the weather, but tonight I'm raw. I'm inside out, my heart exposed, and everything feels sharper.

I settle into my truck but can't manage to point it toward my house. It's stupid. So stupid. Brynn doesn't want to say goodbye. She told me this would happen. She said it would be easier if one day I realized she was gone.

My thumb traces my lower lip, back and forth, thinking too hard about what to do.

"Fuck it," I mutter, and turn on the truck. I didn't fight when Desiree left. I didn't even try, but Brynn is not Desiree.

Brynn is like ivy. She grew around me, slipping into crevices and wrapping around limbs. She infiltrated my body, permeated my insides, devoured my heart.

I didn't fight for Desiree because I didn't need her to breathe.

Brynn *is* my breath.

HER HOUSE IS DARK INSIDE. HAS SHE ALREADY LEFT?

Now that I'm on Brynn's street, I can't make myself park and get out. My truck rolls on and I wipe a palm on my jeans. There's only one other place where she could be right now. One other person getting the farewell she didn't give to me.

"What do you want?" Walt grimaces at me when he opens his front door.

I don't have time or patience for the old man tonight. "Where's Brynn?" I bark. If I had the capacity for humor right now, I'd laugh about how I sound like Walt.

"She's not here," he says unwillingly, as if telling me she's not there is a betrayal.

"Fuck," I yell, slamming my hand against the doorframe. I look at Walt, open my mouth to apologize but stop when I see the look on his face. For one, he doesn't look offended. For two, he looks proud.

"She hasn't left yet."

"How do you know that?"

"She promised me she'd say bye."

I stare at him. I cannot tolerate his bullshit right now.

He chuckles. "I take it you didn't get such a promise."

"Don't rub it in."

He waves his hand. "Don't take it personally. You're the one she can't stand to say goodbye to."

This makes me happy. Actually, it makes me really fucking ecstatic.

"Have you tried her house?" He steps out and I move aside for him. He walks farther out onto his porch and peers down the street.

My hand skims over my hair. "It's dark inside."

"So?"

"She likes light."

Walt doesn't speak. He juts out his chin and squints, scrutinizing the dark. "Damned old eyes." He bats the air in frustration.

I join him where he stands a few feet away, searching the dark alongside him. "What are you looking for?"

He points, and I gaze out in the direction of his finger. As far as I can tell, there is nothing to see.

"What's the make of that car over there?"

I squint too. I can't tell from here. It's across the street and one house down from Brynn's. Quickly, I walk down the steps and out to the sidewalk. "Mercedes." I tell him, raising my voice as I turn back.

The old man's eyes widen.

"What?" I ask.

"Nobody in this neighborhood drives a Mercedes."

"So?"

"It's out of place."

My eyes strain with the effort it takes me not to roll them. "Walt," I say calmly, like I'm talking to a child. "What aren't you saying?"

Walt keeps his eyes in the direction of the car, even though he can't see much of it. "I don't like it. I keep tabs on this neighborhood and I can promise you"—he jabs a finger in the direction of the car—"that car has never been on this street."

My heart begins to race, but I'm not sure why. Maybe it's Walt's serious tone, or his ominous implication. Maybe it's my knowledge of Brynn's tenuous situation.

"What do you think is happening?" I ask.

He ignores me and hurries inside as quickly as he can.

28

WALT

ALL THE LOVE IN THE WORLD COULDN'T HAVE SAVED DAISY. Not even mine, and I'm certain a man has never loved a woman with such ferocity.

Daisy, with her staunch belief in right versus wrong, and her disdain for housework, but love of lists. She waited patiently for me to return from Vietnam. We had a good life, me and Daisy. A few hiccups along the way, but I suppose that's to be expected.

When the cancer came, it barreled down on us like an avalanche. There was nowhere to run, nowhere to hide, and it happened so fast we hardly knew what hit us.

I couldn't save Daisy, but I'll try my damnedest to save Brynn.

I knew something was wrong with her from the beginning. For starters, she was jumpy. I'd take a step and she'd respond by moving her own body, even though she wasn't near me. Like she was always poised to make a break for it. Whatever hurt Brynn, she still fears it. Her eyes betrayed her fear even when her mouth spoke kind or cheeky words, or her shirt was printed with something that would've made my grandmother faint. There were times when I thought she'd collapse under the weight of her shoulders. Whatever she holds on them, it's burdensome. Too much for a girl her age. Ahead of her should be a lifetime of happiness and heartbreak, good fortune and failure, laughter and tears.

If Brynn needs to go, I'll let her, but I don't think she does. Daisy left once, when her low was so low she couldn't look herself in the mirror any longer. She needed to get away from our house, our things, even me. What she really wanted was a new body, one that could do what her heart longed for. She ran because the pain was too great, the need to punish herself too strong. I let her go because sometimes a person needs to run away. Left in a confined space, they might explode. Out in the open, their pain might leak out and have room to spread, thinning and eventually evaporating.

The difference between Daisy and Brynn is that Daisy wanted to leave. Brynn's departure feels forced.

And that Mercedes on the street made the hairs on the back of my neck stand up. Something isn't right.

I can't call the police because I don't like a car on my street. Poorly concealed laughter is all I would get from a phone call like that. I freaked out once, albeit in a pretty bad way, and I became infamous. I don't mind the whispers too much. Besides, it's a hell of a lot easier to growl at people and keep them away.

Except for Brynn. She wouldn't let me shun her.

I slide my foot into my second shoe and stand. "You can stop pacing now," I tell the boy. I know he has a name, but I rarely call him by it. Keeps him wary of me, and that's a good thing when he's dating the young lady I care about.

I grab a flashlight on the way out the door. My knee has been giving me trouble lately, and my back too, but right now I can't feel the pain as acutely. Adrenaline, I guess. Not that anything is actually wrong. Brynn is probably going to answer the door and laugh at the two of us.

Brynn's house isn't far, but I'm damn proud of myself for keeping pace with the boy. He falters when we get there. I stop, irritated. "What?"

He points at her living room window, where the drawn curtains are backlit. "A light is on."

"So?"

"I guess she's home after all." The boy sounds like someone took his favorite toy away.

"So?" I repeat, hoping to get a real explanation this time.

"She didn't come tonight. To my opening. She chose not to come." He looks back at his truck. "I'm going to leave. I can't do this anymore. If she wants to leave without saying goodbye, then fine. I won't make her do something she doesn't want to do."

I don't know what this talk of an opening is, but I do know when I see a man with his heart on the outside of his body. The boy loves Brynn. He also understands that sometimes letting people go is the best way to love them.

I nod. The boy claps me on the back a few times.

"Maybe one day you and I can get together for a beer, and I can get to know you a little better. You must not be that bad if Brynn managed to crack you." He grins at his joke.

"Brynn is like a ninja. She slips in before you notice her, and later realize you never gave her permission."

The boy chuckles and backs away. He tucks his hands in his pockets, and for a few moments, I watch him. Part of me wants to ask him to fight for her, and the other part of me wants to commend him for allowing Brynn the space she needs. I have all the channels on my TV, I see all the reality shows with the so-called men stomping around acting impulsive and selfish. The boy is not like that. Maybe I'll start calling him Connor.

I walk up the driveway and to the house, pausing on the landing. In front of my house, Connor steps up to get in his truck and pauses too, sending me a wave. I wave once and knock.

The door opens halfway, enough for me to walk in.

Odd.

I step in, my gaze going straight ahead to the kitchen. "Brynn," I call.

The door closes behind me at the same time I hear her say in a defeated voice, "I'm right here."

The overhead light picks up the tears tumbling down her cheeks, makes them glisten. First I see the zip-ties on her ankles and wrists, and then the wetness on the front of her jeans.

Something round and cold touches the base of my skull.

"You'll do," a man's voice says from behind. With a hand on my lower back, he gives me a small shove toward the couch. "Sit down."

AT THIS POINT, I'M THINKING IT WOULD'VE BEEN NICE IF Brynn would've told me her real name and what happened to her in Phoenix during a good dinner of crab cakes and French fries. That would've been much more pleasant.

Instead, I'm finding everything out with a gun pointed at my head.

"What do you think of your friend now?" the guy asks

after he finishes telling me about Brynn. Or, Elizabeth, I guess. That's what he calls her. He's standing at the far end of the couch, a spot where he can make Brynn or me his target with a swing of his gun.

He doesn't look like a killer. Not that they all have the same look, but he doesn't strike me as evil, and I've seen evil. He looks anguished. His eyes are lifeless. He's obviously vengeful, but to me, it's an act of desperation, not a true desire to do harm. Instead of grieving, he has channeled his devastation into anger and focused it on the person he believes is to blame.

Brynn is innocent. I read all those articles. Not just the slapdash, sensational headlines a simpleton teenager could've written. I read the meat of the story. It fascinated me. How could one woman erase from the world what my wife and I agonized over?

"Eric, please," Brynn pleads, shifting. She winces and looks down at her bindings.

Rage fills my vision, tinging it scarlet. The first thing I noticed about Eric is that he doesn't know what to do with a gun. The only advantage he has is that he has possession of it. The second thing I noticed is that he looks like a Mercedes driver. His appearance is rumpled right now, but the sheep embroidered on his polo tells me he isn't a thug. On a normal day, in a normal life, this behavior wouldn't come from him, and that is where *I* have the advantage.

"Eric, I'm Walt. I'd say it's nice to meet you, but at this exact moment, meeting you isn't so great. You understand." He eyes me, suspicion in his gaze, but I continue. "I'm very sorry about your wife and child. I read about it. Devastating." I shake my head. "My wife and I suffered a miscarriage once. It broke our hearts."

"Not the same thing," Eric grits through clenched teeth.

I raise my hands in front of me. "No, of course not. What you experienced was worse."

He swings the gun over to Brynn. She covers her face with her bound hands. "Clearly," Eric says. "I'm going to have to kill you both. My plan, as Elizabeth already knows, was to torture her by killing you in front of her, and that's still my plan." He glances down at me. His eyes are wild. "But you did surprise me. I thought someone else would be standing at the door." He looks at Brynn. "I guess your boyfriend doesn't care about you after all. Can't say I blame him. You're an alcoholic whore baby-killer."

Brynn doesn't even flinch. If his words hurt, she doesn't show it.

I'm angry enough for the both of us. I take my eighty-two years, my bad knee and back, and combine it with my red-hot fury. Before that little prick knows what's going on, I've stood up and grabbed ahold of the front of his shirt. He raises the gun above us, and I reach for it too. I have a hand on it, and I'm trying to take it without accidentally getting off a shot. His finger's on the trigger, which is another example of how untrained he is. I have only one idea, and it's something I've never done. Not to any man, ever.

I lift my knee and drive it right between his legs.

He grunts, automatically grabbing himself with two hands. I reach for the gun, but Eric keeps it against his body. I'm trying my damnedest to keep it pointed away from Brynn, and me, but the guy's staggering and he's so inexperienced that the hand holding the gun flops around like a fish.

A crack of thunder fills the air. An explosive blast bounces around the room, ringing and buzzing fills my ears. My hands are wet and red.

Suddenly I'm exhausted. I slump, falling into the couch.
Screaming. I think it's Brynn.
My name, over and over. Who's saying it now? Connor?
Sirens wailing.
I'm so tired.

29

BRYNN

"Ma'am, do you know this man?"

"How long were you tied up?"

"When did he arrive?"

"Is the gun his or yours?"

"Are you hurt in any other places?"

Two police officers ask me these questions. Responses fumble around my mouth. I think I answer, but it's hard to know if the voice I hear is my own. One of the policemen walks me to an ambulance and helps me climb inside.

Red and blue lights flicker around me. Other ambulances. First responders, trying to gauge the situation. More policemen and women arrive, descending, digging, determining fault. The sky is dark, not light, but I'm transported back to that morning anyway. *You need to come with us,* they said.

Not tonight. Tonight I'm clearly the victim.

"Where's Walt?" I ask the paramedic moving around in the ambulance behind me. I'm sitting at the end of the bay, the hard floor beneath me. If I had a blanket draped around my shoulders, I would look like a scene from a movie. Reality is alarmingly different.

The paramedic comes up beside me and steps down off the truck. She stands in front of me and asks for my wrists. "Who's Walt?" she asks. I watch her turn my wrists over, and examine them. Her name is printed beneath an emblem on her shirt. *Lori Turner.*

"The old man. He was in the house with me." I look at my house. Ginger's house. The place that was supposed to be a safe haven for me.

She swipes a wet cloth over my wrists. "He's being examined in another truck. No obvious injuries, just typical stuff that goes along with advanced age."

I nod. Such a simple response that understates the swell of relief inside me.

Lori glides ointment over the abrasions on my wrist. She kneels and starts on my ankles.

"And the... other man?"

Lori looks up at me. "You mean the shooter?"

Another nod from me.

"They took him away already. He'll likely need surgery."

Eric Prince. Deranged. Despondent. Grieving. He needs help.

Lori finishes and stands. "You're good to go. The abrasions on your wrists and ankles will heal. You'll need to follow-up with your doctor, and tell them if any new symptoms arise. Take it easy for the rest of the weekend. The first few days following a traumatic event are difficult."

In my case, it has really been the first twelve months.

Lori reaches for my shoulder to help me stand. She keeps a hand on me while I get my bearings. My legs are weak, I think more from shock than muscle failure.

"Thank you," I tell her, stepping out from the protection of the partially open back doors of the ambulance.

Like Lori said, Walt sits in the back of an ambulance to my right. A paramedic listens to his heart. Walt spots me over the paramedic's shoulder. His eyes close and his chin dips. It's a gentleman-like nod, and it brings tears to my eyes. Growling, grumbling, junk-hoarding Walt wrestled a gun from someone's hands. *For me.*

The paramedic starts talking, and Walt turns his attention to him.

"Brynn."

A strangled voice reaches me. Soaked in fear. Dripping with relief. How can one word, *my name*, convey both those emotions? I turn, and the sight of him rips through everything I felt tonight. Suddenly I'm sobbing, and then I'm in his arms, burying my face in his chest.

"Connor," I cry.

He brushes a hand over my hair. I look up at him. His eyes tell me the story of the terror he experienced tonight too. He cradles my cheek, his lower lip trembling. "I can't believe... Tonight... That guy..." He shakes his head and doesn't say anything else.

"I know. I know."

Connor presses his lips to mine. It's raw, a kiss between the wounded, the battered, the injured.

"All right, break it up."

I pull away, very nearly smiling. I've never been so happy to hear someone's voice. Stepping out of Connor's arms, I step right into Walt's. I hug him gently, even though I want to squeeze him tight.

"Thank you," I whisper.

"You're worth it," he whispers back.

I'm crying again, and just when I think Walt's going to

tell me to quit blubbering, he extends a hand. I step back but keep an arm around Walt's shoulders.

"Connor," he says. "I'm glad you didn't listen to me."

Connor shakes Walt's hand and grins. "Just because you're old doesn't mean you're wise all the time."

Walt wheezes a laugh. "Only most of the time." He looks down the street to his house. "This old man needs his bed. Going to take a while to recover from tonight's excitement."

"We'll walk you home and help you," I say, adjusting my arm so that I have a hold of his elbow.

He sends me a playfully derisive look. "Brynn, I just beat up a guy half my age. I don't need help getting into bed." I let my raised eyebrows do the responding. Walt sighs. "Fine," he grumbles. Connor waves a hand at a police officer standing in the open door of his car.

"Is it okay if we take him home?" He points at Walt. "Do you need anything more from us?"

The police officer walks over. I don't recognize him, but I don't think I'd recognize anybody from those first few moments after they burst into the house, guns drawn.

"You all are free to go. We may have more questions tomorrow, but we'll call it a wrap tonight." He hands me my purse. "This yours?" He nods at Connor. "He thought you might want it."

I thank him and take it. A thought occurs to me. "In Phoenix, there's a detective who worked with me about Eric. The, um..." I pause, not sure what to call him. Lori called him *the shooter,* but I can't bring myself to say that. "Eric Prince."

"You told us already, ma'am. It was one of the first things you said. You were actually quite helpful."

"Oh." I don't remember any of that.

"Don't worry. It's normal not to recall what you said.

Over the next few days, some things will come back to you."
He hands me a card. "If there's anything you think of and
you're not certain you told us, give me a call." He passes out
cards to Walt and Connor. "You guys too," he says, backing
up. "Try to get some rest. Sleep will come easier than you
think."

"Let's go tuck you in, Walt." Connor starts down the
sidewalk.

"Sounds good, Connie," Walt fires back, tucking an arm
through mine.

Connor's shoulders shake with laughter while we follow
him down the street, and into Walt's house.

At the entrance to his room, Walt stops us. "I'll take it
from here." He kisses my cheek and says goodbye to Connor.
"Brynn, there's an extra house key on top of the fridge. Take
it and lock up behind yourself. I don't want the key back."

I smile. "Okay."

I follow his instructions, tucking the key into my back
pocket alongside the officer's card.

Connor wraps his hand tightly around mine as we walk
down Walt's front steps. The ambulances are gone, the
police car has driven off, and the street is quiet again. The
neighbors who poured from their homes with the commo-
tion of the night have gone back inside. Vaguely, I see
Cassidy's face in my memory. Perhaps things will come back
to me as the seconds continue to tick past.

Suddenly I remember something. "Did you get a
message from my phone? Is that why you came?"

Connor looks at me, his eyes illuminated by a streetlight
we're passing under. "I was just about to drive away from
Walt's house and looked at my phone. I saw your message
and knew it wasn't from you. It didn't sound like you."

"So you walked over—"

"Ran," he corrects. "I was coming up your steps when I heard the shot." He shakes his head. "Worst moment of my whole life. Not knowing."

"Everything is okay now," I remind him, even though my wrists and ankles burn with the memory.

We reach my house and he pulls me into his chest. "Stay the night with me," he murmurs into my hair.

"Only if you promise not to let me go."

He pulls back, looking down at me. "I'm never letting you go, Brynn."

I've never really been in love, but I always imagined it feeling like floating. I was wrong. My heart, my core, my soul, my essence, has been connected to the earth, to the solid and stable surface it needs, to Connor, the man who would have let me go to keep me safe.

My hands wind around his neck. "I hope you mean that. I don't want any more question marks between us. We have a period at the end of our sentence now."

He answers me with a scorching and needy kiss. It takes my breath away, and almost my mind too. Luckily I remember I need to change my clothes. It's embarrassing, but I tell Connor what happened.

"If it makes you feel better I will pee right here, right now." He points at the yard. "On the grass, I mean."

I laugh. "That's the nicest thing anyone has ever said to me."

"You can shower at my house. I have an oversized t-shirt with your name on it. You left some clothes at my place, too. I found them yesterday and had no intention of giving them back to you." He grins impishly.

Connor takes my keys and locks the front door. He slips a hand in mine and leads me to his truck in front of Walt's house.

Oh no. The car service for tomorrow morning. While Connor drives I type out a quick message to the guy who's supposed to pick me up.

In the morning I'll deal with canceling my flight. For now, I want to close my eyes and forget tonight happened.

"It doesn't look the same without your paintings." Connor's living room is barren without the canvases, drab without the addition of their color. The empty easels are skeletons. I stop in the center of the room and turn back to him. His t-shirt hangs down to mid-thigh on me, but it's soft, and clean, and I feel a little better now that I've showered.

"I'm sorry I missed your show."

Connor strides to where I stand. His gaze is intense, his chest heaves once with a massive breath. "Later, Brynn. I'll tell you all about it." He grabs me and hoists me into the air. I wrap my legs around his waist and snuggle in.

His nose brushes against my nose, his lips drifting over mine. "You have no idea what it was like to walk in on you tonight. Bound," he chokes on the word. "The look on your face... It was awful. I don't think I'll ever forget it."

"I'm here. *We're* here," I whisper against the corner of his mouth. "Forget everything. Let it all go. We didn't think we'd have tonight, Connor." I graze his lower lip with my teeth. "Let's make the most of it."

Connor's groan fills my mouth, runs down my throat, slides into every inch of me. I wriggle to get closer, but there isn't any space to overtake. The only way he'll be closer is if he's inside me.

He cradles the back of my head with one hand, using the other to hold up my ass. Carefully, he lowers us as one until we're seated on the drop-cloth covered floor. I pull back, only long enough to pull off his shirt, then dive back in for more. He tugs on my shirt, lifting it as high as it will go. Again, I stop only long enough to lift my arms and be rid of my top.

Arms under my shoulders, he lifts me a few inches and buries his face between my breasts. "Brynn," he says in a voice muffled by the valley he's immersed in. "I love you."

I look down, opening my mouth. Nothing comes out. I have no words. He said it before, in my birthday card, but hearing him say it is different. Connor peeks up and grins. Gently he tugs my hair and forces my chin to point up at the ceiling. He lowers me inch by inch back down onto him, as he kisses and licks his way up the valley, over my collarbone, and straight up my neck to my jaw.

His eyes meet mine. My hands run through his hair, down his neck and over his chest. How did he sneak past my defenses? How did all my seconds get better when I thought they never would? I stepped in front of his truck, and he stepped into my heart.

"This week was painful, Connor. A pain I don't want to feel again. The last year has been hell for me. The ugliness of what happened felt suffocating. I never thought I'd find someone who wouldn't hate me when they learned what happened."

"That was a tragedy, but it doesn't define you. I see you, Brynn." One side of his mouth turns up as he runs a fingertip over my cheek. "You're funny and kind. There's light inside of you. When I first met you, I thought your eyes held a storm, but even then, I could see color in them."

My eyes widen. "The painting? The one of the eye?"

A rosy hue sprouts up on Connor's cheeks. "Yeah," he admits.

I laugh. "I'm the buyer."

His eyebrows form a 'V' in the center. "What?"

I laugh harder. The movement makes my breasts bounce and Connor looks down, appreciation softening his features. He lays me back, climbs over me, and I hear the rustle of his pants sliding down his legs.

He pushes inside me, and my breath leaves my chest at the unbelievable feeling of fullness. He rocks above me, his pace a steady rhythm, and in my head, I say the words in time with him.

I.

Love.

You.

I love you.

I love you.

"I love you," I whisper, heightened emotion and incredible feeling sweeping my voice.

Connor pauses, suspended in the air above me. My hips roll, trying to get more of him, until he pushes all the way inside me, stills, and lowers his face to mine. His lips drink my soul and devour my heart. He is a thief, and he has absconded with all of me.

He doesn't stop again. He doesn't stop until I beg him to, until my legs go limp and I can't take another crescendo.

When we come down, when he's carried me to his bed and we've wrapped our limbs around each other, he kisses me softly. "Will you stay tomorrow?"

I kiss him back with all the strength I can manage. It's not much. He has drained me. Between Connor and the other events of the night, I'm depleted.

"If you let me, I'll stay forever," I murmur, as I fade off into sleep.

30

BRYNN

I wake first. Connor sleeps soundly, his bottom lip drawn away from his top. His snores are soft, his breath a steady rhythm.

Everything about last night tumbles to the forefront of my mind. How could so much awful and so much amazing fit into one six-hour time period?

Carefully I extract myself from the forearm Connor has laid across my torso and creep out of the room, going straight for the kitchen. I need coffee like nobody's business.

When the coffee is brewed, I step outside. The sky is already bright, not because we slept in late, but because it's the peak of summer, and the sun rises at an hour that feels closer to nighttime. I sit down on a chair and close my eyes, listening to the chattering birds. Feel the heat creep over my skin. Smell the bitter scent of strong, black coffee.

I thought I'd be getting ready to leave for Phoenix by now. This afternoon I was supposed to be in the air. I still need to cancel my flight.

What will happen to Eric?

He should be held responsible for what he did. I know

that, but I don't want him to lose more of his life. I can't say for certain, but I think he had a psychotic break. A disconnect from reality brought on by profound grief. I looked him up after the accident, combing through his social media profiles. He was a normal guy before everything happened. Upper-middle class. Doting father. He probably worked too much, didn't see his wife slipping away. The disconnection in her didn't raise a flag in him.

I want him to get what he needs to be better, and that is not a jail cell. How can I make that happen? Setting down my coffee on the floor beside the chair, I go inside to grab my phone.

I find three texts from my mother. Two voicemails. One notification from the yoga person I follow on YouTube.

Settling back down in the chair, I pick up my coffee, fold my legs underneath me, and click on the notification. I need some good before I tell my parents what happened last night. It's a new video. I press the little arrow on the screen, and see the yoga instructor, Ember.

"Hey, guys." She smiles and waves from a cross-legged position on a lawn. She looks tired, but her eyes sparkle. "It has been a while since I posted a new flow, and this"—she reaches for something off-screen—"is why. Meet Jonas." She angles an infant toward the screen. Her husband comes into the frame and settles down behind her. His chin resting on her shoulder, he wraps his arms around hers so that he cradles the baby too.

My lips purse and I try not to cry, but it's useless. The tears sting. I blink a few times and let them roll. Ember has in her eyes what Amy Prince did not when I saw her that day. Utter devotion. Joy. No fear, or emptiness. Her husband is attentive. It's obvious even in these few, precious moments she's sharing with her followers. As Ember talks to the camera, he presses his nose against the space behind her ear and closes his eyes briefly. He is a man in love with his wife, his baby, his *life*.

Maybe we all are responsible for what happened to Amy. Her husband, for being closest to her, and not seeing her desperation. Me, for not reaching out that day in the bookstore. Her parents? Her friends? Whomever else, for seeing her but not recognizing her illness. Postpartum depression is treatable. When someone is sick like Amy was, they can't always help themselves. It's the responsibility of everyone around them to help them, and we all fucking failed her. We all failed her baby. Eric Prince most of all.

I hit pause on the video. It freezes on a moment so beautiful I almost want to take a screenshot. Ember, still sitting on the ground, baby Jonas extended. Her husband crouched beside her, taking the baby. The beautiful part? They are beaming at one another.

It rips me in half.

I was dragged into something that day. Amy Prince and her baby crossed my path. I still don't know why. The spiral it sent me down hasn't finished yet. I'm still on it, but I think I'm near the end. I pray that I am.

Before I can step off, before I can figure out a way to help other women like Amy Prince, I need to see Eric.

Connor walks out. He is shirtless, the shorts he pulled on after waking hang low on his hips. He is glorious in the morning light. All male. All mine.

"Do you still love me in the morning?" I shield my eyes with a hand and look up at him.

He grabs my hand and pulls me up. Brushing my hair back from my face, he nuzzles his rough cheek against mine. "I will love you on a plane and on a train, on a boat and in a moat. I will love you anywhere and everywhere between here and there."

I squeeze his shoulders, running my hands down his arms. My brain searches for a good response, but I come up empty. "I can't think of a rhyme for *there*. How about... I love you in the light of day, in every single way?"

I feel his laughter in his chest. "I'll take it, and I'll take you. Right now. In my bed." He reaches down and swats my behind.

I squeal and wriggle in his arms. "I'll join you in bed, if you'll join me somewhere else after."

"Done," he says, taking my hand and pulling me into the house.

THERE ARE TWO POLICE OFFICERS POSTED OUTSIDE ERIC'S door when we arrive. They stand tall and serious, like sentries.

Before we left Connor's house I called the police officer who gave me his card last night. He okayed my visit this morning, and said he'd let the men standing watch know to expect me.

Coming to a stop in front of them, I give them my name and they nod at me. One of them reaches for the door and opens it. Pausing, I glance at Connor.

"Do you want me in there with you?" He asks.

I consider it briefly, then shake my head.

"He's cuffed to the bed, ma'am."

I'm not sure which officer spoke, but I nod and say thank you in their general direction.

Squeezing Connor's hand, I give him a quick kiss on the

cheek. "I'll be out soon." Then I take a deep breath and slip into Eric's hospital room.

The door falls softly into the jamb behind me. I hover near the entrance, uncertain now that I'm here. He lays in the bed, looking a fraction of the angry man he was last night. His eyes are closed. His hair is still a mess. The bed sheets cover his lower half, so I can't see what his leg looks like. As gunshot wounds go, it wasn't as bad as it could've been.

There was a terrifying moment when I thought it was Walt who'd been hit. There'd been blood, the two men pressed against eachother, and they fell together. When Eric rolled away, screaming, I saw the hole in his thigh, and the red that poured from it.

He opens his eyes when I take a step. Stares at me. Aside from blinking, he doesn't move.

Memories of last night come to me. His indignation. His hatred. The feel of a gun pressed to my head. My hands begin to shake, and I look at his handcuffs. *I am safe.*

I take a few steps inside, grab the chair from the corner, and drag it closer. Sitting down, I cross my legs. Uncross my legs. Fidget, and clasp my hands on my lap.

"Elizabeth," Eric says.

My head snaps up. I've never heard that voice from him. So...normal. He has only ever snarled my name.

"Hello, Eric."

The inside of my cheek is captured by my teeth. I'm not sure what to say now that I'm here. In his presence, I feel frightened, and though I anticipated the feeling, the reality is different. I gaze out the window while he says nothing. The absence of sound is louder than if a marching band paraded through here.

He finally speaks. "Why are you here?"

My eyes meet his. I'm thinking a hundred things and nothing at all. So many words swirling around, and I need to choose the right ones. Are there any right words?

I take a deep breath, letting it slide from between my lips. Pushing all those words aside, I open my mouth and let my heart speak for me. "You failed Amy. I know that's not what you want to hear, but it's the truth, and maybe the truth is what you need to face."

Over and over, his cheeks tug and fall back into place as emotions dart across his face.

I don't stop. He's a captive audience.

"Amy was likely battling postpartum depression, and perhaps you already know that. Perhaps you've hidden that truth from yourself so that you don't have to be responsible for missing it." I lean forward. "I want to make something very clear to you. Every day, I struggle with what happened. Life is not the same for me. And yes, I was a mostly worthless person before. My job was to help people party. Not very fulfilling. But I didn't deserve what Amy did to my life that day. Nobody did."

Tears roll freely. I can't stop them, and I don't even bother wiping them.

"I'm sorry. I'm sorry from the deepest, rawest, barest part of my soul. You mourn your wife and child every day, but you're not alone. I mourn them too. I wish they were back with you. I wish you weren't so hurt. I wish you could handle your grief, because I don't want to be stalked and threatened. I want you to stop."

My breath is ragged, making catching it almost impossible. Eric's eyes pour tears like mine, except he has no way to wipe them.

"I'm not planning on pressing charges." My voice is shaky as I continue. "I can't say the same for Walt, the old man you hurt, or the state, but I won't. All I ask is that you get help. You need grief counseling. Badly. You're a smart person, Eric. I'm sure you know this psychosis cannot continue."

He nods, licking tears from his lips. "I want to hold my baby again. I want to hold my wife. I didn't tell her goodbye the day she died. I left early in the morning to play golf, and she was sleeping. I didn't know... I didn't know...," he sobs, chin tucked to his chest, with no way to help himself, or cover his face.

Tissues are on the counter beside the sink. Plucking a few from the box, I come up alongside his bed and hold out a hand with a tissue gathered in my fingers.

"I would like to help you," I say tentatively. "Please don't bite me."

His eyes hold shock. "You think I would—" He shakes his head. He must be remembering what he did last night. "I won't bite you."

I reach out cautiously, the same way I would pet a wild animal. His eyes close as I gently swipe the tissue against them. He reopens them when I'm done, his gaze on me as the tissue moves to his cheeks, then on to his chin and lips.

"Would you like to blow your nose?" It's not something I particularly want to do, but I don't think I'd like it if I were restrained and had snot clogging my nose.

"No," he murmurs, his face coloring. "The nurse can do that."

I toss the used tissues in the trash and go back to the foot of the bed.

"I'm going to leave now, Eric. Good luck with everything." I turn, but his voice stops me.

"I'm sorry Amy ruined your life. I'm sorry I made it worse. I can't forgive you for what happened... Not yet." His voice catches, a sob on the verge of breaking through. "I don't even know if there is anything to forgive."

"You'll figure that out in counseling, Eric." I muster a smile, but I'm certain it's the saddest smile to ever grace my lips.

I leave.

I walk out of Eric's hospital room and straight into Connor's arms.

"You all right?" he asks against the side of my head.

I nod. I'll be okay. Now that I'm no longer running, I can rebuild.

We leave the hospital and climb into Connor's truck.

"Where to?" he asks me.

"A plane. Maybe a train. I'd like to sail on a boat and swim in a moat. We can go anywhere and everywhere between here and there."

Grabbing my hand, he kisses it. "You're free now. Do you want to be Elizabeth or Brynn?"

"Brynn," I say with confidence. Elizabeth isn't someone I want to be anymore.

Connor winks. "Brynn suits you." The trucks roars to life as he puts it in drive and turns around, heading back to his house.

We drive through the town that somehow became my home. Connor has one hand on the steering wheel. The other holds my heart, my soul, and my whole future.

EPILOGUE

CONNOR

"I don't know, man." Anthony makes a face and shakes his head. "It's muggy as fuck here."

"Yeah, you've said that a few times since we got off the plane."

Panic rises as I sift through my suitcase. I push aside shirts and send shorts flying. Of all the fucking things I could possibly forget, how could I make it all the way to Brazil without the one thing I actually need? This trip means everything to Brynn. This is where she came as a child. The beach outside our hotel room is the same beach she planned to come to when she thought she needed to escape. This is where she wanted to celebrate our two-year anniversary. Her parents arrive tomorrow, for fuck's sake. She doesn't know they're coming, and now when they arrive, it's going to be the biggest letdown in the history of letdowns.

Oh, yeah, I invited your parents and Walt for no reason. Certainly not because I was planning on asking you something and now I can't!

Anthony's hand touches my flailing arm. "Connor, chill. The ring is in your carry-on."

I grunt and rake a hand over my forehead. "Thanks. I'm just nervous."

Grabbing the carry-on, I quickly locate the ring box and open it. A cushion-cut diamond glints back at me. I've saved money since the day I knew Brynn would stay in Brighton. Every portion of a painting sold went into the ring fund, and another portion went into the house fund.

Anthony fills a glass with water from the bottle the hotel left on the dresser. "What do you have to be nervous about? You know she's going to say yes." He picks up the paper coaster the bottle had been standing on and throws it at me like a frisbee. It falls short, landing on the bed.

I snap the ring box shut and lock it in the in-room safe. "Quit acting like you weren't nervous when you proposed to Julia." I snatch the coaster off the comforter and toss it in the trash.

He scoffs. "I had that shit on lock."

"I'll make sure to tell her that," I say, pulling a clean T-shirt over my head.

"Please don't." The desperate words tumble from his mouth. He grins, and I laugh too.

"Come on." I grab the keycard and stride to the door. "The girls are waiting for us downstairs. I'm starving."

Brynn

Connor has been acting weird all day. Jumpy. Forgetful.

Truth be told, I'm having a hard time too. I wanted this vacation more than anybody else in our group, but when it came down to it, leaving my work was harder than I thought it would be. Planning an event like the one I've been working on takes careful preparation and attention to detail. Oh yeah, and a keynote speaker. I've been searching, but I'm being met with reluctance at every turn. So far, nobody has wanted to talk about their experience with postpartum depression.

My non-profit aims to provide resources for women dealing with this illness, but how can I advocate for them if I can't get someone to share their experience and demystify it? If I want the shame of the condition stripped away, I need someone who can speak from personal experience. I don't need someone with a case as advanced as Amy Prince's, I just need *someone.*

I'm trying hard to lay on this beach chair and read my book, but I keep losing my place. Finally I give up and set it down beside me. My eyes fall closed and I let my mind wander. I'm almost asleep, thanks to the calming, rhythmic sounds of the ocean, when my eyes fly open. *I* am the person who should speak. Of course. *Of course!*

Excited to share my epiphany, I turn to where I last saw Connor on the beach. He'd been tossing a football with Anthony, but he's no longer there. When I don't immediately spot him, I pull my sunglasses down my nose and scan the area. No Connor. Actually, nobody from my group is anywhere to be found.

My phone buzzes on the table beside me.

Connor: Can you come up to the hotel? I need help with something. Thanks, babe.

I get up, throw on my white cover-up, stow my book in my little beach bag, and sling it over my shoulder. Pausing outside the lobby entrance, I reach down to swipe sand from my feet.

"You make a fine sight, Ms. Montgomery."

I smile, straightening, and reach for Connor. He's wearing his navy blue swim trunks and a white t-shirt. "You aren't too bad yourself."

Taking my outstretched hand, he leads me away from the entrance and around the front of the hotel.

"What do you need help with?" I ask. Connor doesn't answer. He pulls me along behind him, up a flight of stone stairs, and then we walk for another minute. My black slides smack the floor loudly with our steps.

"Connor, what is going on?"

"You'll see."

We round another corner, and come onto a stone terrace with a curved balcony. Beyond it, the sea sparkles. Connor walks me to the balcony wall.

"It's incredible, right?"

I look out. The water sparkles, crashes, and rolls back out to do it all over again. "It's breathtaking."

Connor stands behind me, wrapping his arms around my waist. My whole body relaxes into him. It's still and quiet, and then Connor speaks.

"I love the tan on your skin, and the freckles that dot your chin. I love you so much, I don't know where to begin."

Turning my head against his chest, I peer up at him. He winks and nods, encouraging me to play.

I look back out to the ocean, thinking. "If I were a mermaid, I would grow a purple fin."

His chuckle rumbles against me. "You're one-of-kind, I'm glad you're not a twin."

I smile. "Me too. I call that a win."

Connor shifts, lowering his lips to my ear. "Will you marry me, Brynn?"

I make a sound. Something like a squeal and an intake of breath. My hands are at my face, my fingers shaking.

Connor drops his arms and I whirl around. He reaches into his pocket, pulls out a ring, and starts to bend down.

I grab his arms on his descent and pull him up. "Yes. Yes a thousand times. Don't get on a knee." I stick out my hand. "Put that ring on my finger and kiss me. Kiss me until I can't breathe."

Connor listens. He slides the cool metal over my warm skin, and slips a hand through my hair until it stops at the back of my head. Dipping me back slightly, his face looms over mine and he pauses, his eyes roaming mine. He lowers his lips, and kisses me the way I asked to be kissed. He steals all my breath, just like he already stole my heart. *Thief*.

Somewhere nearby, a throat clears. Connor brings us upright and my eyes open.

"Dad?" Shock rolls through me as I take in my dad, and the people standing next to him. "Mom? Walt?" I laugh, and tears prick my eyes. Julia and Anthony smile, and Anthony kisses the side of Julia's head.

I look back at Connor. "This is amazing. I can't... How..." I shake my head. My body feels light and airy, like I could just float away at any second. "You did good."

Connor squeezes my waist. "I only did what I've been planning to do since the day your shirt told me to fuck off."

I laugh and snuggle in closer.

"Okay, okay, I want my daughter," my mom calls. Reluctantly, I peel my body off Connor's.

There are countless hugs, many toasts, a dinner I hardly remember. Inside I'm soaring, high on emotion. At the end of the evening, we say goodnight and go to our room.

Connor peels off my clothes, lays me on our bed, and with the patio door flung open, and the sound of the waves crashing against the shore, he pushes into me slowly. Our pace is unhurried. The tempo set by the knowledge that we'll be doing this with each other for the rest of our lives.

Two years ago, I thought I would come to this beach to get lost.

But, no.

I came here, and I was found.

The End

Thank you for reading The Time Series! Turn the page to read the first chapter of Good On Paper.

ALSO BY JENNIFER MILLIKIN

Hayden Family Series

The Patriot

The Maverick

The Outlaw

The Calamity

Standalone

Better Than Most - preorder, releases October 5th, 2023

The Least Amount Of Awful

Return To You

One Good Thing

Beyond The Pale

Good On Paper

The Day He Went Away

Full of Fire

The Time Series

Our Finest Hour

Magic Minutes

The Lifetime of A Second

Visit Jennifer at jennifermillikinwrites.com to join her mailing list and receive Full of Fury: A Full of Fire novella, for free. She is @jenmillwrites on all social platforms and would love to connect.

Turn the page to read the first chapter of Good On Paper!

GOOD ON PAPER

Sign it.

Such a simple task. Pick up the pen and sign your name on the line. A few strokes and my name will join his.

Paper bound us, and paper will cement our ending.

Three years ago, on our paper anniversary, Henry handed me a roll of toilet paper. On it, he'd written *I love the shit out of you* in brown Sharpie.

"Mrs. Shay? Do you need a moment?" The attorney we chose has a voice like gravel and kind eyes. That had surprised me. Before him I thought all divorce attorneys were callous, hardened to the emotion spilling out in front of them. My parents' attorneys had dull, lifeless eyes. I assumed years of client theatrics had immunized them to personal anguish.

A deep breath fills my chest, passing slowly through my lips on its way out. I look up into eyes crinkled at the corners. Mr. Rosenstein, our attorney, is dressed in a starched white shirt, navy suit, and plaid bow tie. He may work in New York City, but his outfit says genteel Southerner.

Clearing my throat, I manage to push words past the lump that has formed. "I'm okay. Thank you."

I pick up the pen, its coldness a sharp contrast to my heated palm. My thumb extends, covering the end, and I both hear and feel the click. The sound is thunderous, somehow louder in volume than any of our fights.

How did it come to this?

It's a silly question. I know just how it happened. Epic showdowns decreased in ferocity until the air between us held only silence. Hearts that beat red faded into an unassuming, neutral shade. Eventually we became spectators in the demise of our marriage.

The pen scratches across the paper, my hand making the familiar loops. I dot my *i* and cross my *t,* imagining it as a headline.

Natalie Shay has just signed her divorce papers.

This was a monumentally bad idea.

I should've said no when Henry suggested it, but of course not. Isn't that one of the reasons I left him? His personality was so big, so overwhelming, so *infiltrating* that I lost my voice. It's hard to stand up and breathe when waves are keeping you down, and that's what Henry became. Wave after wave, big ideas and thoughts and criticisms, rolling over me incessantly. I was choking on my desire to be myself. It was either stay and die, or run. I chose.

Out of habit, or maybe guilt, I agreed to meet him after I signed the papers. My hand dips into my purse, closing around the small box. I've done that at least a hundred times since I placed it there this morning. For four years I wore the contents of the box on my left hand and I didn't touch it this much.

Henry is late. He's probably mentally preparing for this moment. He'll come in swinging, expecting recrimination of all the ways our divorce is his fault. He's a natural-born arguer. I used to joke that he missed his calling as a litigator. In every joke there is an element of truth, and what I was really saying hid behind the jest. *Please stop arguing with everything I say. Please stop listing the reasons why acupuncture is a sham when I just told you how good it makes me feel. Please stop trying to make me feel small.*

My eyes are on the door when Henry walks in. We've been separated for five months, and still my heart jumps up, settling into my throat. He looks good. Softness settled into his middle a couple years ago, but it's gone now. My departure kick-started a new fitness regimen. Out of boredom? Or is there already someone new? The thought makes me uncomfortable.

Henry scans the small coffeehouse, spots me, and though his eyes light up in recognition, he doesn't smile. He comes my way, saying *excuse me* over and over as he squeezes his large, tall frame through tables of seated people.

When he reaches me, I open my mouth to say hello, but his words are faster. "Did you choose a table at the back just to watch me bump into people?"

His voice is smooth, his volume normal, but his words cut.

I choose to ignore him. There's no use pointing out that I chose the high-top table so he would be more comfortable. "Hi. How are you?"

He settles onto the stool opposite me and props his elbows on the table. His shirtsleeves are rolled up to reveal muscular forearms. In college, he threw footballs and pretended to bench press me. I was happy and convinced we were meant for one another. Funny how things change.

Henry settles his chin into his cupped hands and gazes at me. "I'm good, Nat. Did you sign?" His expression is neutral, and stupidly I wish there was some emotion there. Where is the anger? Where is the sadness?

"Yep," I say curtly, reaching into my bag. Suddenly I can't wait for this to be over, for him to be gone. "Here." I slide the box across the small space. He takes it, careful not to brush his fingers against mine. Tears swim in my eyes, and I pray they don't spill over. Why am I crying? It's over. It's what I wanted. I initiated it.

My gaze sweeps the room, seeing but not really seeing the long line of people waiting to order. The feel of his stare on my face makes me want to melt into a puddle and seep into the ground.

"Natalie, I—" he pauses, his voice softened by a tinge of regret. "I'm not sure what to say. I don't know how to do this."

"Me neither," I whisper, swiping at my eyes.

"Thanks for giving the ring back to me."

My right hand reaches for my ring finger, rubbing the bare flesh. "It was your grandmother's."

Henry stands, pushing the stool back under the table. "Well, I, uh... I'll see you around. Call me if you need anything." He turns, stops, then shakes his head and laughs disbelievingly. "Never mind. You won't need anything. Aidan is here. Like always."

I lean left and peer around Henry.

Aidan is early. Aidan is always early, but on a day like today, he probably hustled in from Brooklyn after school was finished.

"Shay," Aidan nods at Henry. Calling him Shay is a relic from college.

"Costa." Henry's voice has dropped an octave. He looks back at me, his glare full of meaning, silently hurling his accusations at me, as if they haven't been flung a million times before.

Henry stomps out, bumping into people as he goes.

I look at Aidan. His eyes are on me, his gaze soft. He comes to me, folds my head into his chest, and blocks me from view while I fall apart.

ACKNOWLEDGMENTS

The Time Series has come to a close. I can't believe it. Eighteen months ago I dreamed up a three-part series that would encourage people to think of the powerful moments of their lives. Why was that hour, minute, or second important? How did it change them? Many people are to thank for helping bring my dream to completion.

My husband, Luke. My biggest supporter, my biggest fan. Your never-ending words of encouragement have kept me afloat at times. I love you.

My beta readers, Kristan, Julia, and Crystal. You have kids. You have crazy, busy lives. Still, you read my books and provide the feedback I need to make my work shine. Thank you, thank you, thank you.

A shout out to my editor, Ellie McLove, at Gray Ink. Thank you for handling this book with care and love.

Murphy Rae at Indie Cover Designs, you made three beautiful covers and I'm forever grateful. The Time Series came to life because of you.

Thank you, Officer Alex Dyer of Scottsdale Police Department, for advising me on the judicial portion of this story.

Readers- THANK YOU! Thank you for reading, for loving, for spending your time on my work. Thank you for telling your friends, leaving reviews, connecting with me on social media. I love the messages, the posts, the emails. They make all the blood, sweat, and tears of writing a novel worth it.

ABOUT THE AUTHOR

Jennifer Millikin is a best-selling author of contemporary romance and women's fiction. She lives in the Arizona desert with her husband, two children, and Liberty, her Lab who thinks she's human. Jennifer loves to cook, practice yoga, and believes chips and salsa should be a food group.

facebook.com/JenniferMillikinwrites

instagram.com/jenmillwrites

bookbub.com/profile/jennifer-millikin

Made in the USA
Middletown, DE
19 August 2023

36987006R00163